STARLING

Kirsten Cram

HIGHWAY SIX PRESS

Copyright © 2021 by Kirsten Cram

All rights reserved. No part of this book may be reproduced, scanned, or distributed in any printed or electronic form without permission.

ISBN: 978-0-578-97985-4

to Nature,

to the balm of friendship,

and the saving grace of books.

CONTENTS

Chapter 1 11

Chapter 2 21

Chapter 3 31

Chapter 4 45

Chapter 5 57

Chapter 6 67

Chapter 7 79

Chapter 8 93

Chapter 9 107

Chapter 10 125

Chapter 11 139

Chapter 12 147

Chapter 13 161

Chapter 14 179

Chapter 15 187

Chapter 16 191

Chapter 17 197

Chapter 18 215

Chapter 19 229

Chapter 20 239

Chapter 21 251

Chapter 22 261

Chapter 23 275

Chapter 24 285

Chapter 25 297

Chapter 26 305

Chapter 27 311

Chapter 28 321

Chapter 29 327

Chapter 30 335

Starling, B.C.
1976

CHAPTER

1

When Penny Quinn decided to move closer to her job at the glass plant, she did not tell her daughter Alice until the day before it was to happen. The move entailed leaving the town of Caribou for Starling, a smaller community ten miles down the road. Heading north on a two-lane highway, a direction known as *into the bush*, it was not uncommon to pass through Starling while failing to note its existence. The signs of life were sparse, dimpled across pastures and shrouded by trees–a battered, communal mailbox set askew by an eroding ditch, bottles smashed and gleaming in the weeds, a lone house in the distance with no discernible driveway leading to its step. The looming forest grew everywhere, eager to reclaim the advances made against it, flanking roads and farmland; an ominous distinction between civilization and the wilds. A chorus of coyotes howled across the valley at night, calling to each other in thin yips and barks. Cougars left their tracks in the soft mud along the periphery and bears came down from the mountains, enticed by fields of corn to be made into fodder, not fit for human consumption.

Unless they had reason to do otherwise, most people drove through the area without stopping. Something about the place–the remoteness, its intense, shadowy beauty–was at once seductive yet provoked a troubling urge to step on the gas. The feeling soon passed and was forgotten; after all, families lived and worked in Starling, it was where their kids went to school, and the local men had banded together to form a volunteer fire department. But none of this was known to the casual passer-by; along the stretch of highway that ran through the area, only a gas station called Red's was visible from the road.

Though an official count was never taken, about three hundred residents were tucked away in the far corners of their land. Few people are drawn to country living to nurture a sense of proximity, after all. They were mainly old, grizzled farmers and workers at the plant or mill, though a good many more declined any form of industry whatsoever. Some fancied themselves mechanics, their yards littered with car parts, legitimately or otherwise procured. Less apparent was the quiet yet thriving pot industry secreted in basements and backyards, or growing between skunk cabbages down by the creek. Beyond this, the remainder could more or less be categorized under some variation of the word *drunk*: mean drunk, crazy drunk, lonely drunk, and in certain cases a combination of all three.

Starling was perhaps best suited to those who had always lived there, as the locals, leery enough of each other, disliked strangers even more. An outsider would always be an outsider and so would his kin, excluded for generations from a sense of belonging that did not exist in the first place. A strange inertia wove through the area, a stifling airlessness that belied the passage of time, stretching an afternoon into the eternities yet stealing a life in the blink of an eye. The highway rolled on, past fields and meadows, winding like a ribbon through the trees. It disappeared into the distance, not with a sense of possibility but with the bleakness of being left behind, for no one ended up in Starling who had somewhere better to go.

The community was a hiding place for secrets, cloaking all manner of behavior in the grand tradition of looking the other way. Children showed up to school with bright, shiny bruises and adults shook their heads but kept their thoughts to themselves. What more was childhood, after all, than a momentary flight before someone rubbed the dust off its wings? Such sanctuaries were fleeting, and it seemed a particular cruelty to prolong that which had no hope to survive. There were harmless enough folk and there were others, but everyone kept quiet who lived in that place. When storms came through the valley, buffeting houses and felling down trees, they lingered over Starling, shrieking and moaning what could not otherwise be said.

Alice, who was ten years old, walked to school on her last day in Caribou keeping one foot exactly in front of the next. While the other students horsed around before the second bell rang she sat at her desk and rested her head, scratching the letters *AQ* into her seat with the sharp end of a compass.

"Are you okay, Alice?" asked her teacher.

The girl looked up and nodded, not trusting herself to speak.

That afternoon Alice and her mother drove out to her new school, following the highway into a valley shored up by steep, timbered hills. The land along the road was a tangle of growth overshadowed in places by towering pines. Barbed wire sagged between old fence posts, a bygone attempt to establish order now lost and rusting in the weeds. A sign riddled with buckshot hung askew so that Alice had to cock her head to read it. *Thou shalt not kill* it said in faint, hand-lettered script, a subsequent line scrawled through the word *not*. The girl sat up sharply after that, scouring the brush for further illumination, but in this she was disappointed.

Starling Elementary was a flat, single story structure established for the learning of the first through seventh grades. It looked like a series of shoeboxes stuck together with no apparent vision for the overall design. Penny took the registration papers from the secretary and handed them to her daughter, then went outside for a smoke. Alice sat on the edge of her chair, balancing the clipboard on her knees. She filled in her name and birthdate. Where it said *mother,* she wrote *Penitence*. Where it said *father,* she wrote *Ernest* and in the space allotted for his occupation, *sea captain*. In reality, Alice didn't know the first thing about her father, but she loved how the official nature of a form could make almost anything seem true.

By Thursday, the Quinns were settled into their new home. It was a small, weathered clapboard on the edge of a pasture overrun by thistles and weeds. The pasture sloped up a hill that turned into a forest, and beyond this loomed a mountain range with balding peaks named for parts of the female anatomy. A creek ran through the property, its current weaving a conversation over swirling pools and carpets of slick, mossy stones. Ponderosas towered above thickets of birch and hedgerows sprang up, casting long, fearsome shadows in the late afternoon. Ferns, nettles, and skunk cabbage spread low over the damp ground and willow trees kept vigil along the banks of the creek. A narrow lane connected the house to the road, passing a smaller cottage on the way. Train tracks ran parallel along the other side of the highway and further down a tall, angular house listed slightly, shreds of tarpaper exposed and flapping in the wind.

The next morning Alice got ready for school and walked to the bus stop. In the distance she could make out the figure of a boy crouched over an object on the ground. As she drew near she saw he had stuffed his shoelace into a bottle filled with clear liquid and was striking matches, trying to light the other end like a fuse. So intent was the boy upon this effort that he didn't notice Alice until she was standing directly in front of him.

He looked up, squinting into the early morning sun and saw the halo of a girl wearing knee socks and an ill-fitting brown dress. There was a sash over one shoulder, a change purse belted at her waist, and she was fiddling with a locket that hung around her neck. The boy scrambled to his feet and the two children regarded one another.

"Are you the new girl?" he asked.

Alice tilted her head, taking him in.

"That depends on your point of view," she replied.

"Ms. Kemp said there was one coming."

"Then I guess the cat's out of the bag," she said, her gaze even and cool.

"What are you wearing?" he asked, "It looks kind of official."

The girl gave a twisted smile and straightened her shoulders.

"For your information, it's a Brownie uniform. I'd call that official."

"Are you a Brownie?"

"Technically no, but I'm hoping to join the local chapter."

A light breeze picked up, coaxing the tendrils of her hair, and a truck drove by hauling pigs meant for slaughter.

"Did you earn all those?" he asked, nodding at the badges attached to her sash. Alice did not respond, staring at the boy with an inscrutable expression as if trying to make up her mind on some fundamental point of concern.

"Not exactly," she said.

The bus pulled up and the doors hissed open.

"What's your name, anyway?" he asked. The girl fished

through her change purse and presented him with a small white card. *Alice Quinn* it said, in handwriting that made liberal use of curlicues and stars.

"That's nice," he said, "Mine's Remy. Stay close."

The kids who rode the bus to Starling Elementary were an uncommon lot. Collected from the far reaches of the community, from remote, patched-together dwellings left unfinished both outside and in, they were easily distinguished from the neighborhood children who lived close enough to walk. The bus kids appeared half wild, like the dogs that skulked at their doorsteps–unkempt, mangy, and mean. They averted their gaze and walked with a permanent flinch, as one who expects to be kicked at any moment. The stench percolating from within the depths of the bus was a combination of dirty clothes, fetid armpits, rotten breath, and the searing reek of farts released at intervals by the Gorsma twins.

The boys were hulking and overgrown, with oily shocks of hair falling across their faces. They wore work boots and jean jackets, the rough fabric softened by a glaze of filth accrued from years of having never been washed. They packed their lips with tobacco, spewing dark treacle out the window or onto the floor of the bus. A few stared blankly at nothing in particular, picking their zits until they ran with pus and blood. Their mouths hung open in a dull expression, an impassive mask that kept the rest of the world at bay. In some cases this was a fair indication of their faculties, but either way–better to be branded a waste, a no-good, a troublemaker in Starling than to be known as someone with thoughts and interests, a genuine curiosity to learn.

The girls wore t-shirts like sausage casings, making painfully apparent their ample cleavage or lack thereof. They cursed loudly and made lewd gestures across the aisle, ravenous for attention and willing to do anything to get it. Fights occurred on a regular basis–brewing jealousies that erupted in kicking, slaps, and scratches; clumps of hair yanked out and brandished like trophies in the air. Black liner ringed their eyes and they laughed excessively for no reason–a harsh, braying guffaw that served as distraction from the knowledge they were headed for ruin like cabbages gone early to seed.

Some kids passed around cigarettes, sneaking a puff. Others hunched over dirty comics, jabbing at the pages and sniggering together. A few listened to heavy metal on transistor radios, the volume turned so loud there was feedback buzzing through the bus like a blender on the fritz.

Alice felt dizzy. She tried to stay close to Remy but the lurching of the bus and the gauntlet of knees and elbows made this impossible. Someone kicked her ankle and pushed her from behind.

"*Slut*," hissed a voice as Alice fell, clawing the air on her way down.

Laughter and the smell of stale urine wafted over the girl, and for a moment she panicked, thinking she couldn't breathe.

Remy turned around in time to see this happen. He clambered back and reached for Alice's hand, pulling her to her feet.

"I told you to stay close," he said, ushering her to an empty bench.

"Someone tripped me," she muttered, staring straight ahead.

"It was probably Mona Gorsma. She's psycho. If it wasn't her, then it was probably one of her stupid cousins," he replied.

"Does her eyeshadow make her look like a Chinese dragon?" she asked.

"I dunno," said Remy, intrigued by the notion.

"Well, she smells," the girl said softly, trying to fix the barrette in her hair.

"Like what?" Remy leaned forward.

"I don't want to say," she replied.

"Like piss?" he suggested.

"That's one way of putting it."

There was a stretch of silence as the bus drove down a gravel road, heading for the highway. The boy pulled an object from his pocket. It was a small, rectangular rock in variegated shades of brown, a weathered increment of juts and ridges.

"Here," he said, "You can have this."

The girl said nothing and Remy snuck a look at her from the corner of his eye. She was pale and thin, staring at the seat in front of her as if it might, by her will, open to reveal an escape.

"It's petrified wood," he continued, "From a tree that lived a million years ago. It hardened over time, like a rock. Stronger than a rock, even. Nothing can destroy it. You can't chop it. You can't burn it. Nothing."

The bus rolled on, pitching and jerking over the bumpy road.

"And they call it *petrified*? As in scared stiff?" she finally said.

"Yeah. Kind of funny, now you mention it. Scared or not, nothing can break it."

He set the offering on Alice's knee. The relic sat there a moment, untouched, then she picked it up and put it in her change purse.

CHAPTER

By the time Remy and Alice made it to their classroom, stopping first at the office so the girl could check in, the second bell had rung. Its harsh, incessant noise grated on the nerves of their teacher, Ms. Kemp, who was already in a foul mood. By way of explanation, it could be said Ms. Kemp was not a morning person, nor was she wont to rally at any given point during the day. She was perhaps a "glass half-empty" type, disinclined toward sunny dispositions in general. But these theories merely distracted from the heart of the matter, which was an intense, seething contempt for her students.

Ms. Kemp hated children. She loathed their trusting faces and insipid questions, their roundabout way of doing things. She couldn't abide their easy optimism and simple delights, their natural curiosity and inability to remain still. Yet to question her choice of employment was to call upon a logic foreign to these parts. People did what they did; they were what they were.

Most livelihoods emerged through a process of default, by nothing else happening to get in the way. To question the sense of an outcome, to probe the reason behind a result, to ask why someone who detested children would end up in a classroom full of them was to channel a higher way of thinking. It opened the door to conjecture, notions of autonomy and change–ideas not especially familiar or welcomed around Starling.

Ms. Kemp looked up as Remy and Alice stood in the doorway, noting the girl's pale face. Already she didn't like her. There was something about the child–a delicate, ethereal air that often inspired one of two reactions in others: to protect or destroy.

Loretta Kemp wanted to destroy.

"Take your seat, Mr. LaPierre," she said, "You're late."

Remy hesitated.

"This is Alice," he said, "She's the new girl."

"Oh, *is* she?" exclaimed Ms. Kemp, "The *new* girl? And all the way from Caribou, I understand. How lucky we are you decided to join us!"

Ms. Kemp's voice made the hair stand up on the back of Alice's neck. The teacher seemed to be waiting for a response, but it was unclear to the girl exactly what she was supposed to say.

"Thank you," she mumbled.

"No, thank *you*," said Ms. Kemp, smiling in a way that

exposed a brace of curiously small teeth, "I'm sure *we're* the ones who are graced by your presence."

Ms. Kemp took a piece of paper from her desk and called Alice to the front of the room. The girl wavered on the threshold, as if some alternate course of action might present itself. Of course there was nothing to be done but comply and she stepped forward, the narrow corridor of desks springing up before her like the jaws of a steel trap.

"Class, this is Alice Quinn. Can we all give her a big, warm welcome?" announced Ms. Kemp.

The students stared at Alice. No one said a word.

"Alice comes to us all the way from Caribou," she continued brightly, "Isn't that exciting? But that's not the half of it. Her father is a *sea captain!* A real, actual sea captain. Isn't that right, Alice?"

Alice looked at Ms. Kemp. The teacher waved the paper and raised an eyebrow as the girl stared, stiffening with recognition.

It was her registration form.

By all accounts Alice was a timid child, the spark of protest having long since been extinguished by a series of earlier defeats. Yet somewhere there exists, even in the meekest of souls, a line that is not to be crossed. To trespass that limit is to step on hallowed ground, awakening a force that is blind to consequence and fearsome to behold.

For Alice, that line was her father.

"Yes, that's right," she said.

Ms. Kemp's eyes narrowed. She had not expected a challenge.

"Really? How *fascinating*. Why don't you tell us where your father is right now?"

Alice stared ahead as if the classroom had become a vast, unfathomable space.

"Surely you know?" persisted the teacher.

"He's in Ceylon," said Alice softly.

"I beg your pardon?" said Ms. Kemp.

"I said, he's in *Ceylon*. Surely you know where that is?" said Alice, her hand clenching the piece of petrified wood.

A deathly silence settled over the room.

"It's off the coast of India," continued the girl, "A tiny island shaped like a pearl, only now they call it Sri Lanka. But I'm sure you knew that, too."

She stood like someone expecting a wave to crash over her head, but the look on her face was resolute.

Ms. Kemp was trembling when she reached for the girl. She spun Alice around, her pale eyes inflamed with rage. In so doing, she happened to notice the locket around the girl's neck. She picked it up and said, "Is this a gift from your father? Did *this* come from Ceylon?"

Before Alice could respond, Ms. Kemp yanked the necklace, causing the chain to snap and dangle from her hand.

"This is what happens to children who talk back," said Ms. Kemp in low, menacing tones, "Go to the front of the room and stand with your nose to the wall until you're ready to apologize for your behavior!"

Alice approached the chalkboard without knowing it was there. She could not see or hear, nor was she aware of anything except the point on her neck where the chain had snapped. The necklace was not a gift from her father, after all; it was just a trinket she'd found beneath a bench at a bus station years ago. But as time went on, she convinced herself it was in fact a family heirloom, passed down through the generations from an ancestor who'd managed to smuggle it out of revolutionary France.

Throughout the morning, Alice remained at the board where Ms. Kemp had written the words *sea captain's daughter* over her head with a piece of white chalk. The girl stood straight and tall, but as the day wore on the strain of her punishment became evident. Her shoulders drooped. She swayed on occasion and had to reach for the ledge to regain her balance. Remy did not take his eyes off her. Ms. Kemp watched as well, but the teacher could not be bothered to spend the greater part of her day in the classroom. She went in and out, taking smoke breaks in the teachers' lounge, refreshing her cup of coffee, and pausing in the doorway of Mr. Bouchard's classroom to call out a greeting and laugh excessively at his response.

During one of these excursions, Remy got up to sharpen his pencil and made a detour past the chalkboard. He set a slip of paper and a round, yellow jawbreaker on the ledge.

"Thank you," Alice whispered, but the boy was already halfway back to his desk. She unfolded the note, which contained an elaborate diagram of the classroom riddled with arrows and the words: *watch for my signel!! I'm gonna bust u out!!*

The girl nodded and was about to raise the candy to her lips when it multiplied before her, blurred, and faded into darkness.

Ms. Kemp returned to the classroom in time to see Alice faint. The teacher watched her crumple and heaved a sigh, as if her lot in life had just been made manifestly more difficult.

Remy reached the girl first.

"Alice!" he exclaimed, nudging her shoulder. He rolled the girl onto her back where she lay blinking at the crowd of children who huddled over her. Someone brought a pile of wet paper towels and Remy plastered them across her forehead until she looked like a wounded soldier returning home from one of the great world wars.

"Get her in a desk," snapped Ms. Kemp, incensed by the notion a mere fainting could undermine her authority, "And push it over to the chalkboard. She's still in detention. Unless, that is, you have something you'd like to say to me, Miss Quinn?"

Alice opened her mouth, but no words came out.

"She's trying to speak!" screamed Corrine LeRoy, who could always be counted upon when the moment allowed for hysterics. The students leaned closer. Ms. Kemp waited expectantly as the girl held out her hand, beckoning to the teacher.

"*Give…it…back*," she croaked.

When the bell rang at the end of the day, Ms. Kemp dismissed the entire class except Alice, who was still sitting in the desk by the chalkboard. She waited until the room was empty and the hallways were clear, then got up from her desk and walked over to the girl, leaning in until there was not five inches between them.

"Listen to me, you little brat," she hissed, her breath a cesspool of coffee grinds and cigarettes, "I don't know how they run things in Caribou, but out here children mind their elders or they learn it the hard way!" She clamped her hand on Alice's arm, digging her fingernails into the girl's flesh.

Alice did not move. She could not speak or breathe.

Suddenly, there was a terrific crash at the window. The girl and the teacher whirled around in time to see a dead cat slide down the glass pane, leaving in its wake a streak of blood and guts.

Ms. Kemp screamed. Footsteps clattered down the hallway and Mr. Bouchard rushed into the room.

"What's the matter?!" he exclaimed.

Ms. Kemp pointed to the window with a trembling finger. Mr. Bouchard strode across the room and peered at the carnage.

"Holy crow!" he whistled, shaking his head, "Would you look at that? Those damn kids, those crazy sons of guns!"

He turned to Ms. Kemp, making a gesture as if to offer comfort when he noticed Alice sitting in the desk nearby.

"Why not let your student run along and we'll get to the bottom of this," he said, raising his eyebrow in a manner that was not lost upon the girl.

The only thing that could have possibly convinced Ms. Kemp to release her captive was just such an offer. She straightened the waistband of her skirt and reached back to smooth her hair.

"Get lost," she muttered, not even bothering to look at the girl.

Alice hurried down the hallway and pushed the school doors open, stepping out into the afternoon sunlight. The air was gentle yet crisp at the edges, a reminder the season was on the verge of change. The playground was empty. The bus had long since departed and Alice's mother was at home, sleeping off her shift. For a moment the girl stood frozen, not knowing which way to go. An owl hooted in the distance and she lurched forward, setting off in the direction of the highway. The hooting grew increasingly more shrill until the girl finally stopped and turned, scanning her surroundings. All was calm except for a stately maple that stood next to the playground, its branches shaking as if in the eye of a storm. The girl folded her arms and stared as Remy peeked from the foliage, making urgent gestures and nearly falling out of the tree.

"Shhh," he hissed, "Don't let them see you looking at me!"

Alice retraced her steps and bent over to tie her shoe.

"What are you doing up there?" she asked.

"I said I was going to bust you out and I meant it," he replied.

"That was *you* with the cat?" she asked.

"Yeah, I found it on the road over by Red's."

"Was it dead?"

"What do you take me for? Of course it was dead!"

"Let me get this straight–you walked all the way from the gas station holding a *dead cat?!*"

Alice tugged at a knot in her shoelace.

"Don't worry, I made sure no one saw me," said the boy.

"All things considered, that's the least of my concerns!"

"Well it worked, didn't it?" he said, "I got you out, didn't I?"

"Yeah, but you threw a dead cat at the school!" she exclaimed.

"*Shhh!* What did the cat care? It was already dead. And I needed to create a diversion. Besides, you're free now, aren't you? Doesn't that count for something?"

Alice looked at the gouge marks on her arm.

"Yeah, it counts. It counts for a lot."

From his perch in the tree, Remy looked down upon the girl. She appeared smaller and somehow more vulnerable, her arms thin, her elbows pointy and sharp. Wisps of silvery blonde hair escaped her braids and floated in the breeze. For the second time that day he thought he was seeing an angel.

CHAPTER

On Saturday morning Alice struggled against her blankets, trapped in the space between wakefulness and sleep. Her dreams had been hounded by a faceless man who kept finding her hiding places, drawing so near the girl could hardly breathe. Alice kicked off the covers and curled into a ball, a sob catching in her throat. She rocked back and forth, her breathing ragged as she opened her eyes and made herself take in the room.

The house was quiet but the girl could tell her mother was there, sleeping off her shift. She did not have to verify this by opening Penny's bedroom door; it was just a sense she had, knowing when she was alone. In the kitchen she found some bread and peanut butter, rummaging through the drawers for a knife. She sat at the table with her sandwich and looked out the window, discerning the shadowy outline of a boy on the fence post, hunched over in the appearance of sleep. The girl froze, as if motion might dispel this curious find. When she counted to ten and nothing changed, she slipped on her shoes and went outside.

"What are you doing here?" she said, tearing her sandwich in half and offering part to the boy.

"Thought you might wanna go fishing," said Remy, jumping down from the fence and gesturing at the ground. A shovel, bucket, and battered tackle box lay beside him in the weeds.

"At this hour?" Alice folded her arms and shivered.

"No better time."

He handed her the tackle box and the children trooped through the wet grass to a fallow section of land behind a bank of wild rosebushes. Here the boy stopped and kicked at the dirt.

"This is where we dig," he announced.

He grabbed the shovel and raised it high in the air. Plunging it into the earth, he jumped on the blade with both feet, rocking back and forth until it was buried to the hilt. The boy looked at Alice and raised an eyebrow.

"Watch this," he said, prying a clump of meaty, black soil from the ground. Alice stared at the slew of corpulent worms lodged in the dirt, waving like the serpents on a gorgon's head.

"Holy crow!" she breathed, crouching down for a better look.

"Yep. Looks like we hit the jackpot," he said, straightening up and shaking the hair out of his eyes, "Let's put 'em in the bucket."

Alice lifted the clump from the shovel and let it crumble in her hands. The worms writhed on the ground, shape-shifting in signs and symbols. She picked them up one by one and placed them in the bucket, mesmerized by their contortions.

"Add some dirt so they don't dry out," said Remy.

"I never would've thought of that," she replied, squinting up at the boy.

Remy cleared his throat and turned away, throwing his weight with fresh vigor into the excavation of a new hole. He scowled when his shovel hit an obstacle and fell to his knees, scraping at the earth, intent on some riveting, new discovery.

"Look," he exclaimed, "Potatoes!"

He held one up for her to see. Alice took the object from his hand and brushed the dirt off its pale, golden skin.

"They're perfect!" she exclaimed.

"We could build a fire and roast 'em," said the boy.

"This must have been a garden once," said Alice, looking around, "I bet it's been years since anyone was here."

"We found it," declared Remy, "That makes it ours."

"Yes," said the girl, warming to the notion, "A secret garden, like the one in the book."

"What book?" asked Remy.

"Oh, just this story," said Alice, "About a girl living in India whose parents die from a fever. She ends up getting shipped back to England to live with her rich uncle in his creepy mansion, and all she does is act like a royal pain."

"What does she do?" asked Remy, who had stopped digging for potatoes.

"Oh, you name it—this girl makes a fuss over every little thing. She knocks her breakfast tray off the bed because she doesn't like the food, she demands help in getting dressed, but the worst part is when she slaps the maid!"

Remy stared, unable to comprehend a scenario that involved a maid.

"Then what happens?" he said.

"Well…she makes friends with a boy who lives nearby and they discover an abandoned garden and bring it back to life. As time goes on, the girl smartens up and stops being such a brat. But there's also a mystery in the house because she keeps hearing someone scream, except the servants won't tell her who it is. Turns out she has a cousin hidden away in a secret bedroom who's one hell of a crybaby. He's all sick and pasty, and keeps complaining he can't walk. The girl hates him at first, but little by little they patch things up. She starts sneaking him out to the garden in his wheelchair so he can breathe the fresh air and get stronger. Then one day he decides to try and stand up, and guess what? Turns out he can walk, after all."

"What about the boy?" asked Remy.

"Which boy?" said Alice "There were two of 'em."

"The *first* boy. The one she made friends with. What

happened to him after the cousin came onto the scene?"

"Oh, I'm pretty sure they stayed friends," said Alice.

"You're *pretty sure?*" Remy said, leaning on his shovel and squinting at the girl, "Didn't the story *say* so?"

"I can't remember exactly," admitted Alice, "It's been awhile since I read it. But I'm almost certain that's what happened."

"Well," said Remy, jabbing his shovel into the earth, "Sounds like the cousin came along and messed the whole thing up."

"Not really," said Alice, "If anything, it was good for the girl to find out she had all this extra family. Don't forget, her parents were dead."

"Good for the *girl*, maybe," said Remy, setting the potatoes in the bucket, "But I bet her friend wanted to strap that kid into his chair and roll him down a hill."

"You didn't even read the book," said Alice, tossing her head, "So you don't know what you're talking about."

"Don't need to read the book," said the boy, "I know what I know."

He was about to dig another hole when Alice suddenly jumped to her feet.

"Wait here," she said, "I have to get something for the potatoes."

The girl ran into the house and peeled some wrinkled sheets of tinfoil from a ball she kept in the kitchen. The warmth of the bungalow made her skin prickle and she tiptoed to her room for a sweater, listening in the hallway until she could hear the sound of her mother's breath.

The children made their way down to the creek. Remy scoured the area, kicking at dead undergrowth until he found what he was looking for–a sturdy pair of branches no more than three feet long. He opened his tackle box and retrieved a spool of fishing line, fastening a length to the end of each branch. To the end of the line he attached a hook, threading the plastic cord through its eye and tying a detailed knot. The knot was a thing of beauty, an exquisitely woven coil, and as Alice watched the boy work the unruly strand into its elegant design she had the feeling if she called his name, if perhaps even a clap of thunder were to split the sky, he wouldn't so much as blink. He wound the line around the branch until it was taut, imbedding the tip of the hook into the bark, then repeated the procedure with the second branch, not pausing to look up.

"Here," he said when he was finished, handing the branch to the girl, "This one's for you."

"Thanks," she said.

"C'mon," he stood up, carrying his fishing pole and tackle box, "Let's go catch some fish."

Alice picked up the bucket of worms and followed along.

The crisp air was like a draught of good luck and the morning sun, still on the rise, sparkled across the water where dragonflies lit on the surface, resting a heartbeat before whooshing away. Here and there a rustling in the bushes exposed the flight of some small creature, startled by this sudden invasion. The twittering birds and gentle current wove a canopy of song as the children walked on in silence, climbing over fallen logs, weaving through the grass, taking care not to brush against stinging nettles or catch their hooks on the branches overhead. They stopped at a bend in the creek, the water pooling around the roots of a massive willow that leaned over the bank. It was the boy's favorite fishing hole.

"Look," he whispered.

The dark shape of a trout hung motionless in the depths of the pool. A smaller fish drifted by on the current, as if it was too taxing to summon the least shred of resistance.

Remy reached into the bucket and pulled out a worm, piercing its fleshy end with the hook and threading its body several times through.

"Oh!" winced Alice, "That looks awful!"

"Nah, it doesn't hurt 'em." The boy shook his head.

"How do you know?" she persisted, "Do you have any way of proving that?"

Remy shrugged.

"It's just a worm, Alice. Their brains are the size of fly poop."

He gestured for her fishing rod.

"You want me to bait yours?"

The girl hesitated, examining the lint on her sweater.

"I think I'll just watch," she said.

The boy lowered his hook into the pool, the worm a pale turban of flesh sinking through shafts of light until it disappeared in the shadows. Alice stood motionless as a butterfly sailed through the clearing, lighting on a milkweed bloom. It opened and closed its wings, then lifted and flew away. The girl sat on a nearby stump and watched Remy's fishing line drift across the water, cutting through clouds of gnats and pond skaters on the surface of the pool. Birdsongs filtered through the treetops, a repetitious exchange with intervals of silence measured between. Alice hugged her knees and lifted her face to the sun. She opened her eyes and smiled at the boy, who blinked and looked away.

A sudden shiver went up the line, tugging at the pole. The boy gave it a slight jerk and a fish sailed out of the water, flashing in the sunlight.

"You got one!" cried the girl, scrambling to her feet.

Remy lowered the fish to the ground where it thrashed in the weeds, a futility of struggle. With expert ease he removed the hook and held it up for Alice to see.

"Look!" he said.

The fish was indeed a beauty–a plump, shimmering trout big enough for the boy to hold with both hands. The scales were speckled and steeped in olive green, a horizon of blush streaking the sides, its belly soft and pale.

"It's a keeper!" crowed the boy, "Twelve inches at least!"

He noted the expression on the girl's face.

"Maybe you shouldn't watch," he added, "You might not like this part."

"It's okay," said Alice, her words running together, "Just because I've never been this close to the food chain doesn't mean I should pretend it doesn't exist. I mean, this is the circle of life, right?"

Remy stared at her.

"I have no idea what you just said."

"Never mind," she waved her hands, "I get this way when I'm nervous."

The boy held the fish by the tail and whapped its head against a rock.

Alice covered her eyes and turned away.

When the fish was dead Remy found a forked branch on the ground and stripped the bark with his jackknife, paring one of the tips to a point. A breeze came into the clearing and aspen leaves, like yellow coins, fluttered through the air. Remy took the trout and threaded it by the gill onto the sharpened branch.

Alice held out her hand.

"Here, I'll hold it," she offered.

"You sure?" asked Remy.

"Yes," she said, gazing at him with a fervent expression, "I can't believe you actually caught a fish!"

Remy turned away, alarmed by the sudden bolt of energy surging through him, the grin that appeared without warning and felt like a foreign direction on his face.

Alice held the branch aloft like a torch and followed the boy, stepping where he stepped, ducking where he ducked, wading, climbing, and moving exactly as he did.

By late morning the children could hear their stomachs growling. They scrambled up the creek bank and found a clearing in the midst of an aspen grove that seemed a suitable place to cook their fish.

"Where are we?" asked Alice, scanning the landscape in every direction.

"Just a ways upstream from your place," said Remy, pointing toward the Quinn's bungalow in the distance, "This here is Anderson's field. He won't mind if we use it, long as we don't burn anything down."

"You sure?" said Alice, biting her lip.

"Yeah," nodded the boy, adding, "Pretty sure," under his breath as he turned to gather kindling for the fire.

The girl stood watching him, lost between wonder and alarm for this apparent lack of concern. She gazed across the pasture once more, at the vast space and the mountains beyond, then got to work digging a pit in the center of the clearing and lining it with stones. She took the potatoes to the creek and scrubbed them in the water, emptying the bucket of remaining worms where the earth was soft and black. When she returned, she saw the boy had dragged a dead log into the clearing and was seated before a crackling blaze.

"Here," he said, handing her his jackknife, "Poke some holes in'em so they don't explode from the heat."

Alice marked the potatoes carefully, covering them in patterns of dots and stars. The boy leaned forward, watching over her shoulder.

"Looks like Easter eggs," he said.

"Exactly!" she nodded, delighted he saw it. She wrapped the potatoes in tinfoil and set them by the fire, and the boy buried them in the coals using a paddle of bark.

Remy picked up the fish and turned to leave.

"Make sure you keep the fire going," he said to the girl.

"How am I supposed to do that?" she asked.

"Easy. Just poke it with a stick."

The boy gutted the fish where the creek ran shallow, watching the innards slip over the rocks and wash away in the current. He stripped a branch off a sapling and let it soak in the water, then took it back to the clearing and wrapped a section in tinfoil. Next, he found a forked branch similar in size to the one used to carry the fish and jammed them into the ground on either side of the fire. Draping the trout over the foil-covered stick, he rested each end on the branches.

Alice watched from where she sat, her arms clasped around her legs. The boy kept his eyes on the fire, mesmerized by the flickering flames.

"How long have you lived here?" she asked.

"I dunno. Pretty much my whole life, I guess," replied Remy.

"What do you mean, you don't know? Were you born here?" pressed the girl, who was drawn to the notion of stability like a mirage in the desert.

"Well, I was born in Caribou, at the hospital. But we always lived here."

"Who's *we?*"

"My dad and my brother."

"You have a brother?"

"Yeah."

"Older or younger?"

"Older."

"What's his name?"

"Simon."

"And your dad? What's his name?"

"Gilles."

"What about your mom?"

"She's dead."

The children sat staring into the fire, adding pieces of wood as the boy deemed necessary. Alice dug the potatoes out of the coals and poked them with a stick.

"I think these are done," she said.

She pried the tinfoil from the steaming vegetables while the boy removed the trout from the fire. The skin had shriveled and charred in places, but the meat inside was soft and pink. He set the fish on a piece of foil, lifting the delicate bones from its flesh. Alice adorned the food with a wreath of dandelions and the boy wiped the knife on his jeans, cutting the potatoes in fours. They ate in silence, burning their fingers and tongues, the smoky trout and roasted potatoes tasting better than anything they had eaten in their entire lives.

CHAPTER 4

The next morning was Sunday. Alice woke up and went into the kitchen. She looked out the window and saw Remy sitting on the fence. His head hung down and she stepped behind the curtain, gripped by the thrill of watching without being seen. Before long, however, the vantage point felt onerous so she made two peanut butter sandwiches and took them outside.

"Hey," she said, offering one to the boy.

He took it, nodding.

"How long have you been out here?" she asked.

"I dunno. Not long," he said.

"You look frozen," said the girl.

"Nah."

"Well, my mom is sleeping or I'd ask you in," she said.

"It's okay."

The song of a lark announced its safe passage through the night and the girl ate her sandwich, stealing glances at the boy.

"What happened to you?" she finally asked.

Remy's eyelid was swollen, a faint bruise seeping beneath the skin.

"Nothing," he said.

Alice stared at the ground, a tightness in her throat. A breeze ruffled the weeds and a ladybug tottered up a tall blade of grass.

"Well, what do you wanna do?" she said.

"Let's go get some candy from Red's," the boy replied.

"Do you have any money?" she asked.

"Yeah, about a dollar."

"Wait here a minute," said the girl. She tiptoed into the bungalow and took her mother's purse from the back of the kitchen chair. Rummaging through its contents, she found some loose change at the bottom and went back outside.

"I have about a dollar, too," she said.

The children walked down the lane toward the highway. As they passed the second bungalow Alice asked, "Who lives there?"

"A lady named Madame Voisine," said Remy.

"What's she like?"

"I dunno. She's old. Some people say she's a witch."

"Who's *some people?*"

"My brother. The kids at school."

Alice turned to look at the bungalow. It was covered in vines and nestled amidst lilac bushes, its doorframe crooked, the windows small and dark. The girl folded her arms.

"Do you think she is?"

"What, a *witch?* I dunno. She *is* pretty creepy."

"Being creepy doesn't make someone a witch."

"Yeah, well it doesn't exactly help her case, either."

Alice cast a backward glance at the bungalow.

"Maybe she doesn't know she's on trial," she said.

The children crossed the highway and walked along the train tracks. It had rained the night before and the wooden ties lay soggy between puddles of water shimmering in shades of purple and green.

"Is that where you live?" asked Alice, as they passed the tattered house.

"Yeah," said Remy.

"Which one's your room?"

"Up there." He pointed to the only window on the second floor, then hunched his shoulders and turned away.

The house was tall and narrow, a whim of assembly. It was weather beaten grey, with splintered boards and sheets of plywood tacked over tarpaper and insulation bleached white by the sun. There was a slight tilt to the structure and cracks like fault lines spread across the windows, held together by pieces of electrical tape. The muddy yard was carved deep with tire tracks, the territorial domain for a pack of lean, ragged dogs. Alice blinked. For a split second it seemed as if the house was watching her, not someone inside but rather the structure itself–watching and waiting, content for the moment to bide its time.

The girl shivered and looked away. She peered at her reflection in a puddle but this was also unsettling and she withdrew, kicking a shower of pebbles into the water. The sun disappeared behind some clouds and she took off running, taunting the boy as she passed him, though he had no idea why she started the race.

"If you could fly or be invisible, what would you choose?" she called out, hopping from one tie to the next. Remy looked up. The girl stood on her tiptoes, nimble and light, and for a moment he forgot to answer the question.

"Well?" she held up her hands, waiting.

"I'd fly," said the boy.

Alice stopped and spun around.

"How do you know?!" she exclaimed, "How can you decide so quickly?"

Remy shrugged and looked at the ground, trying not to smile.

"I dunno. Easy, I guess. Just pick one and go with it."

"That kills me!" said Alice, "I spend *hours* thinking about these things and I can never decide. I can't *bear* to make up my mind!"

She took a few more steps then paused, balancing on one foot.

"How about this," she continued, "Which would you rather have–the power to breathe underwater or see in the dark?"

"See in the dark."

"Remy! You didn't give that a second thought. You're just trying to show off!"

"I am not!" protested Remy, shaking his head yet refusing to look her in the eye.

"Yes, you are."

"No, I'm not!"

"Then why are you smiling?"

"I'm not!"

"You are, too."

Alice turned around, skipping backward on the ties, tilting her face to the sky and breathing deeply as the boy went on protesting his innocence in a way that made the air smell sweeter, still.

The walk to Red's took the better part of the morning. The children meandered, picking foxtails to tickle late season grasshoppers caught sluggishly awaiting the sun. They lingered over spider webs beaded with dew and filled their pockets with rocks deemed too marvelous to leave behind. Alice discovered a tiny nest in the weeds that looked like spun sugar and Remy found the tail feather of a hawk. The white sun burned through the low hanging clouds and cleared a tenuous peephole in the hastening sky.

    Red's was something of a watering hole for the old-timers in the area. It was both a gas station and convenience store, with a lunch counter off to one side where farmers hunched over cups of black coffee, cocooned in dirty barn coats and woolen mackinaws. They wore trucker hats pulled low over whiskered faces, their pleasantries limited to grunts, nods, and silence. The children came into the store, swinging the door wide. No one paid them any attention and they headed for the candy aisle.

    The candy aisle at Red's was nothing short of hallowed ground for the children of Starling. It inspired hours of meditation, of scrutiny and debate, of yearnings, epiphanies, and in some cases a deep, trance-like state. There were boxes of penny candies, of blue gummy sharks and cherry flavored feet with oversized toes. There were fizzy jawbreakers, miles of licorice whips, bottle caps, and blistering, atomic fireballs. Heavy glass jars containing butterscotch buttons, candy necklaces, and Swedish berries lined the shelves, and a barrel filled with jellybeans sat next to them on the floor.

    Frog bombs were highly prized–those massive, rubbery gumdrops that alternated flavors during consumption, turning one's tongue to glorious shades of purple, orange, and green. Even better were the honey slugs–hardened candy shells containing a coiled, gelatinous strip that unraveled to the length of a garden hose and took two days of solid eating in order to be consumed. Marshmallow putty, sour strings, and taffy licks came next, and beside these sat a careful arrangement of tiny wax bottles filled with neon syrup, bearing the imprint of a skull and crossbones. The bottles held a particular appeal, as the only way to open one was by biting off its cap. Candy cigarettes were popular with the younger children, especially during winter months when they could pretend to smoke outside and watch their breath billow up like clouds in the air. Bubble gum came in every flavor, in dime-sized balls stacked in colors of the rainbow and bright pink rectangles wrapped in comic strips printed on wax paper. Best of all, the pixie sticks contained a sugary dust that, if inhaled properly, could make a child sneeze until blue liquid dribbled from his nose.

To be in the presence of so much sugar, to observe it refined into an endless array of colors, shapes, and flavors was both a balm and an elixir, bringing reverence and ruin to the young minds who beheld it. It was like being warmed by the sun in one moment, then consumed by its glory the next.

Remy watched as the girl stood motionless before this display. She seemed weightless, transfixed by the splendor. He could see it had eclipsed her point of reference, that she was no longer walking on a mortal plane, and he fought the urge to take her by the hand. Instead, he busied himself with pulling a small paper sack from a pile on the shelf and snapping it open it with a flourish.

"Let's put all our candy in one bag," he suggested, "That way we can share it…if you want."

Alice nodded absently, her attention drawn to the container of candy necklaces on the bottom shelf. She crouched down to inspect them, a shadow flickering across her face.

"I want it *back,*" she whispered.

The boy heard this and stood up straight, clenching his fists.

Nearly an hour later, when all the combinations and permutations of two whole dollars to be spent on candy had been thoroughly exhausted, the children took their sack to the front counter in order to make their purchase.

There were two ways for this transaction to occur. If Mr. Redchenko happened to be working, he would eye the sack dispassionately and ask how much was owed. The money would then be laid out in a grubby array of coins which he'd scoop into his palm and scatter in the till. If, on the other hand, his wife was at the counter, the exchange went down like a ruthless interrogation from the cold war.

Mrs. Redchenko's real name was Olga, but the children secretly called her the Warden. The nickname stemmed from a long, jagged scar on her cheek which Kevin Olenski claimed she got during a prison riot, where she'd been an inmate on death row. According to Kevin, the injured woman killed a guard during the mayhem and stole his uniform. In the ensuing chaos, she was mistakenly escorted to freedom in the back of an ambulance that was later found at the bottom of a ravine, burned to a crisp. What became of the driver? No one knew, but a hiker in the area reported hearing the bone-chilling screams of a man begging for his life. Of course, the hiker went missing soon after that.

Were there holes in this story? Not if you asked the children of Starling. Given the nature of their association with Olga Redchenko, it was the only theory that added up, the only explanation that made any sense.

The Warden established a baseline of fear with her young customers before they could even approach the register to make a purchase. She had them stand off to one side like a subset of society, a lower class, forbidding anyone to approach until she'd ignored them for what seemed like an eternity. When a child inevitably lapsed into distraction, the Warden would make a sudden, guttural noise and fix her budding patron with a glare that could liquefy the bones of a grown man.

She then demanded the children spill the contents of their sacks onto the counter and tally the candies before her. This was an exercise in psychological warfare, for if a child faltered beneath her gaze and lost track of the count, he had to begin all over again.

To complicate matters, the Warden had a lazy eye. Worse yet, no one could agree which eye it actually was. Peter Kowalski claimed it was her left eye while Kirby Chambers swore it was the right, but no one was willing to find out for sure.

However nerve-wracking it was to count out one's candy beneath the Warden's blistering gaze, the ordeal was made ten times worse if she said something that necessitated eye contact. For what could be more terrifying than trying to remember which eye was the safe one to look at? What could trump the fear of realizing, too late, that the wrong choice had been made as the Warden's eye began to drift like a boat out to sea, taking the child's horrified gaze with it?!

As luck would have it, Olga Redchenko was working the cash register that day. Remy automatically stepped to the side but Alice, being unfamiliar with this practice, marched straight up to the counter and plunked the bag of candy upon it.

There was a dreadful calm wherein nothing happened at all. Then the air began to pulse and quiver, gathering tension, as in the moment before lightning strikes. Suddenly, the Warden reared up and shook herself like a dragon roused from slumber. Alice cringed and made a gurgling sound as the boy watched in panic, unable to move. The Warden began to expand, her bosom swelling to such immense proportions it seemed she would either levitate or burst into smithereens. Remy gasped and lurched forward, wrenching out of his petrified stupor. He tried to snatch the bag of candy from the counter as if to turn back time, a vain attempt to erase the past few moments so the universe could go on without knowing what it was to incur the wrath of Olga Redchenko.

It was a heroic effort, doomed to fail. The Warden's hand whistled through the air like the blade of a guillotine and fell upon the boy's arm, trapping it in a vise-like grip.

"What do you think you're doing?" she barked in a voice thick with a guttural, faraway accent.

Remy looked up into a face that was fleshy and pink, anchored by a button nose and pendulous at the jowls. In spite of his horror, he was gripped by a fatal curiosity, a reckless compulsion to stand fast and take in every detail.

The Warden's lips glistened and lay open to reveal a set of sharp, uneven teeth. Her eyebrows had been plucked into oblivion and penciled high overhead, giving the effect of permanent contempt. A fine sheen of sweat beaded the mustache on her upper lip and the infamous scar spread across her cheek like a thick, pulsating worm. When she looked at the boy, her eyes pierced his defenses and broke off a piece of his soul.

"I said, what do you think you're doing?!"

Remy stared at the Warden, unable to stop himself from fixating on one eye then the other, back and forth in a frantic attempt to negotiate safe passage.

"I'm s-sorry," he stammered, "She's new here. She didn't know."

The Warden leaned closer until she was not ten inches from the boy, her nose wrinkled as if it detected something foul. Alice cowered between Remy and the counter, frozen by this harrowing display of trench warfare.

"You filthy little brats," hissed the woman in low tones, her breath smelling of pickled eggs and onions, "Someone should lock you up and throw away the key!"

To Remy's dismay, the Warden's eye began to drift like a driver asleep at the wheel. It rolled aimlessly at first, picking up speed, listing to one edge of its socket at the apparent mercy of some inner, gravitational pull. He watched without blinking, without breathing, like one unable to rouse from a terrible dream. He felt Alice shudder beneath him and knew she was watching, too.

A loud crash jolted the Warden from her inquisition and the children spun around to behold an elderly woman bending over a bottle that had shattered on the floor. She wore an enormous fur coat that was moth-eaten in places and her hair billowed up like storm clouds on a hot summer's day. The woman stood with regal bearing amidst the broken glass and rivulets of wine, her presence made somehow more formidable by the surrounding chaos and debris. Clearing her throat, the woman locked eyes with the Warden and waved a jagged bottleneck in her direction.

"Leave those…kids…alone." Her speech was unmistakably slurred, but the tone was not to be trifled with.

It was the Warden's turn to gasp. She sputtered and choked, clawing the air, unable to convert her outrage into words. Remy saw his chance. He opened his fist and released a handful of change onto the counter. Grabbing the bag of candy in one hand and Alice's arm with the other, he dashed out the door and took off running.

"Who was *that?!*" gasped Alice, trying to keep up as they reached the school and cut across the grounds.

"That," he replied, "was Madame Voisine."

CHAPTER 5

With the gas station safely in the distance the children slowed to a walk, making their way along a fence line that led down to the creek. Remy pried the barbed wire apart so Alice could pick her way through, a delicate maneuver that involved snagging her t-shirt on the rusty, sharpened spurs. She made it across and turned around, preparing to hold the wire for the boy when he grabbed a post with one hand and vaulted like a cat burglar over the fence.

"I didn't realize that was an option," she said, arching her brow.

"If you didn't realize, then it wasn't," he replied, ducking out of reach and hooting with laughter when the girl scowled and tried to push him.

The children meandered through the pasture, following the creek downstream. The late summer sun felt distant in the sky, the air devoid of chill yet no longer offering a warm embrace.

"Follow me, I wanna show you something," said the boy. He crossed the creek on a series of stones jutting from the water, scrambling up the bank into a jungle of growth. Here the terrain was dark and dense, woven with tangled saplings and ancient fir trees presiding overhead. Damp pockets of earth oozed between moldering logs and pale mushrooms shot up in patches across a layer of brilliant green moss. Remy made his way to higher ground, falling to his knees and parting the foliage to reveal a smooth, dry clearing hidden beneath a cluster of giant ferns. Alice crawled inside and sat down.

"It's a perfect, secret world," she whispered, gazing at the lace canopy as it filtered patterns of sunlight across her face. Watching her, Remy could not remember a time when he felt so calm.

He opened the paper sack and withdrew a candy necklace.

"Here," he said, "I got this for you."

"Oh!" said Alice, a crooked smile tugging at her lips.

She held the offering in her hands, deeply moved.

"I'm gonna get the real one back, too," he continued, "From Ms. Kemp."

Alice looked at the boy and her shoulders dropped.

"Remy, be serious. That's impossible! How are you going to do it?"

"I *am* serious," he said, scowling, "I don't know how I'm gonna do it, but I'll find a way."

The girl continued to stare at the boy, but he returned her gaze steadily until she looked away, shaking her head.

"That reminds me of a story I know about a lady who borrowed a necklace this one time," she said.

"What happened to her?" asked Remy, popping a cherry toe into his mouth.

"Well, she was young and beautiful, always wishing she had a better life–more money, nicer clothes, richer friends. She went around sulking all the time and it sounded like she was a real pill. One day her husband came home from work with tickets to a fancy ball, thinking this would make her happy."

"Did it?"

"No, just the opposite. She threw a fit because she had nothing nice to wear."

"*Women*," muttered the boy.

"*Please.* As if you know what you're talking about," said Alice, tossing her head.

"I'm just kidding. Go on."

"So…her husband gives her the money he was saving for a hunting trip and tells her to go buy a new dress. But does that make her happy? *No.* Instead, she starts in about needing some jewelry to go with it."

Alice paused and looked at the boy.

"*What?* I didn't say anything!" he protested.

"No, but I can tell what you're thinking."

"Alice. I just wanna hear the story. I promise."

"Well, there was no way they could afford to buy any jewelry. But then the husband remembered his wife had a childhood friend who was filthy rich. So the woman, whose name was Mathilde, visits her friend and asks if she can borrow something for the night of the ball. As it so happens, the friend has an entire *closet* full of jewels and Mathilde goes through the pieces one by one, trying them on. Finally, in the very last box, she finds exactly what she's looking for: a diamond necklace."

Remy looked up, riveted.

"*Solid* diamond?" he asked.

"Yeah."

The boy let out a long, low whistle.

"What happens next?"

"You don't wanna know."

"Alice!"

"Okay, but don't say I didn't warn you. Mathilde is finally happy as a clam. She wears the necklace to the ball and for one perfect evening her life is everything she'd dreamed it to be. No one could get enough of her. All the men want to dance with her and the ladies whisper behind her back, jealous of her beauty and wondering who she is. When the ball ends it's past midnight and Mathilde goes home with her husband, who'd fallen asleep while waiting for her. She gets inside the house and takes off her coat, looking in the mirror to admire herself one last time when suddenly, to her horror, she realizes…the necklace is gone!"

"Are you serious?" asked Remy, his mouth hanging open.

"Of course I'm serious! Why would I joke about a thing like that?"

The boy shook his head and cursed.

"I *know*," said Alice, "But trust me, it gets worse. They go all over the city retracing their steps and can't find the necklace anywhere."

Remy dropped his head into his hands.

"So now the heat is on and they have to scramble. Mathilde writes a note to her friend, stalling for time. She makes up a lie that the clasp on the necklace broke and they need to get it fixed. Meanwhile, the husband goes out and borrows a ton of money from loan sharks. They take the cash and hire a jeweler to make a new diamond necklace exactly like the one Mathilde lost, which she boxes up and gives to her friend."

The boy exhaled loudly, his face a war zone of emotion.

"What?! You're kidding me! Didn't her friend notice the difference?"

"Nope. That's how rich people are. She got huffy about the late return and all, but she didn't even bother to open the case and check."

Remy rummaged through the bag for a taffy lick,

confounded.

"Was that the end of the story?" he said.

"No way! The writer doesn't let you off that easy. He drags you through the next ten years of Mathilde's life. You have to watch her take these crummy jobs scrubbing people's floors and doing their laundry, until she's all beat to hell and her smooth, lady-like hands look like they've gone through a meat grinder."

Remy lifted his head to stare at Alice then dropped it again, cursing under his breath.

"But here's the kicker. One day, after Mathilde and her husband have paid off every last cent of their debt, she goes walking down the street and sees her friend, the one who lent her the necklace in the first place. Curiosity gets the best of Mathilde, and she makes up her mind to stop for a chat."

"Oh boy," muttered Remy.

"It turns out the friend hardly recognizes Mathilde, that's how much she's changed from all those years of stress and hard work. Meanwhile, the friend still looks like a million bucks."

The boy snorted at this.

"Anyway, Mathilde decides to tell her friend the truth about the necklace. At this point, what does it matter? She's got nothing to lose. But as she tells the story, her friend's expression changes from polite interest to one of utter dismay."

The girl's eyes widened and she seemed to hover in the air, suspended by the immensity of her impending revelation.

Remy looked up from the taffy lick, his tongue shades of orange and green.

"*Why?!*" he exclaimed.

"*Because*," said Alice, savoring the last few moments of this reign of omniscience and lowering her voice for effect, "It turns out…the diamond necklace she let Mathilde borrow wasn't real. It was just an imitation, a complete and total *fake*."

The horror dawning on Remy's expression washed over the girl like a glorious drug.

"Holy crow! Ho-ly crow!" he said several times, shaking his head back and forth, "I did *not* see that coming. Man, if that doesn't punch you right in the gut!"

"I *know*," she nodded, biting the end off a licorice rope, "I feel sick just from telling it."

The boy gazed at his candy, his brow furrowed.

"Just one thing," he said, squinting at the girl as if trying to verify some critical point of concern, "Her hands…you say they looked like they went through an actual *meat grinder?*"

"Pretty much, yeah."

Remy cursed and resumed eating his taffy lick, deeply sobered.

"What kills me, though," continued Alice, clamping the licorice between her teeth and pulling until it snapped, "Is that one perfect evening when Mathilde was so happy, but she had no way of knowing the complete disaster waiting right around the corner."

"What kills *me* is the lousy friend who lent her a fake necklace!" exploded Remy, "What kind of jerk does a thing like that? Do you think she ended up giving the real one back to Mathilde?"

"I don't know," said Alice, twirling the licorice between her fingers, "To be honest, I don't think that's quite the point."

"Not quite the point?!" cried the boy, rearing up on his knees, "What other point could there possibly be? Hey, I know–why don't we ask the lady with hamburger hands? Why don't we get Mathilde's two cents on the matter? I wonder if she'd like the necklace back? Or do you think she'd just shrug her shoulders and say: *nah, that's not quite the point?*"

Alice put her head down. It looked as if she was crying and for a moment the boy fell silent until he realized she was, in fact, giggling uncontrollably. This also caught him off guard. He'd never seen the girl laugh like that before. She looked different, helpless in a good way, and it made him want to do whatever he could to keep it going.

"Yeah, how about that?" he continued, soaring like a lark on the breeze, "Let's ask Mathilde how she feels about her dopey friend tricking her into wearing a fake necklace! And those ten long years spent scrubbing everyone's dirty ginch to pay for the mistake? I wonder what she thinks is the point of all *that?!*"

Alice was shaking. She looked at Remy with tears in her eyes then dropped her head again, laughing for the first time at a story that had, until this moment, kept her up at night, staring into the darkness. She didn't know how to say it, that she was laughing as much from some immense relief as from his humor, she was laughing at something greater than even all of that. She wished there was a way to tell him, but she didn't understand it herself. Instead, she fingered the candy beads around her neck and let the tears flow.

CHAPTER 6

It was Remy's birthday the following week, but on the appointed morning he did not show up for school. Alice stood at the bus stop, hawk-eyed, watching for the boy to emerge from the LaPierre house. The house was dark and still, like a scratch on the horizon, and the girl was both afraid to look at it and afraid to look away. She kept closing her eyes and counting to ten, but still the door did not open. When the bus appeared around the corner heading toward her, she panicked and scrambled into the ditch.

A storm culvert ran beneath the highway, draped with the silken remains of old spider webs. Alice crawled inside and huddled in the gloom, waiting for the bus to pass overhead. When it was gone and she determined the coast was clear, she dusted herself off and hurried back home.

Penny sat at the kitchen table, smoking and staring at the floor.

"I think I missed the bus," said the girl, when her mother did not acknowledge her presence.

The woman looked out the window and swore.

"Great. That's all I needed today," she said.

"You don't have to take me," said Alice quickly, "I'm not feeling that good anyway."

Penny took a long, last drag on her cigarette and closed her eyes as she exhaled.

"I'm tired," she said, "That was a weird shift."

"Do you like working there?"

The woman gave a brittle laugh.

"What kinda question is that?" she said, burying her stub in the ashes. She got up from the table and passed the girl without looking at her, shuffling down the hallway and closing her bedroom door.

Alice rummaged through the top shelf of the cupboard and retrieved a cake mix, purchased for the occasion. She stirred the ingredients together and baked it in a bread pan. When the cake was done, she broke open a pixie stick and drizzled neon sugar over the loaf, topping it with Swedish berries and a blue gummy shark.

At lunchtime she set off for Remy's house, carrying the cake. As she passed Madame Voisine's bungalow, the door opened and the old woman came out onto the front step.

"Is that for the boy?" she asked.

Alice kept her eyes on the cake.

"His name is Remy," she said.

"I know his name. I know who you are, too."

The girl blinked and glanced at the woman involuntarily, clutching the cake to her chest.

"Is it because you're a witch?"

Madame Voisine threw back her head and laughed, a soaring cackle that did little by way of reassurance.

"More likely a drunk," she said, "Though I can tell you something of magic."

"Like what?" asked the girl.

"Well, for starters, everyone has magic but few learn how to use it."

"How do you *know* if you have it?"

"It comes when you need it, and in that moment there'll be no doubt.

"Is that the only time magic comes, just when you really need it?"

"Certainly not. Magic is everywhere–inside of you and all around. But people have a way of forgetting to see it, just as they have a way of forgetting who they are, and this can make the magic harder to detect."

Alice paused to consider this.

"But what *is* the magic?" she said.

Madame Voisine tilted her head and watched a bumblebee crawl inside a hollyhock.

"I would say it's courage that comes from the deepest part of love."

The girl's expression dimmed and she shook her head.

"I don't have any courage," she said.

"Nonsense! Courage is what happens when love is put to the test, and *that* I can see you have in spades."

Alice stared down the highway which was eerily still for the middle of the day.

"I hope you're right," she said.

"You'll see for yourself," said Madame Voisine, nodding briskly as if this was beyond dispute, "Now, would you like a candle for your cake?"

"Yes, but I can't go inside your house," said the girl.

"In the event I really am a witch?"

"You never said you weren't."

Madame Voisine laughed again.

"Wait here," she said.

The woman returned bearing a white taper candle, wizened from use.

"This was the best I could find," she said.

"Thank you," said Alice, "It's just the right touch."

She took the candle and went on her way, heading for the LaPierre house with her face set like a shield.

Upon reaching the property, however, all confidence fled. A pack of dogs came tearing across the yard, incensed by the sight of an intruder. They stopped short at some invisible line and commenced a frenzy of barking, as if no greater audacity could be conceived than the presence of one small girl. Alice held her ground like a reed in the storm, looking as if she might blow away at any moment.

Presently the door banged open and a stream of profanity preceded a shirtless young man onto the front step. Alice did not flinch. Such language was common in Starling, as unremarkable as the passing of gas or the picking of one's nose. It was absorbed and cultivated at an early age, often comprising the building blocks of a toddler's first words. Swearing was so prevalent people actually stopped hearing it, the way one might tune out the sound of rainfall in a place where it always rains. They used expletives to modify every part of speech—nouns, verbs, and adjectives—a practice that had evolved over the years until profanity became so embedded in the local patois it accounted for nearly every other word that came out of anyone's mouth. In most cases, the use of foul language was less an attempt to offend as it was to facilitate conversation or nudge along a thought. Perhaps it *was* a crutch or sign of ignorance, but it was also a way to bleed out feelings no one had the means to otherwise express. Whatever the reason, swearing flowed easily, even poetically, and the residents of Starling would have been altogether lost without it.

"What d'ya want?" growled the young man, squinting at the girl while hawking the contents of his lungs onto a nearby patch of weeds.

Alice forgot herself and stared. At first glance, Simon LaPierre was the spitting image of his younger brother–slightly taller and perhaps stronger in build, but almost identical in coloring and features. Upon closer scrutiny, however, there was something about the young man, a shadowy impression that cankered the resemblance altogether. It was as if he bore the mark of a counterfeit, a lesser form, lacking Remy's curiosity and intelligence, the unpolished refinement of his soul. Simon leaned against the house with an expression like the flat side of a blade, menacing without effort.

"You two could be twins!" exclaimed the girl.

Simon spun around.

"What'd you say?" he growled, taking a step toward her. He was high from smoking weed, but this did nothing to curb the malice that was inherent to his nature.

"Nothing," she mumbled, as if speaking indistinctly could lessen the offense, "It doesn't matter."

"If it don't matter, then keep yer mouth shut," said the young man, his lip curling into a sneer beneath the fuzz of a dubious mustache.

The girl looked down, feeling as if she might crumble into a fine sheen of dust. She reached into her pocket and felt the piece of petrified wood, clenching it with all her might.

"Where's Remy?" she said, her voice rattling like a pebble in a drum, "I have something for him."

"He's sick," said Simon.

"It's his birthday," she replied, "And I'm not leaving until I give him this cake."

Simon looked at the girl, his bloodshot eyes narrowing to slits. An incoherent bellow sounded from within the house and he cursed beneath his breath.

"Suit yourself," he said.

"What about your dogs?"

The voice bellowed again and the dogs turned, slinking back to their run.

It took Alice a moment to adjust her eyes to the interior of the LaPierre house. She stood on the threshold of a large, open room with a staircase built at odd intervals against the far wall, the top step ending abruptly at a closed door. The windows were covered with newsprint, yellowed with age and smeared with the frass of moths and flies, whose desiccated remains piled like furrows of dirt in the sills. The smell in the house was suffocating–thick with the stench of sweat and the lingering haze of a pungent, bleary smoke. The walls were unfinished, the frame of the house exposed in places with tufts of insulation peeking out between gaps in the wood. Off to one side, a table sagged beneath the weight of a dismantled transmission and a cat rubbed against it, its bottle-brush tail twitching in the gloom.

Dirty dishes filled the sink and congealed in stacks along the counter and floor. Pornographic magazines scattered across the couch and a television set nestled amidst beer cans and ash trays on a nearby coffee table. There was a wood-burning stove and next to it the bathroom, the words *shit hole* spray-painted over its doorway and a gaping chasm kicked through the wall.

A man sat at the table, smoking. His shirt was unbuttoned, exposing flaccid breasts that sagged over a barrel gut carpeted in coarse, white hair. His grizzled face hung low, like a death mask, and he did not look up or acknowledge the girl in any way. Simon yelled for Remy, kicked a dog that was underfoot, and flopped down on the couch. After a long moment, the upstairs door opened and a shadowy figure emerged at the top of the steps.

"Remy, it's me," said Alice, squinting through the gloom, "I brought something for your birthday."

The boy did not respond so she held the cake aloft, waving it like a distress signal. When he still didn't speak or move, she lowered the offering and stood there, helpless, not knowing what else to do.

"Remy, it's *me*," she said again.

"Go away," he muttered.

The girl looked around the room. The smell of it pressed

against her and for one terrible moment she thought she might claw the air to keep from sinking beneath some dark, invisible surface. She pressed her lips together, shaking her head.

"I can't," she said.

Silence hung like a curtain in the air. Finally, the boy's shoulders dropped and he began to shuffle down the stairs. When he reached the bottom step, Alice caught sight of his eye and gasped. It was bruised and swollen, like a glossy, polished plum.

"Remy," she whispered. Her voice caught in her throat and she stepped backward, feeling the room shift beneath her feet. There was a loud crash and she gazed down at the birthday cake lying in pieces on the floor. From out of nowhere a dog appeared and began to eat it, sneezing at intervals on account of the pixie dust. Alice looked at Remy, stricken, and said, "That was meant for you."

From his place on the couch, Simon burst out laughing.

For a moment, it seemed the girl did not hear him. She stood silently as the dog went on rooting about the pan, a peculiar, almost absent expression on her face. Simon caught himself watching her and turned away, annoyed. He was used to having the upper hand, but something about the girl brought an uneasy shift to this balance. Her stillness was like a presence, so intense it seemed the entire room moved toward her, catching him in the pull. Alice felt it, too. She straightened her shoulders and began to breathe more deeply.

It was just as Madame Voisine had said—a strange energy was coursing through her body, filling her with a momentum that made her at once both bristling and calm. Simon turned and pawed through the cushions, searching for the distraction of his cigarettes. He found a crumpled package and put one in his mouth, then looked up to see the girl standing over him, a burning match held aloft in the air. He startled and cursed, trying to play off the shock, but his cigarette trembled when she offered him the flame.

"You think that's funny?" she asked, her eyes gleaming in the firelight, "As it so happens I still have a gift to give, one that comes by way of Madame Voisine."

"That old witch?" scoffed Simon, though he squirmed in his seat and did not meet her gaze.

"The very one," she said, staring intently at the boy, "She asked me to tell a story and said it was for all to hear."

The girl pulled the taper candle from her pocket and touched it to the match, which crumpled to dust as the wick burst into flame. When she spoke, her voice was like the ocean, hushed but filled with an untold force.

"Once there was a girl who lived with her older brother. Their parents were dead and he was all she had left in the world. The boy found amusement in being cruel to others, but for his sister he reserved his greatest contempt. One day he coaxed her into the cellar, then ran upstairs and locked the door. He leapt about the room as she cried, spurred and roused by her terror. After a time the boy grew hungry and left the house, forgetting what he had

done. The girl huddled on the cold, earthen steps, unable to see her hands in front of her face. She beat on the door, begging for help, scratching the heavy panel until her fingers bled. A terrible fear clutched her throat, reaching inside until she could take it no longer. Her soul split in two, leaving half to keep the girl just barely alive and the other half to roam the country, looking for the brother who had done this thing to her.

Years later she found him in a faraway tavern, drinking with a boisterous crowd of his friends. The girl came forward and sat beside him, but the brother couldn't see her. Looking into his eyes, she saw there was not even the faintest hint of contrition or regret. The girl put her hand on his arm and shuddered, feeling more forsaken than ever. In that moment, all the fear and suffering left her body and the brother's arm began to throb with a searing pain, an agony that was to endure for the rest of his days. He gazed at his flesh in horror—it was bloody and gouged, as if scratched by a set of fingernails trying desperately to hold on."

The room was silent when Alice stopped talking and the candle flickered, casting shadows against the wall.

"Make a wish," she said, offering the flame to Remy.

The boy stared at her, then leaned forward and blew it out.

"Is that it?" asked Simon, unaware he was whispering, "Is that how the story ends?"

"Funny you should ask," said Alice, turning to the brother, whose drug-addled brain was fertile ground for paranoia and suspense, "I happen to know the girl is still out there, roaming the countryside. She doesn't stop to eat or sleep. She's looking for anyone who would do harm to others and when she finds them, she settles the score!"

"What does she do?" quavered Simon, his eyes wide as if someone had him by the throat. Alice gave the boy a long, hard stare then stamped her foot, making him yelp.

"Let's hope you never have to find out," she said.

Simon cringed as she took a step forward, but the girl only moved past him and went outside, closing the door behind her. The late afternoon sun flattened the shadow of the house into a narrow crease against the gravel and mud. A low growl rumbled from beneath the steps, but the girl did not acknowledge the dogs and they did not renew their grievance. When she reached the edge of the property, Alice paused. She took two more steps and began to tremble like a leaf.

CHAPTER 7

With October came the transcendence of autumn. Frost crept in during the dark hours before dawn, dusting the grass in a fine, jeweled powder that blinded as the sun rose like an empress in the sky. The world blazed with color, with one last glorious pulse, and the air was rich with the scent of damp earth and the fallen leaves upon it. There was a feeling of maturity, of a round and complete ripeness as the days continued to revel in a pale, retiring warmth, and shades of crimson, wheat, and ochre rippled across the hills.

The children lingered outdoors, trailing through this dappled band of glory. They walked home from school through the aspens, crossing golden meadows, stopping to raise their faces to the sun and let go of every other thought. They fished along the creek, storing their rods and tackle in the woodshed behind Alice's house. There was the discovery of wild raspberries, late for the season, trees whose branches hung low with apples, and chestnuts in spiked casings that split open when they fell to the ground.

A vigorous debate ensued between the children as Halloween drew near. Alice wanted them to dress up as highwaymen, like the character in her favorite poem, but the boy could not come to a consensus on the matter.

"The whole thing makes me crazy," he said as they walked along the train tracks, laying pennies on the rail, "What kind of person writes a poem like that, anyway?"

"Someone with a flair for drama," replied the girl, balancing on her toes.

"Well it's demented, if you want my opinion. That highwayman had no business shacking up with the landlord's daughter in the first place. I knew it was over the minute he snuck up to her house in the middle of the night. Who goes and whistles at *that* hour, for crying out loud? I'm telling you, I saw the whole thing coming a mile away." Remy picked up a stick and whacked at a patch of weeds.

"You did *not*," said Alice, who'd read the poem a hundred times and still hadn't recovered her shock at the ending.

"Did, too. Listen, I got news for you: when a fugitive from the law gets the bright idea to *whistle a tune* while everyone else is trying to sleep, you can be pretty sure his days are numbered."

The girl frowned.

"It would've been fine," she said, "Except for the stable boy who had to go and ruin it all by ratting on him."

"That's another thing–the stable boy. Why did the poet have to call him an *ostler*? Who says that? Why not call him a hired hand or a servant, or just plain *stable boy*? No one even knows what an ostler is."

"Meaning, *you* didn't know," said Alice, looking sideways at the boy.

"Whatever. Don't pretend like you did, either. And what kind of innkeeper hires such a creep to work for him in the first place? Letting that nosy little snitch run around, lurking in the shadows, is hardly what I'd call good for business. I'm telling you, the whole thing was doomed from the get-go!"

Remy had been preoccupied with these details since the first time Alice read him the poem. As a result, a controversy arose between the children regarding the stable boy's eyes, which the poet had described as "hollows of madness." Remy interpreted this to mean the boy had empty sockets where his eyes should have been, prompting Alice to point out the entire poem hinged upon the boy being able to tell the soldiers what he had seen.

"But it doesn't say he *saw* anything!" Remy had exclaimed, "It says, 'dumb as a dog, he *listened!*'"

"That's because he had to stay hidden!" retorted Alice, scouring the text for evidence to support her claim.

"And I say it's because he didn't have any eyeballs!"

"If he didn't have eyeballs, then what *did* he have?"

"*Hollows of madness*, like the poem says."

The children walked on. Alice stopped to pick a thistle, grey and blowsy, gone to seed. She waved it like a scepter, watching the pale down drift away on the breeze.

"And another thing," continued Remy, "The part about the stable boy's hair, calling it *moldy hay*. Was that really necessary? It's like kicking a guy when he's already down."

"How so?" asked the girl.

"Because he was *blind*, Alice. I'm telling you!"

"You said all that about his hair just to bring up the thing about his eyes again!" said the girl, whirling around to confront him.

Remy looked away, trying not to grin.

"I did not!" he said.

"Yes, you did. I know you, Remy LaPierre. That's exactly what you did."

"I didn't!" he said, but when she pushed him he had the grace not to protest.

"Anyway, my biggest beef is with the guy who wrote the poem," Remy continued, "*He's* the one who made it all happen in the first place: calling the stable boy an ostler, giving him moldy hair. And look what he did to the highwayman: skin-tight pants and boots going up to the thigh? C'mon, Alice, what kind of self-respecting criminal shows up for a job dressed like that? He wouldn't last three seconds in Starling and you know it."

"But Remy," pleaded the girl, "Think how fun it would be

to dress as highwaymen for Halloween!"

"I'm not wearing any lace, Alice. We've been through this already."

"Okay, okay–no lace. Just capes and masks."

"A mask would be cool."

The girl hopped along the rail, smiling to herself.

"And maybe just a hint of lace. A tiny puff."

"No."

It was getting late in the day. A train passed through the valley, its mournful whistle lingering in the gloom. The children collected their flattened pennies from the tracks and held them to their faces, the heated metal leaving discs of crimson on their cheeks. They watched as Alice's mother pulled onto the highway in a rusty green hatchback, heading in their direction.

"Is that your mom?" asked the boy.

"Yeah."

"Where's she going?"

"To work."

"Where does she work?"

"The glass plant."

Remy looked at the girl.

"Aren't you gonna wave?"

The girl watched as the car passed by and shook her head

imperceptibly.

"She won't see me anyway."

The last traces of light faded from the sky, a clear indication it was time to part ways yet the children lingered on the tracks, the pennies growing cold in their hands.

"I know!" Alice spun around, her eyes bright, "Meet me at my house in ten minutes. Can you bring a hammer and nail?"

"Just one nail?" asked the boy, "What d'you need it for?"

"You'll see," she said, skipping off into the gloom.

When the boy appeared on Alice's front step with a hammer in hand, she hid behind the door and ushered him inside. He followed her into a small kitchen, hushed by the absence of clutter, noticing a ceramic ashtray on the table.

"I made that for my mom in kindergarten," said the girl, "It's supposed to be a hand print."

"You did good," said Remy.

They passed through the living room, its walls paneled with laminate wood that had peeled and buckled in places. The carpet, a thick shag, was the color of aged whiskey and looked as if it had seen better days. A couch slumped in one corner beneath a painting on black velvet of an old Indian chief with a tear running down his cheek. Next to this a TV tray balanced on precarious legs and a lamp sat upon it that was missing a shade. There was a television set perched on two milk crates and a rocking chair that had been painted several times over, its current color a drab, olive green. Alice turned down a hallway and opened the first door.

"This is my room," she said, fiddling with a strand of Christmas lights draped over the window. Remy looked around slowly, taking in every detail with a keen eye. The room seemed plain at first, nothing more than a few milk crates and a bed pushed against the wall. The bed was neatly made with a map of the world pinned above it, repaired in places by strips of Scotch tape. A clock radio sat on a nearby milk crate and a row of pine cones lined the windowsill like nesting dolls, arranged by size down to one no bigger than a plum. A garland of leaves hung between two hooks on the wall and in the faint glow hollowed by the Christmas lights, these small evidences of the girl made the room feel warm in a way the boy could not describe.

"It's nice," he said.

"Thanks," replied Alice, disappearing beneath her bed to retrieve a small, weather beaten trunk.

"What's that?" asked the boy.

She looked at him with wide eyes and whispered, "It's a treasure chest."

"Why are we whispering?" he whispered back.

A smiled flashed across her face and without realizing it, the boy leaned in closer.

"Because…it's *magic*," she said, opening the lid.

The contents of the trunk fit together like interlocking pieces of a puzzle. A row of books lined one side, tucked next to a catacomb of small, nestled boxes. There was a plastic hourglass filled with sand, a whistle, a flashlight, an empty perfume bottle, an old key, and a collection of breath mint tins. Wedged between these objects, a bulging pencil case kept everything in its place.

"Neat," said Remy, peering inside.

The girl, watching his reaction, was pleased.

"Look at this," she said.

She withdrew a velvet jewelry box and gave it to the boy, who pried the lid open to reveal a pile of tattered butterfly wings in shades of yellow, pink, and grey. The wings rustled gently beneath the boy's breath, as if they possessed the will to summon one last, resplendent flight.

"Where did you get all these?" he asked.

"Here and there," said the girl, shrugging, "I find them as I go."

"What happened to the rest of their bodies?"

"I don't know," she said, taking the box and peering inside, "It's hard to say for sure."

"Foul play," he suggested.

"Yes," she nodded, looking into his face to gauge for sincerity, "I think you may be right."

Alice held out a stone for the boy to inspect. It was smooth like glass, a rich charcoal grey with ribbons of white passing through it.

"This is a wishing stone," she said, "You get one wish for every ring." The girl looked at Remy, speaking in solemn tones, "I'm saving it for something big."

There were other stones, too: speckled ones, heart-shaped, a rock with a secret hollow, shards of mica, and a brown, fossilized shell.

"These all come from the places I've been," she intoned, arranging the rocks in a circle between them, "And this one stands for us here, right now." Reaching beneath her pillow, she retrieved the petrified wood Remy had given her and set it in the midst of the round.

The boy watched in silence. He fished about in his pockets until he found his favorite shooter marble and placed it next to the relic.

Alice stared at the arrangement as if considering the gesture, then nodded.

After this, she handed Remy a breath mint tin. He opened it and stared, the look on his face causing the girl to smile.

"Holy crow!" he exclaimed. The tin contained the largest bee the boy had ever seen. It was sapphire black and covered in shaggy, iridescent fur, bearing an uncanny resemblance to a miniature buffalo on the verge of stampede.

"It's *blue!*" said the boy, holding the box up to the flashlight.

"I told you," she replied, handing him a magnifying glass, her eyes bright in the shadows, *"Magic."*

The children sat side by side as Remy examined the bee, moving closer until his nose left a smudge on the lens.

"Is that where you keep your poems?" he asked, nodding to the books in the trunk.

"Yes," said the girl, "Would you like me to read you one?"

"As long as it's not *The Highwayman*."

She opened a threadbare book with buttery soft pages.

"This is one of my favorites," she said, reading aloud:

I live my life in widening circles which move out over the things of the world.

Perhaps I can never achieve the last, but that will be my attempt.

I am circling around God, around the ancient tower,

I have been circling for a thousand years,

And I still don't know if I am a falcon, or a storm, or a great song.

Remy closed the tin and set it carefully on the floor. He leaned forward, resting his head against his knees. Alice sat beside him gazing at the book in her lap, letting the words soften and blur. The Christmas lights twinkled overhead and in this cavern of stillness it seemed they had a world to themselves, a million miles away.

Presently the girl asked, "Are you hungry?"

"Yeah," said Remy, feeling suddenly ravenous.

Alice went into the kitchen and put a pot on the stove. She

measured some rice and milk, stirring the mixture as the room grew warm and sweet.

"How do you know how to do that?" asked Remy.

"Oh, I used to live next door to a lady who showed me," said the girl, adding a little salt. She leaned over the pot and inhaled deeply. "She always said there was no better smell in the world than steamed milk. What do you think?"

Remy stepped forward and took a perfunctory sniff.

"No, you have to really breathe it in," said the girl.

He inhaled deeply.

"Well?" she said, watching him.

"Pretty good, I guess…but not the *best*."

"Oh *really*. And what might that be, according to your superior nose?"

"Pine trees after it rains," he said, a bit too readily.

Alice stared at the boy, saying nothing,

"You know, like when the sun comes out," he mumbled, jamming his hands into his pockets.

"Yeah, I got it–pine trees and rain, throw in a little sun–*verrry* interesting," she said, arching her brow.

"What, you think you're the only person around here who notices stuff?!" he blustered, but he was unable to meet her gaze.

"Au contraire," she said and turned back to the business of

stirring, her face hidden by clouds of steam.

When the pudding was ready, Alice filled two mugs and sprinkled brown sugar on top. The children took their food to her bedroom and sat down on the floor.

"This is good," said Remy, shoveling great spoonfuls into his mouth.

"Thank you," replied the girl, "Rice pudding is my specialty."

When they had finished eating, Alice cleared the dishes and said, "Now we need to get busy and make the masks."

She went to the kitchen and returned with an empty carrier for a six pack of beer.

"This'll do just fine," she said.

She turned on the radio and got to work, cutting the cardboard into contoured strips with openings for their eyes. Using a mixture of water and glue she showed Remy how to adhere layers of newsprint to the masks, smoothing them down to create a sculptured effect. When the masks were dry, she placed them on a phonebook and pounded a hole through each end using Remy's hammer and nail. The children laced yarn through the openings and fastened the masks to their faces.

Alice leered at the boy.

"Your money or your life!" she said.

The boy raised an eyebrow as if to consider his options.

The girl laughed, brandishing an imaginary sword. She

made a theatrical lunge and twirled about the room, lurching to a halt when she noticed the clock.

"It's past midnight," she said, staring at the boy through her lopsided mask.

Remy shrugged his shoulders.

"So?"

"So aren't you going to get in trouble?" she asked.

"Nah," he said, looking at the ground, "I'll be fine."

"Are you sure?" The girl peered out the window where she could glimpse the lights from Remy's house in the distance.

"Yeah. My dad'll be asleep. Simon will be out."

"I wish you could stay," she said, feeling her throat tighten, "I wish you didn't have to go."

"I *could* stay," asserted the boy, "I could stand outside your window like the highwayman and keep watch through the night."

"Remy, be serious! That's crazy!" she exclaimed.

The boy shrugged, his face impassive.

A moment later, unable to help herself, she ventured, "Did you really mean what you just said?"

He shrugged again.

"Wouldn't say it if I didn't mean it."

The girl looked away, shaking her head, her heart aching with the fear and longing such assurances always brought.

CHAPTER 8

Halloween was a highly anticipated event in Starling. Children lay in their beds at night, the promise of free candy sizzling their brains until they twitched and quivered like rabid squirrels. For adults it beckoned like a beacon of depravity, when indecent behavior could masquerade beneath the legitimacy of holiday fun. It pitted the women against the singular challenge of having to come up with costumes that were even more revealing than their usual attire, though in this quest they were not to be outdone. Still, most people would agree the main attraction was the fireworks, and all year long they looked forward to this night for the chance to blow things up.

When the sun set on the last day of October, the community gathered at a vacant field next to the school, tapped a few kegs of beer, and used liberal amounts of gasoline to start a bonfire that was kept burning by a truckload of wood. When it got dark enough and no one was left who could walk a straight line, then it was time for the fireworks. The notion of what qualified as a firework was open to interpretation in Starling, loosely applied to any foolhardy soul in possession of a match and something that could explode. More than one missing ear or finger could be attributed to the revelry of that night, which was how Pinky Doucet and Wax Klassen got their nicknames.

As Remy hurried to the Quinn's house that morning he found Alice on the front step, clutching their costumes to her chest.

"Where did you get those capes?" he asked, a trifle dubiously.

"Shhh…they're the curtains from my bedroom. We have to take good care of them," she said, securing the fabric around the boy's neck with a safety pin and tying the mask to his face. Remy helped Alice with her costume. He stood back to survey the effect as she tucked a crumpled piece of toilet paper into the neckline of her jacket.

"For the bunch of lace at my throat," she explained.

"Of course," he replied, as if nothing could be more apparent.

The children had devised their own plans for the evening. Alice told her mother she would be sleeping over at Lori Skinner's house. Remy, for his part, did not bother to fabricate an excuse.

After school they played by the creek until the sun went down, then joined the other kids in trick-or-treating around the neighborhood. When a crowd began to gather for the bonfire, Remy and Alice walked home along the train tracks, their candy stashed in pillowcases slung over their shoulders.

As they drew near the LaPierre house, Alice began to waver. Already forbidding by day, the house was nothing short of sinister in the darkness. Moonlight spilled over its frame, exposing beams and angles which made the girl think of a tall, gaunt man hovering in the shadows. The closer they got, the house itself seemed to come alive, the unlit windows giving the entrance a hooded expression as if feigning indifference, yet all the while not missing a beat.

"Is anyone home?" ventured the girl.

"My dad," said Remy, "But he never turns on the lights. Wait here."

He crossed a weedy patch of land separating his house from the tracks and disappeared into a shed. Alice stood alone in the dark, feeling less like a highwayman with each passing moment.

When the boy returned, he was carrying a knapsack.

"Okay," he said, "Let's get out of here."

"Where are we going, anyway?" asked Alice, moving briskly so the boy had to hurry to catch up.

"To this place I know," he replied, "It's a surprise. The only thing I can tell you is: wear something warm."

The children continued walking down the train tracks, crossing the highway at the lane leading to Alice's house. As they passed Madame Voisine's bungalow, Remy quickened his pace.

"I wonder where *she* is tonight?" he muttered darkly.

"Oh, *brother*–you've got it all wrong. She couldn't be a witch," said Alice.

"Well, Simon said he saw her down by the creek one time with a dog that looked like a wolf."

"*Really?*" said Alice, somewhat torn by this new and compelling piece of evidence.

"Yeah, and when she caught him watching her, she turned into a big black bird and flew away."

"You're kidding me! What happened to the dog?"

"Good question. He didn't mention that part."

"Hmm. This is a pretty serious claim. Then again, it *is* coming from your brother."

"True."

They stopped at Alice's house, where no one was home, and the children went inside. Alice hurried to her room to put on an extra sweater and a toque that had been made for her by a neighbor lady in Caribou. It was charcoal grey and peaked at the corners, and Alice liked to think it made her look like a cat. Zipping up her coat and still wearing the highwayman mask, she returned to the boy who was waiting for her in the kitchen.

Remy stared.

"What? You said *wear something warm*," she said, shrugging her shoulders.

"I see you took me at my word," he replied.

"Well, I didn't think you were fooling around."

"Touché."

The children set off once more, striking out across the pasture beyond the bungalow. They headed toward the tree line that flanked a slope leading up to the mountains on the western side of the valley. The moon hung like a pearl in the sky, casting a bright glow over the children so they could see the pall of their shadows against the ground. When they reached the edge of the forest, Remy took a flashlight from his pack and turned it on.

"Don't worry, I know where I'm going," he said.

Alice looked at him quickly. Until that moment, it had not occurred to her to worry.

They struggled through the underbrush, trudging uphill until the girl had to bite her lip to stop from asking if they were lost. At length the terrain flattened out unexpectedly, opening onto a plateau where the children were able to walk without hindrance.

"Here we are," said the boy, "This is it."

He trained his light on a grove of aspens in the distance. An old yellow school bus sat parked in the circle of trees, the rusted hulk settled unevenly in the ground, giving it a somewhat crestfallen appearance. A few windows were broken, but the presence of the vehicle out in the middle of nowhere was so strange and fantastic the girl could only look upon it in awe.

"How did it get here?" she asked.

"Some hippies brought it to camp in a few years back," said Remy, "I don't know how they got here, probably took some logging road no one uses anymore and then free-styled into the bush, but the bus broke down and they decided to split once the weather turned cold. Anyway, it's my place now. No one else knows about it."

"*Unreal!*" breathed Alice, climbing the steps to peer inside and the boy, hearing this, let himself grin wildly in the darkness.

"Check it out," he called, dizzy with wanting to show her everything at once. Alice followed him to the back of the bus where he trained his flashlight on a rickety ladder bolted to the side.

"I'll go first," he said, scaling the rungs.

He clambered over a guardrail onto the roof, then turned and gestured to the girl.

"Come on up. It's safe!"

When she reached the top Remy clicked off the flashlight and the children sat quietly, taking in their surroundings.

"Look how the trees glow in the moonlight," whispered Alice.

"Maybe we're surrounded by ghosts," said the boy, "Let's hope they're friendly!"

But the girl could not be provoked.

"More like guardian angels," she nodded, her expression serene.

They sat in silence until the girl looked up, breathing sharply.

"Oh, the sky!"

Wreathed in aspens, the heavens seemed to hang low, pendulous beneath the weight of an endless array of stars.

"There's the Big Dipper," said Remy.

The girl reached up, tracing the constellation with her finger.

"So many stars, you could never count them…not in a million years," she said.

Remy watched the girl as she gazed at the sky. She seemed like a creature from the forest, her toque casting a feline silhouette against the milky light of the moon.

"Are you cold?" he asked.

"Not really," she replied.

"Me neither," he said.

The children got to work setting up camp. Remy laid out two sleeping bags from his pack and Alice set the pillowcase of candy between them.

They crawled into their bedding and lay down. Remy popped an atomic fireball into his mouth. Alice fished through the assortment and selected a licorice whip.

"This is the life," said the boy, settling in.

"You can say that again," nodded Alice.

They ate their treats in silence, watching the sky. Remy took the fireball from his mouth and inhaled deeply, trying to cool his tongue.

"Will you tell me a story?" he said.

"Hmm…let's see," Alice tapped her chin with the licorice, considering her options, "Well there's this one I know, but it has a pretty sad ending."

"Let me guess–it's French."

"As a matter of fact, it is."

"What a surprise. Don't you know any happy stories?"

"I have a book about two sisters who get shipwrecked on an island with a boat full of babies."

"And that's supposed to be *happy?*"

"I mean, worse things could happen."

"What's it called?"

"*Baby Island.*"

"Does the title sum it up?"

"Pretty much."

"Let's go for the French one, then."

"Well, it was kind of hard to follow. It takes place a long time ago in France, with this one guy belonging to a filthy rich family that turns out to be quite the haven for scumbags."

"What did they do?" asked Remy, drawn to the sordid details in spite of himself.

"Tons of jacked up stuff. You really wouldn't believe it. But the uncle takes the cake by running over some little kid with his carriage. When his driver tells him what happened, he has the nerve to complain about the nuisance of beggars in the street."

"What is *wrong* with people?" said Remy, taking the fireball out of his mouth and holding it up to the moon.

"You're telling me. Anyway, the story gets kind of confusing. To be honest, I skipped through some of the pages but basically the nephew, whose name is Darnay, is a pretty decent guy. He marries a girl named Lucie whose father was thrown into prison thanks to Darnay's uncle, the one who ran over the kid. There's a bunch of peasants who are sick of the rich people getting away with everything, so they finally decide to take matters into their own hands. Things start to get pretty tense. If you're a rich person, you can pretty much guarantee you're a goner. There's this one lady who's obsessed with revenge, and she starts knitting the names of everyone who deserves to get killed as a way to keep track of things."

"*Knitting* them?" The boy sat up, incredulous.

"Yeah."

"She couldn't just find a pen and write 'em down?"

Alice stared at him, trying not to smile.

"Remy," she began.

"I'm sorry, but you can't tell me I'm the first person to ask this question. I mean, who *knits* a hit list? She sounds like a very crafty villain. What did she do when she needed to buy groceries, I wonder? Knit the words *milk* and *eggs*?"

He popped the fireball back into his mouth and listened to

the girl laugh. Every time she stopped to catch her breath, he feigned knitting and spoke in high, falsetto tones, "Let me see. Sugar? Yes, we need sugar. How about cornflakes? No, that'll take too long to knit. Oh la la, now I have to unravel the C."

Alice buried her face in her hands, shoulders convulsing.

"Do you want me to tell you what happens or not?" she said, coming up for air.

"By all means. Don't mind me, I'm just over here knitting myself a pony. I've always wanted one, you know," said the boy.

"A pony?" said the girl, her smile nearly eclipsing her face.

"Dammit, he kicked me. Down, boy! That's it, now you're getting unraveled, too," he said.

Laughter drifted through the trees, fading into the night.

"Okay, but here's the kicker," said Alice, chewing vigorously on the licorice whip, "Darnay is thrown into prison and condemned to death. But there just happens to be this guy named Sidney Carton who looks like his twin and is also, by the way, in love with Lucie."

"Oh boy," said Remy.

"So Carton, who felt like his life had never amounted to much, visits Darnay in prison and tricks him into taking a sleeping potion."

"Here we go," muttered the boy, shaking his head.

"Carton switches clothes with Darnay, then claims his 'visitor' came down with some super contagious disease everyone's afraid of catching. So the guards back off, thinking all along this is

Carton, when really it's Darnay who's rushed out of the prison, where his friends are waiting to help him escape."

"And Carton?" asked Remy.

"What about him?"

"Alice."

"Trust me, you don't wanna know."

"Alice, you can't go this far into the story and not tell me how it ends."

"To be honest, I'm not sure you can handle it."

"Alice!"

"Okay…okay!" said the girl, grinning wickedly, "If you must know, he doesn't make it."

"What do you mean, *he doesn't make it?!*"

"I mean, they take him to the guillotine and the story ends with him comforting a little seamstress before they both get their heads chopped off."

"What?! A *seamstress?!* What does she have to do with anything?"

"She doesn't. She just shows up at the end of the story."

"But why were they killing a seamstress in the first place? What could she have possibly done to deserve it?"

"Who knows? Maybe she darned the king's undies."

The boy struggled in his sleeping bag to turn and confront the girl, who bent over the pillowcase of candy in a show of great concentration.

"Are you making that up?"

Alice shrugged, deeply intent on her selection.

"Maybe."

"I can *hear* you smiling. You and your stories! You make me crazy, Alice Quinn."

"I am *not* smiling! Anyway, the thing that makes *me* crazy is Sidney Carton. He knew he was signing his death sentence when he went to the jail to trade places with Darnay, but he went ahead and did it anyway. No one forced him; it was all his own idea."

"I know why he did it," said Remy stoutly. He lay back down and was quiet for a moment, "I'd do it, too."

"Do what?"

"Take the fall for someone I loved."

"You would?"

"Yeah, I would."

The children ate their candy and gazed into the night.

"That takes true courage, Remy LaPierre. It means you have a noble heart."

Before the boy could respond, a star fell. It did not burn out quickly, but rather seemed to make a pilgrimage across the sky. It surged and meandered, indulgent in its course, illuminating the heavens with plumes of iridescent gas that curled in its wake like a lustrous, feathery serpent. The children watched in silence, gripped by the wonder of it all. The star blazed on, pulsing shades of radiant green. It came to rest in a cluster of light and burst with color, as if its last moments in existence were an ode to some great, inexpressible joy.

"Alice," breathed Remy, or maybe her name was only a thought uttered in his mind. Either way the girl nodded, lost in an expression of awe that was deepened by knowing the boy saw it, too. The light flickered and was gone, leaving the sky to its original majesty as the children gazed on, caught up in a rapture too hallowed for words.

"Alice," said the boy again, after a time.

"Yes."

"I think you're the song."

"What?"

"From the poem. I think you're like a great song."

A breeze came through the clearing and the trees seemed to rustle and confer as the girl took this in.

"That's quite a thing to say," she replied.

The sky deepened, its twinkling cavern stretching to infinity and Alice blinked at dwindling intervals, trying to prolong the moment, but her eyelids felt heavy and slow.

"I wonder what you are?" she murmured, "I guess maybe the falcon."

But she did not sound sure.

The air was crisp and clear, filled with the antiquity of the season. It was quiet in the clearing and the aspens hovered around the children, keeping watch. Alice burrowed into her sleeping bag and closed her eyes.

"Remy."

"Yeah."

"I'm going to go back and imagine my entire life with you in it."

The boy gazed at the sky and breathed deeply, feeling as if he could see farther than ever before, beyond the most distant star, as if it was all within his reach, or somehow inexplicably inside of him.

"Maybe this sounds crazy," he said, "But it feels like we already did."

CHAPTER 9

Things weren't getting any better at school. Ms. Kemp, for all her apparent disinterest in the classroom, stoked a resentment toward Alice that smoldered like a coal in the ashes. She pounced on any chance to berate the girl, watching her with a fixed intensity as she pretended to grade papers, work with other students, or circulate about the room. Sometimes, the teacher didn't bother to put on an act. She would stand at the chalkboard and stare at Alice while everyone kept their heads down except Remy, who would simulate farting sounds or shoot spitballs at Nikki Kilchuk, as a bird tries to distract predators from its nest.

Ms. Kemp loved to catch Alice daydreaming, stealing up to slam her hand against the girl's desk or bark out her name from across the room. This sudden shattering of the girl's composure, the way the blood drained from her face, made the teacher's stomach clench in a dark and delicious way. It wasn't enough to merely call attention to these reveries; Ms. Kemp insisted upon badgering Alice to give an account for herself until she was reduced to silence, unable to even whisper a response.

It was the sheer whim of the teacher's moods, the peculiar discrimination of her anger that consumed Alice, snatching her from sleep in the middle of the night to leave her trembling in the darkness, her heart beating like a rabbit on the run. In those moments Alice tried to keep still but the dreams were relentless, hounding her from bed into the kitchen where she'd crouch against the refrigerator, feeling its warm hum against her cheek. Sometimes she fell asleep this way and other times she could not stop crying, but Remy came down the lane each morning to walk her to the bus stop and when she saw his figure in the distance, the act of grabbing her coat and going out the door rolled over the girl in a numb, involuntary motion.

"Whose car is that?" he asked one day, nodding to a black Trans Am parked in the driveway.

"A friend of my mom's."

"Is his name Rob Novak?"

"Yeah."

The boy was quiet a moment.

"I don't like that guy," he said.

"Neither do I."

They hunched their shoulders and continued up the lane, the low hanging clouds and wisps of fog thickening the air like a chilled soup. A tapping sound caught their attention as they passed Madame Voisine's bungalow and the children looked up to see the old woman at the window, beckoning them inside. Remy walked on as Alice stood still, rooted to the ground.

"What are you doing?" he hissed, shaking his head, "Are you crazy? C'mon, let's get out of here!"

"Remy, that's rude! I'm just going to see what she wants," said the girl, stubborn on this point. She strode across the yard, regretting her bravado more keenly with each step.

"Alice! Don't do it…she's a witch!"

"Shh!" she scolded, but by the time Alice reached the front porch her legs felt numb, dragging like weights. She wavered a moment, considering retreat, but the door swung open and Madame Voisine stood on the threshold, imperious in a silver kimono that glittered like frost.

"The cold is coming," she said, as if announcing it by her own decree.

The girl stared at the woman, forgetting to speak.

"You'll be in need of something to keep you warm."

"I'm okay," mumbled Alice.

"*Are* you, my dear?"

Madame Voisine held her gaze and the girl looked away.

"Follow me," she commanded, turning and disappearing into the house.

"Madame Voisine, I have to go to school," began Alice, but the woman was already gone. The girl looked back at Remy. He shook his head violently but she shrugged her shoulders and went inside.

The entrance of the bungalow led directly to the kitchen, a small room dwarfed by an excess of large, feathery ferns. An aloe plant sat on the counter next to the stove and tendrils of ivy snaked along the walls. Rubber trees and philodendron hung in macramé baskets at various intervals, and a black cat lounged on the table amidst winter savory, sage, and mint.

Alice stood still, feeling a faint ache stir in her heart. The air smelled fresh and alive, and it seemed she could not breathe enough of it. She leaned forward, trying to take it all in, this secret forest, this vast and miniature world.

"For you."

The girl spun around, startled. Madame Voisine stood in the doorway holding a long, woolen scarf in her arms.

"Red," she said, wrapping it around the girl several times, "For courage."

Alice blinked.

"For me?" she said, fingering the tassels.

"Especially for you," nodded the woman.

"It's so soft," whispered the girl, closing her eyes.

"It will do the trick," said Madame Voisine.

This amused the girl and she could not help but smile.

"You see? Already a little magic," said the woman, "Now off you go before your friend summons the nerve to break down my door."

"Thank you, Madame Voisine," said Alice. She made a little curtsy and turned around, trying to commit the room to memory, though she somehow knew one could spend a lifetime in this house and only begin to make its acquaintance.

Remy was on the front step when Alice appeared at the doorway. His shoulders were braced for impact and he had the look of one preparing to storm the fortress.

"What took you so long?" he said roughly.

"I was hardly gone a minute," she replied, skipping down the steps, "And look what she gave me!"

"It was *way* more than a minute and that thing is probably cursed!"

"Remy, honestly. Don't be such a chicken."

"*Chicken?!*" he sputtered, torn between indignation and the intense desire to be on his way, "Just 'cause I don't wanna hang out with a witch!"

"Oh, for crying out loud! She's no witch," said the girl. She stopped and stared at the bungalow as the boy pressed forward, "But there *is* something rather…unusual going on in that house."

At the bus stop the children stood in silence, watching their breath condense in the frosty air. Remy reached into his pocket and pretended to smoke a cigarette. He took a long drag then doubled over, hacking and pounding his chest. Alice ignored him for as long as she could, though it did little to deter his antics.

"Give me that thing," she finally said.

She grabbed the imaginary cigarette from Remy's hand and pretended to dangle it in the air.

"Easy, Alice," he said, speaking in warning tones.

The girl raised an eyebrow and shrugged.

"Alice, wait! Don't do it! You know I need my morning puff!"

He took a step toward her as she made a gesture to drop the cigarette on the ground and crush it beneath her heel. Remy stared in disbelief.

"I can't believe you did that!" he croaked, "It was my last smoke!"

Alice threw her head back and laughed. It sounded like chimes in the breeze and the boy inhaled deeply, no longer feeling the cold.

"If you could have one of the following powers, which would it be: to predict the future or travel through time?" asked Alice, spinning in circles so that the scarf fluttered out like a brilliant fan.

"Travel through time," said Remy.

"Hey!" she stopped and pointed her finger at him, "You didn't even *think* about that."

The boy scuffed his shoe in the gravel, unable to conceal his smile.

"Give me another one," he offered, "I'll try harder this time."

"Okay. What would you rather have: an invisible tree fort or a tiny, talking turtle?"

"Tree fort," he said, before she could finish asking the question.

"Remy!" said the girl, stamping her foot, "You did it again!"

"Did what?"

"You know."

"No, tell me."

"You rattled off any old answer. It kills me when you do that! You gave up the chance to have the turtle without a second thought!"

Remy stopped scuffing gravel and looked at the girl with genuine curiosity.

"You *do* realize this is a game, right? You don't really expect a turtle the size of a peach pit to appear out of thin air and start telling you a story?"

Alice rolled her eyes and looked off into the distance.

"I *know*," she said stubbornly, shaking her head, "Maybe this sounds crazy but in the moment I'm trying to decide, it seems so real I can hardly bear it."

"That's one thing I like about you," muttered Remy, stuffing his hands into his pockets, "The way you see things."

She turned to him, half hearing what he said, and the boy held her gaze for a split second before they both looked away.

"But let me put it to you like this," he continued hastily, "In the last five minutes I became a time traveler with an invisible tree fort. And what did you get? *Nothing.*"

"Remy!"

Alice swung her knapsack at the boy but he dodged out of reach, calling from a distance.

"Hey! If it ain't real, what does it matter? Either way, you better learn how to make up your mind."

"I *do* know how to make up my mind!"

"Oh yeah? Then what would it be–the turtle or the tree fort?"

Alice paused, her mouth open, and the boy laughed. She yelled incoherently and chased him down the road, swinging her knapsack like a slingshot. When the bus came rumbling around the bend the children straggled back and lined up without speaking, the moment extinguished.

The bus rides to school grew quieter as the cold set in. The children swayed gently in the thin light, staring into space while others closed their eyes and escaped to the irresistible reprieve of sleep. The skunky musk of cannabis emanated from the back of the bus and though the day was just beginning it seemed to be getting darker, the light leaching out of the low, grey skies. There was something mesmerizing, even intimate about the dimness and shadows, the communal body heat, and the jostling motion of the vehicle that allowed its passengers to sit side by side without tension, resistance, or thought.

When they reached Starling Elementary, the children poured out of the bus, moving across the playground like a dark, brackish flood. A sudden holler split the air and those closest to the uproar filed a wide berth around Mona Gorsma, who'd just stepped in a pile of fresh dog crap.

A few older boys issued the standard snickers and jeers requisite in the case of such misfortune, but everyone else knew to put their heads down and keep moving. Mona, who was never one to suffer humiliation without returning it in spades, spun around and grabbed her nearest victim.

It happened to be Alice Quinn.

"You. *New girl.* Wipe this shit off my boots," hissed Mona, shaking Alice by the arm. The girl gasped and lurched forward, mesmerized by the sight of Mona's rotting teeth like two eroded wood chips stuck in puffy, reddened gums.

"Let her go!" called Remy, pushing his way through the crowd.

Mona turned to the boy, caught off guard by this challenge. She raised her eyebrows, the streaks of makeup on her face rendering her somewhere between a corpse and a clown.

"Who's gonna make me, LaPierre?"

"I am."

"Is that so? You gotta thing for the new girl?" Mona simpered, her expression leering and grotesque.

"Just let her go. She can't help you, anyway. You're still gonna stink if there's shit on your boots or not."

There was a collective intake of breath from the kids who had stopped to watch the action unfold. It was a well-known fact around Starling that the topic of Mona Gorsma's body odor was to be avoided at all costs by anyone who entertained a will to live. At Tanis Jerome's slumber party two years ago she'd given Nikki Kilchuk a nosebleed for complaining her sleeping bag smelled like pee, and Sean Burrows had a chunk of graphite imbedded in his shoulder from the time Mona stabbed him with a pencil for pretending to gag when she sat next to him on the bus.

Mona released Alice with lightning speed and spun on Remy, who stood in full cognizance of the penalty he'd just incurred. Her cousins, Buck and Jerry Gorsma–hulking, identical twins sharing the equivalent of half a brain between them–grabbed the boy, twisting and pinning his arms behind his back.

"What'd you say?" said Mona, spittle flying through the gaps in her teeth. Remy did not reply. There was no point in reasoning with a Gorsma, especially this one. Mona was equal parts stupidity and spite, a dull-minded brute of a girl with a voracious appetite for the suffering of others. She took a perverse pleasure in hurting things, in stepping on nests of young field mice, burrowed in clouds of down. The barn cats knew to steer clear of her and even the horses shied away. She threw rocks at swallow's nests, knocking them out of the eaves, mesmerized by the adult birds' impotent, fluttering fear. Last year Mona scratched Mr. Bouchard's initials on her wrist with a razor blade, picking at the wound until it hardened into a fleshy, illegible knot.

"You gotta thing for the new girl, LaPierre? Is that why you volunteered to clean my boots?"

Mona was not five inches from Remy's face, weaving back and forth like a cobra. The boy hung from the twins' grip, his head down. It was useless to struggle and he focused instead on breathing through the molten pain that was coursing down his shoulders.

The second bell rang but no one moved. Mona made a gesture as if to turn away, then spun around and kicked Remy's legs out from underneath him. A piercing scream shattered the air and several kids ducked as if expecting some enormous bird of prey to swoop down upon their heads. In the ensuing confusion Buck and Jerry released the boy and the tide of children surged on toward the school.

Alice rushed to Remy as he lay crumpled on the ground.

"Are you okay?!" she cried, touching his shoulder. He jerked away and struggled to sit up, keeping his back to the girl.

"You didn't have to do that," she ventured, gesturing helplessly.

"Yes, I did," he muttered, wiping his face on the sleeve of his jean jacket.

Alice looked across the playground. A metal swing was wrapped around a pole so that it hung askew, making a clanging noise in the wind. The sky was dim, the lights from the school casting a ghostly beacon through the fog.

"Remy, come on," she said, holding out her hand to the boy though he still refused to face her, "Let's go clean off your pants where she kicked you. We're going to be late for class."

Ms. Kemp was waiting for the children when they came through the door.

"Nice of you lovebirds to join us," she said.

Alice froze and stared at the floor. Remy made a move to explain their delay, but the teacher dismissed it with an airy wave of her hand.

"No, no…that's quite all right, Mr. LaPierre. It's obvious you and Miss Quinn enjoy each other's company *far* too much to be bothered with such trivial concerns as showing up to class on time. And who am I to spoil the fun? Please take your usual place at the chalkboard, Miss Quinn…and by all means, Mr. LaPierre, you may go stand beside her."

Alice walked to the front of the room like a doll with no joints. Remy took his place next to the girl, watching her from the corner of his eye. Ms. Kemp marched up to the children and wrote the word LOVEBIRDS over their heads in bold letters, encasing it in a giant, frilly heart. She stood back to admire her work.

"There now, what a perfect match. What a *devoted* pair. Class, did you ever see such a splendid, adoring couple?!"

The room was silent but Ms. Kemp went on brightly, as if a response was immaterial.

"Isn't it a pity something as dreary as school must come between them? So tiresome. Such a shame. *Nothing* should get in the way of true love!"

The blood drained from Alice's face and she began to tremble. Ms. Kemp saw this and a shiver went down her spine. For the first time in seventeen years she was finally enjoying her job as a teacher.

The morning wore on and the children remained at the board. Alice stood like an animal with its leg caught in a trap and Remy kept glancing sideways, trying to gauge her condition. He did not so much mind the punishment; indeed, there was some part of him that didn't mind it at all, but he could see it had struck the girl a mortal blow.

Ms. Kemp kept them inside during recess, an arrangement she came to regret when Mr. Bouchard dropped by to say hello. Accordingly, she dismissed the children to the hallway and forgot about them, so that they took their seats when the bell rang and the rest of the class came in, red-cheeked and stamping their feet from the cold.

Alice refused to look at Remy for the rest of the day. She kept her head down, wisps of hair covering her face. Marni Pitt caught a glimpse of the girl on her way to the pencil sharpener and told the rest of the class her face was the color of curdled milk.

Ms. Kemp could not be bothered to notice. As it happened, there were more compelling distractions in the supply closet where Mr. Bouchard was having trouble locating the overhead projector.

When school let out, there was the usual commotion. Children streamed outdoors, pushing and shoving, calling out insults and looking for fights. Remy got caught up in a crowd of fourth graders playing keep-away with Wax Klassen's toque and by the time he broke free, Alice was nowhere to be seen. He searched the halls and couldn't find her anywhere. She was not in the cloakroom nor waiting in line for the bus. He circled the school twice before noticing, at the far end of the field, a flash of red disappear into the tree line leading down to the creek.

Remy took off running.

"Alice!" he yelled, when he'd narrowed the distance between them. The girl hunched over and started to run, her knapsack heaving from side to side. They raced through the aspen grove in Anderson's field, a streak of color blurring between the stark, white trees. Alice could hear the boy's footsteps closing in on her. She looked over her shoulder and tripped, rolling like a tumbleweed as she fell to the ground. Her knapsack tore open and sailed overhead, papers fluttering into the air like the scene from a dystopian snow globe.

"Alice!" said Remy, stopping short. The girl scrambled away from him, her eyes wild, gasping and choking for breath.

"Alice," he said again, more softly. He didn't dare go near her. Instead, he began picking up her papers, sneaking glances at the girl as he kept to a cautious distance.

Alice huddled in a ball, knees clasped to her chest, her face lost in the depths of the scarf.

"Alice, look. This is where we made a fire that one time and cooked our fish. Remember? Look, the stones are still here. C'mon, I'll make another one. Watch this–I'm gonna use my homework to get it started."

Remy gathered a handful of twigs and grass. He pulled a worksheet from his bag and rolled it tightly, then struck a match from his pocket and lit it like a torch. He fed the blaze with bigger sticks and continued ripping pages from his notebook, hoping to distract the girl with this brazen display of vandalism.

"Look, Alice. The fire's burning good now. Come over here, okay? Come sit where it's nice and warm."

Remy moved closer to the girl and held out his hand.

Alice lifted her head and stared through the boy.

"I don't love you, Remy," she said, speaking in dead tones, "I don't love *anyone*."

"It's okay," he said, "Don't listen to Ms. Kemp. She's an idiot. She doesn't know what the hell she's talking about."

"Well, I don't. I don't love anyone. I *don't!*"

Her voice broke and she huddled on the ground, fists clenched and eyes tightly shut.

"*Shhh*…it's okay," said Remy, speaking gently though there was a ringing in his ears, "It's just me, okay? Don't let that stupid bag get to you. Dammit, Alice, she's a friggin' idiot. She's nothing but a stupid old bag."

The girl was shaking, her face twisted and unrecognizable as a sound rose from within her, a guttural, keening wail that echoed the bewildered misery of an animal in pain. The boy felt the earth shudder beneath him and he fell to his knees, calling out her name.

"Alice, listen to me!" he cried, reaching out to touch her arm, "One thing you gotta know–I'm not going anywhere, okay? You hear me?"

"Don't say that!" sobbed the girl, struggling away like a bird with a broken wing, "Don't say those things to me!"

"Doesn't matter if I say it or not! It doesn't change a thing!"

"Don't you *read?* Don't you know anything?!" she cried, gesturing wildly, "People only say stuff like that before they end up having to *leave!*"

Remy looked away, feeling his throat tighten. He stood up and wiped his face, breathing heavily.

"Listen to me," he said slowly, his voice fraying at the edge, "I don't give a shit about your books right now. They're just stories. Do you hear me? Friggin' make believe. They aren't real. *This* is real. *You're* real. You're the only real thing to me. Don't you understand? Don't you know that? Nothing else matters. You're the only real thing."

Alice looked up at the boy, stricken, then buried her head in her arms. The dim light of the afternoon faded as her body shook with sobs, lost in the folds of the scarf.

Remy looked up, remembering the fire.

"C'mon, Alice. Come sit by the fire. No one's making you, but just do it anyway. We can stay as long as you want and we don't have to talk about anything. *Please.*"

Alice closed her eyes. She felt like she'd been living a hundred years. But Remy was reaching for her and the fire glowed in the fading light, so she took his hand and let him pull her toward the warmth.

CHAPTER
10

Snow began falling the first day of December. Alice woke up and got out of bed, tiptoeing to the window. She rested her fingers on the ledge and leaned forward, her breath making pale rosettes on the glass. Outside the world was transformed, made smaller and more intimate, spun into a boudoir of veils and fine lace. It was silent like the tomb–a deep, padded stillness whose hushed presence hung heavily in the air.

The alarm clock rang, startling the girl. She hurried down the hallway and into the kitchen, opening the refrigerator door.

"Nice nightie," said Rob Novak who was sitting at the table, watching her with a hooded expression.

The girl spun around.

"What are you doing here?!" she exclaimed.

The man burst out laughing, a dull-witted mirth that loosened a cesspool of phlegm in his throat.

"You should see yer face!" he jeered, "Looks like you seen a ghost!"

"Where's my mom?" asked Alice, her gaze darting between the man and the entrance to the hallway.

"Sleeping. Needs to get up and feed me." Rob stretched back in the chair, scratching his belly, smiling at the girl through half-open eyes as if they were in on a secret joke.

"You gonna make me something to eat?"

"I have to go to school," she said, keeping her head down and ducking out of the room.

"Aw, that's not very nice."

He frowned, stamping his foot and making a move as if to grab at the girl when she passed by. Alice gasped and skittered across the linoleum, sending the man into new spasms of laughter.

"Come back here!" he called, gasping for breath, "Let's see you do that one more time!"

Alice hurried to her bedroom and shut the door hard. She stayed there a moment, feeling her heart beat against the hollow panel. When her eyes began to sting she grit her teeth and pushed on, getting dressed in quick, jerky movements. She reached beneath her pillow for the petrified wood and went to the window, staring at the shawls of thickly falling snow. It was too early for the boy to arrive but she stood there anyway, as if by concentrating she could will him into existence. The floor in the hallway creaked, startling the girl. She fumbled at the latch on her window, slid it open, and heaved herself into a drift.

Remy met her at the top of the lane.

"Hey!" he said, struck by the sight of the catlike creature coming toward him through the snow.

The girl nodded but did not reply.

"Is everything okay?" he asked, taking a step closer, "You're never out this early."

"It's fine," she said, her voice muffled within the depths of her scarf.

The snow stopped falling by the time school got out, though clouds hung low over the valley like the generous bosom of an affectionate great aunt. Remy suggested skipping the bus in favor of walking home along the train tracks and Alice, whose stomach had been growling all day, weighed her hunger against the thought of finding Rob Novak still sitting at the kitchen table, and agreed. The weather was bearable enough as the children started down the road but the winds soon picked up, buffeting and lashing through their coats as if they were wearing nothing at all. The girl stumbled along, her bones aching. She wanted to cry but did not dare, knowing to falter would only make things worse, as if the cold was a tyrant that could sniff out and punish weakness. They trudged past the gas station when Remy stopped short, suddenly intent.

"Wait," he said, pointing to the other side of the road, "What *is* that?"

Alice did not respond.

"Look–sticking out of the snow," he insisted, "That blue thing. Do you see it?"

"Remy, I'm cold."

"Just a minute." He loped across the pavement and floundered through the drifts, crouching to retrieve the object. "You're not going to believe this," called the boy, turning and waving his fist in the air. He made his way back to the girl, "Guess what I just found?"

"No clue."

"Guess."

"Remy, please. It's freezing out here."

"Just one guess."

"Turkish delight."

"What?"

Alice shook her head.

"Never mind."

Remy held up a piece of paper for her inspection. It was a crumpled, soggy, five dollar bill.

The girl stared at the money, her teeth clenched to keep from chattering.

"C'mon. Let's go spend it."

"But what if it belongs to someone?"

"It does belong to someone–*us*. Now c'mon, you're shivering."

The children entered the gas station stamping their shoes, their cheeks red and burning from the heat of the room.

"Let's go sit at the counter," said Remy, leading the way.

"Are we allowed?" asked Alice.

"Of course we are," he said, hoping this was true.

Mr. Redchenko was working the lunch counter that day.

"What's it going to be?" he said, as if there was nothing unusual about the sight of the two children seated before him.

"She needs something hot to drink," said Remy, nodding at Alice.

"We have coffee."

"That'll do."

Mr. Redchenko poured two large cups of the beverage, stirring them full of sugar and cream.

"This one looks like a little *kukla*," he said, regarding the girl. He stood for a moment, then set some pastries before the children–hot, buttery rolls with sausage baked into the center. They stared at the plate and Alice gripped the counter, feeling light-headed.

"What do I owe you?" said Remy, glancing at the man.

"No charge. T'was my pleasure," said Mr. Redchenko, "A gift for the little Russian doll."

Alice took a sip of the coffee, the warmth seeping through her.

"*Spasibo*," she said softly, surprising herself.

Mr. Redchenko roared with delight, clapping his hands.

"And she speaks Russian, too?!" he said.

Alice looked down and pursed her lips, an old longing stirring deep inside.

"No," she shook her head, "Just some words I learned from a neighbor lady who used to take care of me."

Mr. Redchenko moved on, still exclaiming, refilling the cups of two old farmers who'd been sitting at the counter for over an hour and had yet to utter a single word. The children devoured the pastries and drained their coffee to the last drop.

"Let's get some candy before we go," said the boy. Alice looked up, her face rosy and bright.

"You always have the best ideas," she said.

They wandered to the candy aisle and hovered before the display, lost in the rapture of having to make such a splendidly agonizing choice. When they were finally decided the boy looked out the window, noting the lateness of the hour, the soft pats of snow falling sideways in a lavender sky. Instead of waiting to the side, he marched up to the counter and set their purchase upon it. The Warden recoiled as if she'd been struck by a snake, unable to gather her wits before the boy continued.

"There's a dollar's worth of candy in that sack," he said,

"Plus three chocolate bars."

He slapped down the five dollar bill and folded his arms, staring the woman straight in the eyes.

"It's wet!" she hissed, her jowls quivering, the scar on her cheek as dark as a licorice whip.

"It's *money*," said the boy, refusing to look away.

"Where did you get it?"

"What difference does it make?" he replied, smoothing out the bill, "It's cold, hard cash…and when I say cold, I mean *cold*."

Alice, to her horror, burst into giggles.

"You think it's funny?" said the Warden, turning on the girl, "Is this your idea of a joke?!"

From across the room, Mr. Redchenko barked something to his wife in a strident tongue. She slammed her fist onto the counter, responding with a stream of invective that needed no translation. The couple went back and forth, gesticulating wildly, tidal waves of anger rising up and crashing like great orchestral cymbals between them. Finally, the Warden grabbed the bill from the counter and flung it into the till. Nostrils flaring, she counted out Remy's change and stalked off, slamming the door to the family's living quarters behind her. The children took their candy and scurried toward the exit before this fragile truce could be broken. From the corner of her eye, Alice stole a glimpse at the shopkeeper who looked at her and winked.

Once outside, Remy and Alice huddled in a phone booth next to the store. The winds had died down and it was snowing heavily, a thick layer of clouds keeping the colder temperatures at bay. Remy took a mint flavored Aero bar from the sack and handed it to the girl.

"You do it," he said.

She unwrapped the green foil from one corner and the children leaned forward, bumping heads as they breathed in the sublime scent of milk chocolate.

"Here," said Alice, snapping off a piece and offering it to the boy, "You go first. You're hungrier than me."

Remy popped the confection into his mouth and almost swallowed it whole. He closed his eyes.

"Aeros are…everything," he said, after a moment of silence. It was the closest the boy had come to uttering a prayer.

"Have some more," said Alice, "You didn't even taste that bite."

"No, it's your turn." He shook his head, resolute.

Alice nibbled the corner of her chocolate. The pairing of rich cocoa with peppermint melted on her tongue and permeated her senses until it seemed to the girl she was lost in some form of holy communion.

"It's perfect," she said, in the hushed tones one reserves for a church.

"It's *chocolate*," nodded the boy.

He looked up and stared into the snowfall, recalling the gravity of a distant, forgotten concern.

"We should be on our way."

Alice put the bag of candy into the boy's knapsack and zipped it shut. The children turned up their coat collars and pulled down their toques, quiet and grim. Remy wound the scarf around the girl's neck and head, leaving a peephole for her eyes. He slid the door open and the children stepped out, hunching their shoulders as they disappeared into the darkness and the shadowy curtains of falling snow.

It was two miles down the highway from Red's to the LaPierre house, and a little ways beyond to the Quinn's bungalow. The children walked arm in arm on the train tracks, unable to see more than a few feet ahead, reaching their destination past suppertime. The bungalow was cold and dark as they kicked off their wet shoes and hurried to the girl's bedroom. Alice turned on the Christmas lights and went to the kitchen to boil some water, returning with mugs of tea.

"What other books do you have in your treasure chest?" asked Remy, his face hidden in the darkness, hunched over his cup.

"Here, I'll show you," said the girl. She pulled the trunk out from beneath her bed and opened the lid.

"I have *Brighton's Book of Verse*, *Grimm's Fairy Tales*, *The Collected Stories of Guy de Maupassant*, *Baby Island*, and *The Holy Bible*."

"You have a Bible? Where'd you get it?"

"From a church."

"What do you mean, from a church?"

"What do *you* mean, what do I mean? I got it from a church."

"They were handing out Bibles?"

"Not exactly."

"Not *exactly*? You mean you took it?"

"I didn't *take* it. I *found* it."

"Let me get this straight: you *stole* a Bible from a church?!"

"I didn't steal it! It was in the lost and found, and I was the first one to find it."

"How does a Bible get lost in a church, for crying out loud?"

"Search me. But it was in the lost and found box, and you're allowed to take stuff from there."

"Yeah, but I think the idea is you take things that actually *belonged* to you in the first place."

Alice shrugged, as if this detail did not merit a response.

"Have you read it?" asked the boy, seeing she could not be engaged.

"Some. I can tell you, it makes those French stories look like a walk in the park."

"Really? How so?"

"Let me see. Well, there's this one time where God tells a guy named Abraham He's going to destroy a city for being too wicked."

"What?! What does that mean, *too wicked?*"

"I don't know. It didn't give details, but clearly He was not pleased."

"So He decides to go and level the place, just like that?"

"Well, I doubt it was on a *whim*. Anyway, Abraham makes a deal with God to spare the city if he can find fifty good men, and God agrees."

The boy rolled his eyes.

"Sounds like a set up to me," he said.

"Remy, you haven't even heard the story," said the girl, annoyed by this bit of conjecture.

"Fine. Then keep on going."

"Fine. Then quit interrupting. The problem is, there aren't fifty good men to be found. So Abraham goes back to God and asks if they can narrow it down to forty-five good men instead. And God agrees. But it turns out there aren't forty-five of 'em, either."

"I see where this is going," muttered the boy, shaking his head.

"No, you don't. You're just saying that to show off."

"Alice, it's obvious! I mean, who is this Abraham guy, anyway? His bargaining skills are the pits! What makes a person think he can rustle up forty-five good men when he's just been through the town and couldn't find fifty?"

"How am I supposed to know? I'm just telling you what I read. Besides, Abraham *did* know how to drive a bargain. He kept lowering the number and God kept taking the deal. The only problem is they got down to ten good men and Abraham couldn't even find that many."

"So then what happened?"

"God rained fire and brimstone on the city."

"*What?!*"

"That's what it said."

The room fell silent.

"I don't even know where to begin with this!" sputtered the boy, "For starters, how can you believe any of it?"

"What do you mean?"

"I mean, God, the Bible…do you even believe it's real?"

"I don't know," said the girl, hunching over the book. She shook her head and spoke slowly. "I don't know if the Bible's real. I don't know if God is real. But you wanna hear something crazy? I talk to Him all the time."

"What do you mean, you *talk* to Him?"

"I mean…in my head. I have this running conversation going, just whatever happens to be on my mind, and I'm pretty sure I'm talking to God."

"Does He answer back?" asked the boy.

"Not that I can tell," she admitted.

"I don't know if that's crazy or not," said Remy, who was holding up the carpenter bee and examining it through the magnifying glass, "But I think the whole thing's a *lot* to swallow without any proof."

"I go back and forth," sighed the girl, "Sometimes I want to believe He's real, other times I can hardly bear to think of it."

"How come?"

"I don't know. Maybe because it hurts either way."

She flipped through the book and ran her finger down a page.

"*Keep me as the apple of thine eye, hide me under the shadow of thy wings.*"

Alice stared at the words until they blurred before her.

"If God was real, I wish that's how He'd think of me," she said softly.

"I hate to break it to you, Alice, but I don't think He is real," said Remy. The room fell quiet and the boy shrugged, angry he could not offer more. "I will say this much–if there *is* a God, that's exactly how He'd think of you."

The girl hugged her knees and rested her head, her brow furrowed and grave.

"For some reason, it's harder to believe *that* than to think He exists in the first place."

She closed the book and put it back in the chest.

CHAPTER 11

On Saturday morning Alice got up and made rice pudding. When it was ready she spooned some into a cup, wrapped the scarf around her shoulders, and hurried up the lane.

The world outside was covered in snow. Thick, alabaster quilts blanketed the fields, dimpled in places by brambles and weeds, and fence posts wore caps of soft powder. The trees bent in heavy splendor, robed and beribboned in white, and a set of tiny bird tracks crisscrossed the lane, each step like the imprint of an ancient rune.

Madame Voisine's bungalow looked like a gingerbread house buried in sugary peaks, a decadent confection trimmed with dollops and frills. The girl struggled through the drifts and climbed the stairs, knocking on the front door. When there was no response she stood motionless, watching her breath steam the air, gazing at her sneakers that were already wet and cold. Alice stamped her feet and began to shiver. She stared into the distance, pushing back the thought she had nowhere else to go.

On a sudden impulse she reached out and touched the knob, giving it a gentle twist. The door swung open and the girl watched, wide-eyed at the thing she had done.

"Madame Voisine?" she whispered, leaning forward. The house was quiet and warm, bearing the faintest hint of cinnamon. Alice hesitated, then took off her shoes and tiptoed into the kitchen, setting the cup of pudding on the counter. The black cat greeted her with a plaintive meow but did not look up, as if the girl's presence was not compelling enough to rouse himself from slumber.

"Madame Voisine?"

Alice stepped into the living room. It was filled with curiosities, with ornate candlesticks and a giant, creeping fern. An empty nest sat on the windowsill beside a coiled nautilus, and next to the fireplace a large, earthenware vase held a mottled array of feathers. There were books in every direction–lining the shelves, piled high on a coffee table, in stacks on the floor and in the corners of the room. A garland of crystals hung across the front window catching the morning sun; chiseled prisms bending the light into mosaics of color flickering against the walls.

Madame Voisine lay propped on a velvet chesterfield, breathing lightly. Her eyes were closed and she looked like an antique porcelain doll with her rouged cheeks, patchy hair, and fine, spidery cracks on her skin. A goblet containing the dregs of a crimson merlot sat on the coffee table, and beside it a glass dish filled with gumdrops gleamed against the marble surface. Alice took a crochet blanket from the back of a chair and spread it over the woman, tucking the ruffle beneath her feet.

In so doing she noticed an enamel box no bigger than a pincushion lying on the floor. It was the color of the sky in springtime, inlaid with etchings of a sun, moon, and stars. A delicate key lay nearby and when she inserted this into the lock, the box made a clicking sound and opened to reveal a tiny, dimensional scene of a meadow with a brook tumbling over a bed of dark, speckled stones. Sunlight gleamed on the water and a dragonfly hovered nearby, unable to fix upon a landing. Grass rolled across the meadow in feathery waves and bees droned in clusters, nuzzling a carpet of wildflowers. A lark soared overhead, preening in flight, and behind a thicket of brambles, all that was visible of a young fox was its quivering nose thrust into the air.

Alice knelt beside the couch and held the box so close it seemed for a moment she could breathe in the scent of lavender and rose. She gazed upon the scene until she forgot where she was, lulled by the murmur of the brook and the sun against her face, the insistent nose of the little red fox.

Just then, a crash at the window startled the girl and she looked up, nearly dropping the box. She glanced at Madame Voisine, but the old woman slept on as if summoned to another world. The sun disappeared behind some clouds and the girl got up, testing every floorboard as she tiptoed across the room.

She stood at the window, her breath fogging up the glass, then slipped on her shoes and went outside.

The morning light washed thin and grey as the girl floundered through the drifts, searching for the cause of the disturbance. The only tracks leading to the bungalow were her own, but beneath the front window she noticed a small, circular impression in the otherwise pristine snow. Drawing near, she saw a disheveled puff of feathers and held her breath as she reached into the frozen hollow.

A tiny white owl lay cupped in her hands, its body limp and still. The owl was no bigger than a rose in bloom; too little, almost, to be real. Alice held the creature close, trying to shelter it from the frigid air. It appeared lifeless, but when the girl stroked its wing the owl blinked and shook its head, as if trying to knit together the discrepancy of the past several moments. The little bird struggled to its feet and began puffing out its feathers, smoothing them repeatedly with its quill of a beak. When it was finished grooming the owl sat quietly, perhaps lost in thought. The girl kept still, too, nearly forgetting to breathe. Without warning, the bird launched from her hands and shot into the air. It lurched and fluttered, trailing a shower of down, giving every indication of heading for another crash. At the last possible moment the owl righted itself, gained elevation, and flew off into the trees. The girl gazed at the spot where it disappeared, forgetting the cold, losing track of time.

The winds picked up, moaning through the valley. A white feather spiraled through the air and landed next to Alice, who tucked it into her scarf. She stood up and retraced her footsteps through the drifts, leaping from one print to the next until she made it back to the lane. A little brown bird rustling through a withered bush stopped to tilt its head at her, then returned to its squabble with a stubborn pod of seeds.

Alice hurried to the end of the lane and peered down the highway at the LaPierre house, the road flanked on either side with drifts piled high by the municipal plow. The house seemed to lean more than ever beneath the weight of the snow, and bayonets of icicles hung from its eaves like the jaws of a slavering wolf. A bitter gale lashed at the girl and she turned away, catching her breath. She stepped behind a mailbox and counted to one hundred, willing Remy to appear, but the house remained dark and still. The girl closed her eyes, feeling her stomach begin to churn. A semi rumbled by, shifting gears, bound for the mill with a load of logs strapped to its trailer. The girl waited for the truck to disappear around the bend, then sprang forth and lunged across the road.

The LaPierre dogs tore down the driveway as Alice approached and she froze in her tracks, realizing to advance or retreat would be equally catastrophic.

It was Remy who finally came to the door. He called off the dogs but did not venture down the steps toward her.

"What are you doing?" she called, her voice shrill through the distance between them.

"Nothing," he muttered, looking away from the girl.

"I made rice pudding," she said.

The boy was silent.

"Let's go to my place," she continued, "I'll tell you a story. We can listen to music and fold paper cranes. There's the pudding…and I'll make us some tea."

"I don't know," he finally said, "Wait for me by the road."

Remy stepped inside and was gone long enough for Alice to count into the hundreds, flinching at the row she could hear from within the house. When the boy re-emerged, she was standing on the front step.

"I told you to wait by the road," he said roughly, pushing past her.

"You're not the boss of me," she replied, a tremor in her voice.

They started off across the yard–the boy taking long strides while Alice hurried behind him, biting her lip. The winds were relentless and a tight pain rising in the girl's throat ached all the way to her ears. She folded her arms and fought to keep her balance on the slick, frozen mud but at the edge of the property, she jerked to a halt. A dark, ravenous thought of wanting it all to end rolled over her, taking her breath away. She turned in every direction. The sky overhead was desolate and the barren landscape stretched on forever. The girl bent down and picked up a rock, hurling it toward the house with all her might.

"There!" she screamed, her cry caught up and devoured by the wind.

Remy, who was farther ahead, heard scraps of the commotion and turned to see the girl facing the house as if she would throw herself against it and beat it with her bare hands. The winds whirled about her like a dervish, tugging at her scarf and whipping her hair into jagged peaks. The boy saw this and blinked, feeling the air rush back into his lungs.

"Alice," he called, retracing his steps, "C'mon. Let's go to your place and have some tea. I want to hear your story. And we can fold the paper cranes."

CHAPTER 12

On the first day of Christmas break, Remy showed up at Alice's house with a hatchet in hand.

"C'mon," he said, when the girl opened the door, "Let's go get a Christmas tree."

"From where?" she asked, ushering him inside.

"What d'you mean, *from where?*" said the boy, turning to gesture at the hill behind them. "Have you looked outside lately? There happens to be an entire forest in your backyard!"

"Remy, we can't just take one of those trees! They don't belong to us."

"Yeah, we can. It's Anderson's property. He won't care."

The girl blinked rapidly, alarmed by the boy's apparent readiness to swing at whatever stood in his way.

"But they're huge!"

"Some are. There's smaller ones, too."

"So…we just go up there and *take* a tree? Do you even know how to do that?"

"What d'you mean, *do I know how to do that?* Of course I know! You just keep chopping 'til one falls down."

Alice raised an eyebrow. The boy stared back brazenly until he had to turn away so she wouldn't see him smile.

"We never had a Christmas tree before," she said slowly.

"Well, I aim to fix that. Put your coat on. Let's go get a tree of your very own."

The girl shook her head, one corner of her mouth twisting higher than the other.

"You always have the best ideas," she said.

The children set out across the pasture beyond the bungalow. It was an arduous trek through the snow and they lunged like salmon against the current as they climbed the hill. Alice followed the boy, trying to stay in his footprints. When they reached the edge of the forest she gazed up at the towering evergreens, hushed and watchful, like sentinels on guard.

"It feels like we've found the wardrobe door," she whispered.

"What?"

"I mean, like…*Narnia*. Where the white witch is in power and the world sleeps in endless winter."

"What are you talking about?"

"*Shhh,* Remy. Be careful what you say. She has spies everywhere. Even some of the trees are on her side!"

"You're crazy," muttered the boy, annoyed at being left out of the game.

"It's a magical world in this book I'm reading. Some kids find it by crawling through a wardrobe door," said Alice.

She climbed onto a stump and gazed about their surroundings. A jagged cascade of ice hung from a boulder, the remnants of a brook frozen to the faintest shade of blue. Trees bowed beneath lavish fittings of snow, yielding to dormancy–that great, primordial rest which precedes all new things to come. Tapestries of frost laid out over opulent, rolling drifts transformed the landscape into an otherworld of silence and repose. It was beauty beyond longing, and in this realm of stillness the only trace of movement came from the girl's breath making soft clouds of vapor in the air.

"Sounds dumb," said the boy sullenly.

Alice turned, having forgotten he was there.

"No, it's one of the best stories I've ever read. You'd love it."

"What's a wardrobe anyway?"

"It's like an old fashioned closet, I think. People stick their coats in them."

"Well, it sounds dumb to me."

"Not as dumb as saying that when you haven't even read the book."

They walked on in strained silence when Alice suddenly stopped in her tracks, staring through the trees. A young deer stood in a grove of saplings, motionless, watching the children. It was the color of fallen leaves with a soft, white bib and ears like semaphores, rapt with attention.

"*Mr. Tumnus!*" she breathed.

There was a rustle in a nearby bush and a sleeve of snow crumbled off the branch of an evergreen. The deer blinked and slipped away, bounding silently through the undergrowth.

"Remy, I'm not kidding," said the girl, "I think this place is magic."

"Alice, you think everything is magic."

The girl paused to consider this, a half smile on her lips.

"I don't know if I *really* think it or not. But I need to believe in the possibility of it. I need to believe there *could* be magic in this world. Otherwise…"

"Otherwise, what?"

"I don't know how I could bear it."

The children entered the sapling grove and looked around.

"One of Mr. Tumnus's trees would be perfect," said Alice, contemplating a young pine poking out from the snow, "Do you think he'd mind?"

"No, because if there's a witch on the loose, then you have come to rescue him. You are the rightful queen, and taking this tree announces your arrival to the forest."

Alice turned to the boy, her eyes bright.

"You're my best friend in the whole world," she said.

Remy looked away, swinging his axe in the air.

"Same here," he muttered.

They wandered around the grove, examining trees, settling on a lopsided fir that took the boy less than ten minutes to chop down.

"You made that look easy," said Alice.

"That's because it *was* easy."

"Are you kidding me? You just cut down our very own Christmas tree. I've never seen anyone do that in my entire life!"

Remy straightened up and looked around, feeling as if he could chop down the entire forest.

By early afternoon the children started for home, dragging the tree behind them. At the edge of the forest Alice stopped to survey the valley, pristine white and blinding where sunlight caught crystals in the snow. Remy scowled, his eyes trained on a procession in the distance that toiled up the hill toward them.

"What's wrong?" asked Alice, turning to follow his gaze.

"It's the Gorsmas," said the boy, "And they've got their dog."

The Gorsma's dog was a creature of mythical proportion to the children of Starling. Even the very mention of his name–Dagger–could incur in them a brief paralysis, followed by a nervous twitch and an impulse to pee their pants. Some kids said the dog was actually a wolf. Peter Kowalski took it a step further, claiming he'd looked out his window the night of a full moon and saw a man running through his backyard. The man fell down on all fours, writhing in contortions until he transformed into a hideous creature that Peter identified as Dagger. Peter said it was the scariest thing he'd ever seen and that the man looked exactly like Mona Gorsma's father, who'd died a few years earlier in an accident at the mill. Of course Peter had no way of proving his story, making it all the more credible to the local way of thinking. After all, there was no cure for boredom like a good, sordid rumor, and what could be more compelling than a lurid claim no one had any evidence to dispute?

Either way, anyone could see Dagger was no normal dog. The gaunt, overgrown animal was a misfit of anatomy, like a creature forced against its natural design. Having known only hunger, cold, and the heel of a boot from his earliest days, it was as if anything that might have been inherently good in the dog had been kicked and starved out of him long ago.

"Whatever happens," said Remy through clenched teeth, "Stay behind me."

"What will they do?" whispered Alice, all color draining from her face.

"Let's go," he said. There was no way to avoid a confrontation, nor would it do any good to try. The boy understood this and stepped in front of the girl, hoisted his grip on the axe, and kept moving. A few minutes later their path intersected with the Gorsmas, Mona riding a toboggan pulled by her twin cousins.

"What're you doing on this property, LaPierre?" she demanded, holding up her hand as Dagger began to growl.

"None of your business. This is Anderson's property. We're allowed to be here."

"No it ain't. This field belongs to my uncle and that makes you two dirty trespassers."

"This is Anderson's field. Always has been. Anyone who says different is a liar."

Mona struggled to her feet, tipping off the toboggan and floundering in the snow. After a furious struggle she regained her balance, marooned by drifts reaching nearly to her waist.

"Who you calling a liar?" she shouted.

"Who you calling a trespasser? Anderson's house is one field over. We can settle this right now by going to ask him."

"*I* can settle this right now by letting Dagger rip you to pieces," said Mona, folding her arms over her chest with the expression of one who only understands brute force. The dog bared his teeth at the boy and girl, punctuating his low-throated growls with a series of rapid, maniacal barks. Remy stepped forward and brandished his axe in the air.

"Then Dagger better damn well hope it's his lucky day," he said, "'Cause I'm gonna bash his brains in the second he makes a move."

Mona turned to Buck and Jerry but the twins hung back, looking askance, the prospect of facing Remy and his axe rather less appealing than their preferred method of sneaking up from behind. Mona swore and kicked at the snow. She rebuked her cousins with a loud stream of insults but they bowed their heads like beasts of burden, unable to face her yet determined not to move. There was something about the LaPierre boy, an unpredictable grit, the dark mark of lineage, that was not to be dismissed. With her cousins on the verge of mutiny and the added hindrance of the snow, Mona sensed her dwindling advantage and looked to salvage a respectable retreat.

"I'll let it go this time, LaPierre," she said, turning and spitting into the drifts, "But you better never let me catch you on this hill again. And if Dagger ever finds the new girl out on her own, there'll be nothing left of her by the time he's done. Ain't that right, boy?" Mona clapped her hands at the dog, sending him into a new frenzy of barking.

"Her name's Alice. And that dog better not go anywhere near her."

"Oh yeah? Or what?"

"You don't wanna know."

"Oooh, I'm so scared!"

Remy stared hard at the dog, saying nothing. Mona clambered onto the toboggan, cursing up a storm, berating her cousins for letting the sled wobble as they went on their way. The boy watched until the Gorsmas were specks in the distance before turning to the girl.

"There," he said gruffly, "They're gone now. You okay?"

Alice did not respond. She blinked rapidly and turned away, a sharp breeze blowing wisps of hair across her face. Remy stood motionless, scanning the fields before them. From here the children could see the Quinn's bungalow and Anderson's farmhouse in the distance, pocket-sized trees along the creek, and the horizontal ribbon of the highway with cars moving back and forth like quaint, miniature toys. The winds picked up, sweeping bits of ice across the snow in whirling gusts. The boy did not flinch against the sting of the shrapnel but the girl ducked her head, lost in the folds of her scarf.

"Alice," said Remy, "It's cold and we gotta keep moving. I'll take the tree. C'mon, let's get out of here."

The children commenced their trek down the hill once more. As they neared the bungalow, Alice stopped and stiffened. Remy, who was walking behind her, followed her gaze to the black Trans Am parked in the driveway. He paused, waiting to see what the girl would do. When she didn't move, he dropped the tree and scooped up a snowball, throwing it and hitting her between the shoulders.

Alice whirled around.

"Don't!" she said.

"Don't what?" The boy stared back, trying not to blink.

"Don't throw snow at me."

"I didn't!"

"You did so."

"Did not. Maybe it was Mr. Tumnus."

"*Remy.*"

"*What?* You're the one who said he was magic."

"Don't use my words against me."

"Okay, so in the event I threw a snowball, then what?"

"You *did* throw it!"

"I'm not admitting to anything. But for the sake of argument, let's just say I did."

"I *did* just say you did."

Alice glared at the boy, anger welling beyond her ability to comprehend. Remy shook his head and packed another handful of snow, lobbing it in her direction. This time it grazed the girl's shoulder and exploded, leaving chunks of ice in her hair.

Alice's mouth dropped open.

"Are you crazy?!" she exclaimed, "Have you gone and lost your mind?"

The boy began to laugh as if he really was crazy. Alice clenched her fists and made a snowball, throwing it with all her might. Remy ducked out of the way with ease, making an exaggerated show of relief. The girl stood trembling, unable to think or see, heavy breath flaring her nostrils. Something akin to a battle cry erupted from the depths of her being and she lunged forward, ready for war.

A chase ensued, made absurdly sluggish by the knee-deep snow. Remy stayed several steps ahead, just beyond reach, enraging the girl until her mind was emptied of every other thought except the blinding desire for revenge. She charged through the drifts, screaming unintelligibly until she collapsed, lungs ragged, unable to take another step. Remy approached cautiously, calling for a truce. Alice ignored the boy until he sat down beside her, then hit him in the head with her last snowball.

Remy sputtered indignantly.

"But I called truce!"

The girl shrugged, smiling into her scarf.

"Maybe I didn't agree to your terms," she said.

When the snow began to soak through their clothing, the children got up and staggered back to the tree. Remy examined the trunk.

"We need some kinda bucket to keep this in," he said.

"I'll go look in the woodshed," replied the girl.

The woodshed was an old, sagging shack at the end of the driveway, partially stacked with firewood and containing odds and ends left by previous tenants. A few minutes later Alice emerged carrying a rusted pail.

"That'll do," said the boy.

The bungalow was quiet when the children went inside, the evergreen in tow. They tiptoed through the kitchen and into the narrow hallway. Penny's door was closed and the children moved silently in the darkened space. Remy carried the tree into Alice's room where they propped it in a corner and filled the bucket with water. When they took off their coats and hats, static electricity made their hair stand on end and the children smiled at each other, not saying a word.

The rest of the evening was spent making decorations for the tree. Remy took the Christmas lights down from the wall and draped them around the branches. He cut snowflakes from tissue paper while Alice dusted the pinecones from her windowsill with a fine sheen of glitter, looping them with string. They folded paper cranes out of the girl's old homework sheets, placing the birds at intervals in the boughs.

"Do you believe in fairies?" asked Alice.

"No."

"Well, here's a fairy kiss for you." She reached into the jar of glitter and pressed her fingertip against his cheek.

"Very funny," said the boy, though he did not wipe it off.

The room fell into silence and the children turned to contemplate the tree.

"Let's plug it in," said Alice, reaching behind the branches.

The little evergreen lit up, its sudden transformation causing the girl to catch her breath. Tissue snowflakes hung in garlands and the pinecones swayed gently, twinkling in the glow. Paper cranes nestled amidst the needles and the air was filled with the scent of fresh pine. The light from the tree made a cavern in the room, crowned by bowers of darkness.

"Look, Remy!" said Alice, turning to the boy, "It *is* magic! Don't you feel it?"

Remy looked at the girl's face, radiant in the shadows. He felt drawn to her in a way he could not explain for he did not have the words, but it felt as if every day of his life had existed just to bring him closer to this moment, and outside the bitter night never seemed so far away.

"Yeah," he said, closing his eyes and feeling the strange ache of relief flow through his body, "I do."

CHAPTER 13

Snow fell steadily on Christmas Eve. The glass plant shut down for the holiday and Penny drove to Caribou with Rob Novak for lunch at the Buckeye Saloon. Alice trudged up the lane and knocked on Madame Voisine's door.

The old lady answered wearing a tinsel boa draped around her fur coat.

"Come in, my dear," she said, smiling as if they shared a secret, "I was just giving the ferns a yuletide tipple."

"Would you like some help?" asked Alice.

"From the girl who brought me such a marvelous pudding? Nothing would delight me more! Come–make a cozy place beside Minou and tell me something of yourself."

Alice took a seat and looked at the floor, trying to compose her features.

"What would you like to know?"

"Oh, anything and everything…the little details that make up who you are. For starters, if you could spend a day with anyone who's ever lived, who would you choose?"

Alice stared at the woman as she went on watering the plants, young, green tendrils coiling about her as if greedy to slake their thirst.

"Madame Voisine," she stammered, "How did you know? I think about that question all the time."

"Do you?" said the woman, peering at the girl through the fronds of a maidenhair, "Then you must have a good answer."

"That's just it," said Alice, shaking her head, "The more I think, the harder it is to decide."

"Have you narrowed it down at all?"

"Well, I have a few people in mind. There's one I keep coming back to, but I'm not even sure if he's real."

"Not sure if he's *real*? How so? Is he a character from a book?"

"Sort of…but not really."

"A mythical being?"

Alice shrugged.

"Depends on who you're talking to," she said.

"Well, I'm at a loss," said Madame Voisine, gesturing with her free hand, "Tell me who this mystery person is."

"It's God."

"God?"

"Yes. As in…the Great Almighty. Do you think He's real?"

Madame Voisine set down her watering can and the ticking of a clock could be heard from somewhere deep within the house.

"That's quite a probing question, my dear," she said, brushing away some invisible dust, suddenly restless with her hands, "One that hardly hinges on my opinion, to say the least. If such a being as God exists, surely He does so whether I believe in Him or not."

"Yes," said the girl, nodding slowly, "I suppose whether or not you believe would affect *you* more than it would Him. I mean, He's *God*, for crying out loud. But either way…do you think He's real?"

Madame Voisine looked at Alice. Her expression, so naked with longing, was almost painful to behold and for a moment the woman wavered, tempted to say what the child was yearning to hear.

"I don't know," she finally admitted.

There was a heavy silence as the words hung in the air between them.

"So…you're on the fence, then," said Alice, averting her gaze to look out the window.

"That's a rather sharp way to put it," replied the woman, picking up the watering can but making no move to return to the plants.

"Oh, it's just something one of my old neighbors used to

say. She talked a lot about stuff like that. One time she told me there's no such thing as an atheist in a foxhole."

"Is that so? Has she ever been in one, I wonder?"

"I have no idea. I don't even know what a foxhole is."

"Perhaps she doesn't, either."

There was another silence as Alice continued to look out the window.

"I'm sorry if my answer disappoints you," said the woman.

"It's okay. I'm not disappointed," said the girl, trying not to look disappointed, "I just wondered, that's all."

"But what about you, my dear? Why would you choose to spend a day with God if you're not even sure He exists?"

"I don't know," said Alice softly, gazing at the sleeping cat whose whiskers twitched with his dream, "They say He's supposed to really love you."

The woman filled a teakettle with water and set it to boil.

"Who's *they?*" she asked, rather darkly.

"Just…people I know. The lady I was telling you about who lived down the street from us in Caribou. I used to play with her kids. Sometimes I went to church with them."

"And what did you learn of God in their church?"

"A few things, I guess. Mainly I remember the color of the carpet. It was dark red and went on for miles," said Alice, bringing her feet up and clasping her arms around her knees.

"One time I asked the lady if she was afraid to die. She turned to me and said, *death is the reward.* That spooked me a little."

"I should say *so,*" remarked Madame Voisine.

"Sometimes," continued the girl, "I have this dream where I wake up inside a coffin, and the color of the lining is red like the carpet in that church."

"*Bonté divine!*" exclaimed Madame Voisine, throwing her hands in the air and turning to face the girl, "What is this path you've travelled?"

She set a cup of hot cocoa in front of Alice and rested her hands upon the girl's cheeks, looking deeply into her eyes.

"My child, I see you will find what you're looking for. Truth cannot elude one who seeks for it with the wholeness of her heart."

She bent down and kissed Alice on the forehead. The girl closed her eyes and breathed in traces of rosewater and spice. She sat quietly as the woman busied herself in the kitchen, returning to the table with a glass of wine and a plate of gingerbread cookies.

Alice regarded the offering, the cup of cocoa and the spoon she was given to stir it with. She felt strangely removed, as if this was happening to someone else, as if she was watching the scene unfold from a corner of the ceiling.

"Do you like gingerbread?"

The girl blinked, coming back to the moment. There was something about being in Madame Voisine's house that felt like an old dream, perhaps even an enchantment. She could not point to any particular piece of evidence as to why this was so; it was both in the details of the place and in something greater and more elusive altogether. It was in the plants beckoning from their pots and the languorous indifference of the cat. It was in the faint scent of cinnamon and being asked to sit at the table with a cup of cocoa placed before her. It was in the warm shafts of sunlight making cross-sections of the room, and the tone of the woman's voice that filled the girl like a lost memory until it was all she could do not to put her head down and cry.

"Very much," she replied.

Alice set her cup on its saucer and pulled a little box from her pocket, giving it to Madame Voisine.

"This is for you," she said.

"For me?" said the woman, and her eyes sparkled so that the girl lost sight of the years between them.

Madame Voisine removed the lid and grew very still. The interior of the box was painted to look like a pond in springtime. There was a ripple in the water where a tiny frog had vanished from its lily pad, and a thatched nest made of real grass sat amidst the reeds. A paper crane rested there looking pensive and kind, and a chick sat beside her, no bigger than an apple seed.

"*Magique*," she whispered and Alice sat back, hugging herself tightly. The girl could see by the look on the woman's face she was no longer sitting at the kitchen table but rather crouched beside the nest, admiring the baby crane, caught up in the wonder of a glorious spring day.

When Madame Voisine looked up, her eyes were bright.

"Such a treasure," she said.

Somewhere, the clock chimed the hour and Minou shifted, yawning from his post beneath the potted plants.

The woman reached into her coat and withdrew a package, pushing it across the table.

"It's your turn," she said.

Alice looked at her with wide eyes.

"But how did you know I was coming?"

"Oh, I just had an idea," said Madame Voisine, smiling at the girl.

The gift was wrapped in white tissue and fastened with a string. Alice untied the bow and the paper fell away to reveal a crystal pendant hanging from a faded, brass star. She gazed at it with a lopsided smile and the woman watched with a similar expression of her own.

"It's beautiful," said the girl, holding the crystal to the light.

"I thought, perhaps, for the top of your tree..?" the woman suggested.

Alice looked at her quickly.

"How is it you know *everything*, Madame Voisine?" she asked, "Sometimes I think you really are a witch, after all."

The old woman laughed.

"This is Starling, my dear. It would call upon greater powers *not* to know what goes on around this place–now that would be magic, indeed!"

From the window Alice saw Remy walking down the lane toward her house. She tapped on the glass and the boy spun around. He stood there squinting, then scowled.

"I should be on my way, Madame Voisine. Remy's outside waiting for me."

"Won't your friend come in?"

Alice peered at the boy, who was gesturing with his hands and vigorously shaking his head.

"I don't think so."

"Of course. Sometimes it's easier to see what's been put in our heads than what's right before our eyes," said the woman, gazing out the window.

Alice put on her shoes, zipped up her coat, and tucked the crystal into her pocket.

"Let me send you home with this," said the woman, handing her the pudding cup filled with gingerbread cookies.

"Thank you, Madame Voisine. Merry Christmas," said Alice, giving the woman a hug.

"You too, my child. Come again and see me soon."

Alice stepped outside and waved at Remy, who was waiting by the lane, kicking at a snowdrift.

"Hey," she said, floundering across the yard toward him.

"Hey," he said, "What're you doing?"

"I was just visiting Madame Voisine. My mom went to Caribou for the day."

"When does she get back?"

"Tonight. What are you doing?"

"Nothing, really. Simon has some friends at the house."

The children kicked at the snowdrift together.

"Do you want to sleep over at my place?" she asked.

"On Christmas Eve?"

The girl shrugged.

"What difference does it make?"

Alice and Remy spent the afternoon building a fort in the pasture. The snow packed easily and they constructed thick walls, chinking the cracks until it was deemed invincible. When the shadows stretched long across the field and the cold grew sharp, they made their way back to the bungalow and kicked off their shoes, laying their socks out to dry.

Alice opened the refrigerator and looked through the cupboards. There was nothing to eat in the house but she made some tea and that, with Madame Voisine's gingerbread, left them feeling warm and content. Afterward they went into the girl's bedroom where she stood at the window, peering into the darkness.

"When's your mom coming back?" asked Remy.

"I don't know. She said by nightfall."

"Was she with Rob Novak?"

"Yeah."

The girl reached into her pocket and unwrapped the pendant from Madame Voisine. She stared at it, blinking, a frozen look upon her face.

Remy saw this and said, "Do you want help getting that on the tree?

"I can do it myself," mumbled the girl.

"Well, you better step on it. Christmas is coming, you know."

"Very funny," said Alice, looping the string from the package around the brass star.

"Don't fall," said the boy, as she strained to reach for the top of the tree.

"I'm not!" she said, wobbling a little.

"Looks like you might."

"Quit trying to make me!" she snapped.

Remy stepped back with a sense of relief. It was preferable to make the girl laugh when she got this way, but failing that he would settle for chagrin. He plugged in the tree lights and sat down beside her.

"It's the perfect touch," he said, nodding to the star.

"No thanks to you," she replied.

The boy closed his eyes and said nothing. His work was done.

A beam of headlights stabbed the room and played a search across the walls.

"That must be your mom," said Remy, glancing at the girl.

She rested her head on her knees and did not respond.

"You going out there?"

"I will in a minute."

When Alice went into the kitchen she found her mother and Rob Novak seated at the table, eating from a box of fried chicken.

"Hey baby," said Penny, pushing the food toward her, "Want some?"

"No thanks, we already ate," said Alice, shaking her head.

"Who's *we?*" asked Rob.

"Me and Remy," said Alice, keeping her eyes on her mother, "Is it okay if he spends the night?"

"Is that the LaPierre kid? You wanna sleepover with him? Nothing like getting started early, eh?" said Rob, leering at the girl.

Penny threw back her head and laughed, a mirthless cackle that caused the girl to look sharply at her mother.

"Sure, why not?" she said, taking a drag on her cigarette and blowing the smoke through her nostrils.

"Don't do anything your mother wouldn't do," began Rob, leaning back and winking at Alice.

"Rob!" Penny spoke in warning tones, but a hungry smile trembled on her lips. Her appetite for attention was insatiable–anything would do, and nothing could ever be enough.

"'Cause she pretty much does it all!" he finished, ducking as Penny threw a drumstick at his head.

"You pig!" she exclaimed, folding her arms in a mock pout, "She's only a child!"

"Not for long," he replied, keeping his eyes on the girl.

Alice turned and left the room.

"You okay?" asked Remy, when she came into the bedroom. She shut the door and leaned against it, staring at the floor.

"I hate him," she said.

"So do I," nodded the boy.

This simple offering of solidarity washed over the girl like a tonic so that she stepped forward and sat down by his side. It was enough for the boy and he did not move, as one would not turn to look at a wild animal venturing near for shelter. The twinkling lights blurred and the children sat in silence, letting it all run together, failing to notice or register any other thought, which was a form of solace unto itself.

"Remy," said the girl, "who would you spend a day with if you could choose anyone who's ever lived?"

"You," he replied.

"Wait, you didn't listen. I said, *anyone who's ever lived*. That means you can choose from the past or present. It could be *anyone*. Anyone at all."

"I heard what you said."

"Then why did you pick *me?* For crying out loud, we practically spend every day together anyway. You just wasted your wish!"

"I didn't waste my wish. It got *granted*. How 'bout that? Let me guess: you'd pick someone you'll *never* get to spend the day with."

Alice scowled and was silent.

"Am I right?" he asked, cocking his head, "So *now* whose wish just got wasted?"

"Never mind," she said, refusing to look at him.

"Don't be so grouchy," said the boy, "Here, I have something for you. Close your eyes."

Alice stared at him, her eyebrow raised.

"I'm being serious. C'mon…close your eyes and hold out your hand."

The girl finally complied.

"Okay, now…look."

Alice opened her eyes. A wooden turtle about the size of a walnut shell was sitting in her hand.

"Oh!"

She ran her finger over the carving, holding it inches from her face.

"It's perfect," she said, "Such a tiny, perfect thing!"

"Merry Christmas, Alice."

She gazed at the turtle, her eyes shining.

"Where did you get him?" she asked.

"Down by the creek. He was wandering around, looking for a friend."

Alice turned to the boy and smiled so that his throat went dry.

"Is that so? And what did you tell him?" she asked.

"I said I knew just the girl," he replied.

Alice's smile grew impossibly bigger.

"But how did he get there in the first place?"

"From the creek, like I said. I whittled him out of a piece of wood I found down there."

"You *made* him?"

"Yeah."

"Remy, since when did you learn how to do that?"

"I guess you don't know everything there is to know about me, Alice Quinn."

She blinked at the boy several times, then held the turtle up to her ear.

"Does he talk?"

"Only to you."

Alice reached for a package beneath the tree and handed it to the boy.

"Here," she said, "Merry Christmas to you, too."

Remy fumbled with the tissue paper, flustered by the girl's attention.

It was a book. Remy held it up to the tree lights and read the title.

"*The Lion, the Witch, and the Wardrobe*," he said, looking it over quietly, "I've never had a book of my own."

"Well, this one's a good place to start."

He opened the cover.

"*To Remy, where it's always Narnia, from Alice*," he read, leaning in to peer more closely at the page.

"Oh, just ignore the rest of it," said the girl, waving her hand dismissively.

"It says here, beneath some scribbles: *Property of Starling Elementary*," he observed.

"Yeah, well…it used to be," she said.

"*Used* to be?"

"Don't look at me that way. The book was so good I couldn't bear to return it. So I told the librarian it got lost and ended up paying the fine."

Remy laughed.

"Only you would think of that," he said.

When the house grew quiet they rolled out a sleeping bag on the floor beside Alice's bed.

"Shouldn't we unplug the tree lights?" she asked, climbing beneath her covers.

Remy regarded her with a grave expression.

"Santa won't be able to find us if we do," he said.

Alice lay back on her pillow, watching the boy make shadow puppets against the wall. There was a rabbit and a dog, and another shape he insisted to be a pelican, though the girl only laughed harder each time he tried to make it fly.

"Remy."

"Yeah."

"How old were you when your mom died?"

"Eight."

"That was two years ago."

"Yeah, almost three."

"Do you remember her?"

"Sort of."

"What was she like?"

"I don't know. She slept a lot. I used to make sure she had a glass of water by her bed. Every time she woke up I helped her take sips through a straw. Then one day she stopped being thirsty."

"Oh," said Alice. The room was quiet, the shadow puppets gone.

"But I don't remember it very well," said the boy, telling the old lie.

"That would hurt too much to remember," said Alice softly, "Sometimes I change memories so they can't do that to me."

"Do what?"

"*Hurt.*"

"What do you mean?"

"Like…my dad. He's not really a sea captain, you know."

The girl's voice sounded thin and far away and the boy closed his eyes, floating after it in the darkness.

"I bet your mom never wanted to leave you," she said, "I bet that was the hardest part."

"Alice. No one in their right mind would leave you, either," he said, "Not in a million years."

The girl blinked and her tears made a sound as they hit the pillow.

"Here," said Remy, reaching his hand toward her. She reached back and they linked fingers, a lifeline being thrown in either direction.

CHAPTER 14

In the new year, Remy got a job. Mr. Anderson hired the boy to care for his chickens, a daily chore that entailed feeding, watering, and gathering the eggs. For this he was given three dollars a week.

The job would have been simple enough had the flock not included a hulking tom turkey named Ichabod, whose obsession with power rivalled that of the great tyrants of old. All day long Ichabod patrolled the grounds, pestering chickens, tormenting the rooster, and making plain his dominion over a balding peahen who'd built her nest in a crate at the far end of the coop. As time went on the turkey grew more ruthless. Rather than softening with age, Ichabod's lust for control drove him to increasing heights of fanaticism. He lashed out at will, attacking anything that moved, and over the years more than a few kids who came to gather eggs for the farmer feared the last thing they'd hear before departing this earth was the sound of that turkey's blood-curdling gobble.

Each day after school the children walked from the bus stop to Anderson's farm, where Alice stood outside the coop and flapped her arms to distract Ichabod while Remy slipped inside and gained access to the henhouse. At the sight of the girl Ichabod puffed out his chest and paced in mounting fury, beating his wings and emitting sounds of displeasure like that of a ticking bomb. When he looked big enough to burst he'd charge, barreling toward Alice with his head thrust forward like a fireplace poker. Ichabod did not stop short of the fence but rather hurtled against it, beating and clawing the wire with murderous intent as the girl stood not three feet away, unable to feel the bones in her body.

One bitterly cold afternoon Ichabod was nowhere to be found. The children walked the perimeter of the coop, rattling the wire and calling out his name.

"I don't get it," said Alice, furrowing her brow, "He's always out here bossing that poor little peahen."

"Weird," agreed the boy, staring hard at a barrel that lay sideways in the middle of the coop, "You don't suppose he's hiding on us, do you?"

Alice looked at him, wide eyed. Remy laughed.

"I'm just kidding. Have you seen the size of Ichabod's head? They don't call it a bird brain for nothing."

"Ichabod's no ordinary turkey," said Alice softly, "I think he holds a grudge against us."

"Impossible," scoffed the boy, though his bravado diminished considerably when it came time to venture inside the coop.

"Here, I'll go with you," offered Alice.

"No, you stay outside, just in case."

"But Ichabod's *gone*. We've looked everywhere. Maybe Mr. Anderson finally decided to eat him."

Remy disagreed but did not protest when the girl tiptoed in behind him. They picked their way across the frozen yard and opened the door to the henhouse, peering into the gloom.

"Ichabod?" whispered Alice.

"There's no way he'd be in *here*," said the boy, hovering on the threshold all the same.

The smell of old hay and the murmur of brooding hens calmed the children and they went inside, feeling safe in the musty stillness.

"Looks like the coast is clear," said Remy, reaching for the nests.

Just then, a piercing gobble shattered the silence and Ichabod erupted out of the darkness like he'd been shot from a cannon.

Alice froze. Remy raised his arms against the hailstorm of wings beating down on him that seemed to come from every direction.

"Run, Alice!" he yelled, swinging his bucket at the bird.

Alice stumbled out of the henhouse and lurched across the yard, slipping on mud and patches of black ice. She looked up and saw the chicken coop door in the distance, receding like a dark and terrible dream.

"*Run!*" screamed the boy.

Alice ran.

But when she reached the door, it wouldn't open. The old wood had warped against the frame and though she rattled the latch violently, it refused to budge. She turned to see the boy charging toward her with eyes like saucers, his bucket flying behind him in the air.

"Open the door!" he yelled, the turkey bearing down on him like a low flying missile.

"It's stuck!" she cried, banging the latch with her fists and throwing herself against the panel. Remy was five feet away, coming at full speed when the latch finally popped. Alice yanked the door open as the boy ran through, slamming it behind them in time for Ichabod to land with a terrific crash against the other side.

The girl closed her eyes, hardly able to stand. Streams of mucus ran down her face and her hands shook so badly it took several attempts to fasten the latch. When she turned to the boy, she gasped.

"Are you okay?!"

Blood dripped from Remy's hand and spattered in the snow.

"Oh no, he got you! Ichabod got your finger!" she exclaimed, grabbing his arm to inspect the damage.

"What do you mean, he *got* my finger?! He *bit it off?!*" cried the boy, straining to see for himself.

"No! He didn't bite it *off*. But he gave it a pretty good gash. Hang on."

Alice bent down and scooped up a handful of snow. She rubbed it over Remy's finger, trying to determine the extent of the damage.

"I can't make it stop bleeding," she muttered, "C'mon, let's go wash it off in the creek."

The children hurried across the farmyard and scrambled down the bank to a place where the water ran shallow.

"It looks cold," said the boy.

"Give me your hand," Alice commanded.

She submerged his finger in the water, clouds of crimson billowing from the gash and washing downstream.

"It's freezing!" he protested.

"Hold still," said the girl. She pulled off her scarf and pressed it against the wound.

"Now grip this hard and don't let go. We have to get you home."

"What about the chickens?"

"I'll come back and feed them myself."

"No, Alice! We have to do it now. I don't wanna lose my job."

The girl looked at him grimly.

"Okay, but *I'm* going in for the eggs. You keep Ichabod busy over by the peahen's nest."

As it happened, Ichabod was in no need of such distraction. His crash into the chicken coop door had rendered him unconscious and he slumped on the ground, a motionless pile of pinfeathers and down.

Alice stared at Remy.

"Is he dead?" she whispered.

"I doubt it. That thing could survive the apocalypse."

She fed and watered the chickens, gathered the eggs, and left them on the steps of the farmer's front door. As they passed by the coop on their way home, the children saw Ichabod rouse himself and wobble about the yard, a look of bilious incomprehension upon his face.

When the children reached the Quinn's house, they discovered the scarf had fused to the cut on Remy's finger. Alice ran a sink of warm water and soaked his hand, separating the wool from the congealed blood with painstaking care. She got out her magnifying glass to examine the damage.

"It's still bleeding," she observed.

"I could've told you that without a magnifying glass," he replied.

"Very funny," she said, "I can't tell if you need stitches or not. I bet Madame Voisine would know what to do."

"No!" scowled the boy, "You're doing just fine."

"Honestly, Remy," she said, shaking her head, "I don't know why you believe those crazy stories. Madame Voisine may be different, but in the very best way."

She bandaged the wound, cutting a strip of fabric from her bed sheet to use as dressing.

"There," said the girl, inspecting her work, "Your poor finger. I hope it feels better soon."

She bent over and touched it to her lips.

"Yeah," said the boy, clearing his throat, "It does a bit, actually."

CHAPTER 15

The next day, Ms. Kemp's class was scheduled to visit the library. The children trooped into line, jostling for position.

"Do you enjoy library time, Miss Quinn?" asked Ms. Kemp as she walked down the row. The teacher spoke in idle tones, a detail that should have raised flags, but Alice in her excitement looked up without seeing, already browsing the shelves of books in her mind.

"Yes!" she replied, her smile fading as she noted the dour set of Ms. Kemp's expression.

"Well, that's a shame, because you no longer get to go."

"But…but I have to return my books," the girl stammered, clutching the stack to her chest.

"But-but-but!" mimicked the teacher, her hands flying to her face in mock horror, "I *have* to return my books!"

A silence fell over the room and Alice stood still, her shoulders hunched over the precious cargo in her arms.

Ms. Kemp leaned forward, her lips pressed together in a thin line.

"How curious! How very *odd*. Returning your books didn't seem like such a priority last month, now did it?"

The teacher held up a pink library notice bearing the fine for *The Lion, The Witch, and the Wardrobe* and wafted herself with it like a fan.

"But I paid for that," said the girl, barely audible.

"Speak up!" barked Ms. Kemp, "I can't hear you!"

"I said I paid for it," Alice repeated, whispering again.

"Oh, you *paid* for it, did you? I didn't realize the book was for *sale*. Since when did the school library become your own personal bookstore, Miss Quinn?!"

Alice stared at the ground. Ms. Kemp reached out and grabbed the girl by her chin, tipping it up so she had no choice but to meet the teacher's gaze.

"I said, *since when did the library become your own personal bookstore?!*"

Alice opened her mouth but could not speak. There was a fury in the teacher's eyes that seemed to make them quiver and the girl, who'd lost all feeling in her legs, hung like an insect circling the drain before its complete and utter demise.

The silence was shattered by Corinne LeRoy's deafening scream.

"Something's wrong with Remy!" she cried.

The entire class swung around, shifting their attention to the end of the line where the boy was staggering about, his face covered in blood.

"I don't feel so good," he said.

"What in the living hell–," began the teacher, taking a step backward. She wobbled and grasped a chair for support, breathing heavily. Ms. Kemp did not fare so well at the sight of blood.

"Get him out of here!" she yelled at Kevin Olenski, making fluttering gestures with her hands, "Someone take him to the nurse!"

She collapsed into one of the desks as Remy lurched toward her, his eyes rolling up into the back of his head.

"Teacher," he moaned, stumbling. He flung out his hands and grabbed onto the woman in order to break his fall.

Ms. Kemp looked like she was being engulfed in quicksand. Her face turned a chalky shade of green and she began flailing her arms.

"Get him off me!" she screamed, staring at the blood smears on her blouse.

Not to be outdone, Corinne LeRoy swooned and fell to the ground but when no one paid any attention, she scrambled back to her feet and shot dirty looks at all her friends. Ms. Kemp put her hand over her mouth and made a gagging sound that set off a chain reaction, causing three students standing nearby to actually throw up.

The teacher ran out of the room and did not return for the rest of the day. Corinne LeRoy left to find the janitor and halfway through the hour Ms. Benita, the librarian, came to collect the other children. Remy was sent to the school nurse, who took one look at his injured finger and stared at the boy, hard. He put his head down and would not meet her gaze. The nurse pursed her lips and dressed the wound in silence, preferring not to learn more about the incident than she was absolutely required to know.

Before going to bed that night, Alice took out a pencil and piece of paper and drew a girl in the middle of the page. Beside her she drew an extra t-shirt, some jeans, and a pair of shoes. Next to these, a knapsack and a flashlight, a book, a canteen, and a box of matches. Alice stared at the drawing, rocking back and forth until the knot in her stomach began to relax. She folded the paper into a square, turned off the lamp, and got into bed. A few minutes later the light clicked on again and the girl climbed out from her covers, laying the drawing on the floor. Huddled in the shadows, she drew a sweater next to the t-shirt and an apple beside the book. Blinking slowly, she folded the paper and went back to bed.

CHAPTER 16

February did not surface out of darkness. The children walked to the bus stop beneath a starless sky and finished school with the setting of a dim, obscured sun. The cold was relentless, seeping into houses to ice down the bed sheets and petrify the floors. It was waiting for the children when they stepped outside, stiffening their nose hairs and reaching a sadistic fingernail down their throats as if to shatter their lungs. A grim economy took hold of the valley as the residents withdrew into themselves, conserving their movements, becoming as bleak and still as the low hanging clouds. Remy came down the lane for Alice each morning but the children walked in silence, their toques pulled low and fists clenched tight, each step causing their bones to tremble and ache.

After school they did the chores at Anderson's farm, moving slowly, speaking in low tones. Even Ichabod was quiet, hunched into his mantle of feathers, facing away from the flock.

The turkey had never fully recovered from his collision with the chicken coop door and though he looked as ill-disposed as ever, there was a vacant glaze in his eyes that seemed to keep his more hostile aggressions at bay. When the chores were done, the children trudged to the bungalow and huddled over mugs of hot tea. In these moments, the boy often asked Alice to read him a story, sitting back with his eyes closed and shutting out every other care but the sound of her voice.

"I had no idea fairy tales were so deranged," he said one evening after Alice finished reading *Hansel and Gretel*, "Aren't they supposed to have happy endings?"

"I guess so," said the girl uncertainly, "This one wasn't so bad. It says: *then all their sorrows ended and they lived together in peace.*"

"Yeah, with the father who left them to *die* in the woods!"

Alice flipped through the pages, scouring the text for some redeeming piece of evidence.

"Well, it says he didn't have a happy moment from that time forward, so I guess he felt bad about what he did," she said, her voice trailing off into silence.

"I doubt it," scoffed the boy.

Alice frowned, trying to get at the thing that was bothering her.

"Do you believe in happy endings, Remy?"

"Endings? I don't think about 'em. All I know is here and

now."

"But don't you ever wonder how things will turn out?"

"Nah, not really. I don't see the point, " he said, shifting so his hair fell over his face.

The girl gazed at him intently, then changed the subject.

"Anyway, the best part of the story is the cottage made of gingerbread, with sticks of peppermint for the door and windows of crystallized sugar."

"Have you ever tried licking Madame Voisine's windows?" said the boy ominously.

"I'm not going to dignify that with a response." She closed the book with a clap.

"What?! You said yourself there's magic in her house."

"Yes, but…it's not the same thing. There *is* something different about her, in the most odd and wonderful way."

"I bet that's what Hansel and Gretel thought at first, too."

"Honestly," said Alice, shaking her head.

"C'mon. I was only trying to make you laugh," said the boy.

"If you want to make me laugh, then say something funny," she replied tartly.

Remy held up his mug and peered inside.

"I don't think Ichabod's mother hugged him as a baby,"

he said.

The girl smiled in spite of herself and the boy, seeing this, pressed his advantage.

"She *couldn't* have! How else do you explain his crotchety mood…unless it's because of that *thing* hanging over his nose."

Alice laughed.

"It's a beak, not a nose, and for your information that *thing* is called a snood," she said.

"A *snood?!* Well, that explains everything. How would you like to have a snood? How would you like to wake up every morning, look in the mirror, and see that soggy flap of skin in the middle of your face? I'd be bitter, too, if I had a snood."

The girl huddled into a ball, shaking with mirth.

"Stop saying that word!" she cried.

"*Snood.*"

"Remy!"

"What do you call the stuff under his chin?"

"I'm not telling you."

"*Tell me.*"

Alice was laughing so hard she couldn't speak.

"C'mon, Alice. Give it up. So help me, Ichabod has a right to know!"

"It's called…a wattle," gasped the girl, dissolving into a fresh round of giggles.

"A *what*-tle?"

"A *wat*tle."

Remy stared at the girl.

"You've got to be kidding me," he said.

"No, I'm serious."

"A *wattle*."

"Yes!"

The boy sighed and shook his head.

"Alice, let me put it to you this way. If there is a God, I know more about Him by that one turkey alone than from all the stories in the Bible put together."

The girl looked at Remy and smiled.

"I know exactly what you mean," she said.

A warm silence settled over the room and in that moment it felt like nothing else mattered, nothing could even come close.

"Snood," said the boy.

"*Remy,*" said Alice, but her face was happy and light.

CHAPTER 17

Spring came to Starling in signs and wonders. It cast a sharp light over the valley, coaxing from the dormant earth tender shoots of pale, young green. Daffodils peeped through the snow in front of Madame Voisine's bungalow and the lilac bushes dimpled with delicate, closed buds. A skeletal tree at the end of the lane transformed overnight, bursting with velvet tufts, and decrepit orchards along the highway blossomed into ballrooms of frothy, pink gowns. Everywhere the snow was melting, the incessant droplets of water a symphony of percussion beneath the blinding, white sun. Great, conglomerate icicles hanging from the eaves of the LaPierre house gleamed, then cracked and fell like spears into the drifts below.

With each day came new life. Lambs dotted the pastures, their woolen coats pristine against hillsides of fresh grass. Calves blinked at the world with wide eyes, turning to nuzzle their mothers with clumsy, ardent resolve. A chestnut foal, born hours ago, wobbled to stand on stilted legs, kicking and skittering by the end of the day. The children became more animated, too. They walked home from the bus stop along meandering paths, leaping over puddles and gesturing broadly as they talked. The light hurt their eyes and the air burned their lungs but they went about looking at everything, breathing deeply, unable to take enough of it in.

As they walked down the road after school one day Alice stopped short, holding her arm out in front of the boy.

"Shh! Did you hear that?" she said.

"Hear what?"

"That noise! I keep hearing a weird sound, like a *sssss*."

The children stared at each other, waiting.

"I don't hear nothing," said Remy, "Maybe you're going crazy."

"Very funny," she said, looking around.

They resumed walking, the girl scuffing at the gravel beneath her feet.

A few moments later, she stopped again.

"There it is! Did you hear it?"

"Alice, I'm serious. You really are losing it now."

"*Shh!*"

The girl bent over, staring at the ground.

"*Oh!,*" she gasped, discerning a small, furry creature mixed up in the dust and debris.

"Remy, look!" she said, kneeling for closer inspection, "What *is* that?!"

Remy crouched down beside the girl.

"Looks like a bat," he said.

"I think he's been hurt!" cried Alice.

The bat hissed at her.

"I don't think he likes you," remarked the boy, "You've only been kicking him down the road for the past few minutes."

"Remy!" exclaimed Alice, her voice heavy with anguish.

"I'm just *kidding*," he said, "I wonder how he got here? Poor thing looks pretty young. Must've swooped too low and got clipped by a truck or something."

The bat, indeed, had seen better days. One wing folded properly at his side while the other stretched out at an odd angle.

"Oh, Remy! We have to do something! We can't let him die!"

The boy took off his jean jacket and held it flush to the ground. Using a twig, Alice gently excavated the creature from the gravel and nudged him onto the coat. The bat struggled and hissed, wrinkling his snoutish nose to reveal fangs like tiny shards of glass.

They carried the creature to Alice's house and put him in a berry basket lined with newsprint.

"Let's take him to Madame Voisine. Maybe she can help us," said the girl.

Remy scowled.

"Why would *she* know anything about bats?" he said.

Alice gazed at the creature nestled in the bedding.

"I just have a feeling she will."

They walked up the lane, the girl leading the way while the boy dragged his feet. As they approached Madame Voisine's doorstep Remy hung back, unable to meet Alice's withering gaze.

"*Honestly,*" she said, marching up the stairs and knocking perhaps louder than was necessary. A distinct thud preceded a silence, then the door swung wide open. The old woman winced in the sunlight, weaving slightly, her eyes ringed with dark liner and hair piled high like snowdrifts, secured by a fortress of tortoise shell combs.

"You come bearing gifts, I see," she remarked, peering into the basket.

"We need your help," said Alice, "We found him by the road on our way home from school."

"He's just a wee one," said the woman, "Barely left his mother."

"That's what *I* said," asserted Remy, folding his arms.

"Takes a sharp eye to see it," said Madame Voisine, tilting her head at the boy, who quickly looked away.

She stepped back and ushered the children inside, scooping the cat from his perch beneath the potted mint and setting him on the floor. Alice placed the basket on the table while Remy looked around the room with its profusion of greenery, his eyes wide and mouth slightly ajar.

The old woman put on a pair of gardening gloves and inspected the bat.

"This doesn't look good," she said, "The wing is broken and he's in a state of shock."

"What's going to happen?" asked Alice, her voice so soft it frayed in places.

"I don't know. It's rare for a little creature to survive such an injury…though not unheard of," she added, the girl's expression moving her to venture onto the thin ice of hope.

"It's all my fault," whispered Alice, her eyes beginning to shimmer.

"It's *not* your fault," asserted Remy stoutly, "For crying out loud, since when does anyone check to see if they're kicking a *bat* down the road?!"

Madame Voisine pursed her lips at this and looked away.

"But he wouldn't have been as badly hurt," said Alice.

"You were the one who discovered him," interjected the woman, speaking in official tones, "Without you, he'd still be on the highway–helpless and in danger. You came to the rescue, you brought him to safe haven. You did well, my dear, very well, indeed."

More than the torment of self-incrimination or the anguish of watching the bat suffer, it was this unexpected kindness that rushed through the girl, breaking her last resolve. She closed her eyes and tried to swallow, hot tears sliding down her cheeks.

A logging truck passed on the highway, causing the bungalow to rattle and hum. Alice wiped her face on her sleeve as Madame Voisine withdrew behind a fern and began rummaging through the kitchen cupboards. Remy looked away, helpless at watching the girl cry, so that when the old woman returned bearing supplies he was actually relieved to see her.

She handed Alice a pair of gloves and said, "Are you ready to help me set this wing?"

"But I don't know what to do!" cried the girl, turning to Remy who stepped back, relieved to be overlooked for the mission.

"It's okay," he said, nodding vigorously, "You'll do fine."

Alice put on the gloves but did not move.

"I don't want to hurt him," she said.

"This is his only hope," replied Madame Voisine, "He must pass through greater suffering if he's to have a chance to survive."

She laid out a tea towel and a roll of gauze, picking up the bat who wrinkled his nose and hissed so weakly the sound could hardly be heard. He made a brief struggle then slumped in surrender, closing his eyes as if he could no longer bear to know what was happening. The girl saw this and stepped forward.

"Hang on!" she whispered, tears streaming down her face. Madame Voisine placed the bat on the towel and commenced working the injured wing to its proper position. Alice could not bear to watch, but the universe offered no escape from the knowledge of this small agony, and there was nothing to be done but stand her ground as the woman moved the joint back and forth, holding it in place with her finger.

"Give me some gauze," she said to Remy, "And Alice, extend his good wing so I can fasten the dressing around his middle."

Madame Voisine set the wing, wrapping the gauze several times before securing it with a piece of tape. Alice folded the healthy wing back into place and returned the bat to the basket. The creature lay motionless, the pink membrane of his ears pointed and alert though his eyes remained steadfastly shut.

"Drape this over the basket and keep it away from Minou," said the woman, handing Alice the tea towel. She rummaged through a drawer and found an old medicine dropper.

"This will help him to drink," she said, "Keep the gloves for as long as you need them and be careful not to get bitten."

"What about feeding him?" asked Alice.

"You can mix a little sugar into his water. Eventually he'll take insects, but the greater concern is to keep him alive through the night."

"It will be a miracle," whispered Alice, peeking beneath the towel.

"You could say that," nodded the woman, watching the girl hunch over her tiny ward.

As the children walked down the lane Remy said, "I better get over to Anderson's and do the chores."

"I'll take Pip home first, then come and help you," offered Alice.

"You already named him?" Remy glanced at the girl.

"Why not? It fits perfectly," she said, clutching the basket as she went on her way.

Alice arrived home to find Rob Novak at the kitchen table, eating a fried egg sandwich. Penny sat across from him smoking, her cup of coffee untouched.

"What d'you got there?" he said, looking up from his plate.

"Nothing," said Alice, trying to slip by.

"It's not nothing. I watched you from the window, peeking beneath that towel. Let's have a look." Rob leaned forward, sucking food from his teeth, and held out his hand. Alice stared at it but did not move.

"Show me," he commanded, relishing the look on the girl's face.

Penny hunched over her coffee and took a drag on her cigarette.

"It's *nothing*," mumbled the girl, putting her head down and rushing through the kitchen. She slipped into her bedroom and closed the door, barricading it with a stack of milk crates.

"Hello," she whispered, removing the towel from the berry basket.

The bat wrinkled his nose, too weak to manifest any greater sign of discontent.

"I'm sorry for kicking you," she said.

Alice tiptoed to the door and put her ear against it, then slipped into the bathroom for a cup of water. She filled the medicine dropper, squeezing the bulb until a droplet appeared. At first the bat did not respond, failing to register the liquid until it was dribbling down his chin. He shook his head and made a belated attempt to drink, so that when Alice tried again he opened his mouth and swallowed. The girl's hand trembled as he took another drop, and then another.

"You did it, Pip! You *did* it!" she cried and her heart leapt, surging into the atmosphere on this meager spark of hope. The girl felt almost dizzy with relief. She clasped her hands and fell to her knees, glancing at the plastered ceiling overhead. There was something grim about its network of patches and cracks but Alice closed her eyes and said, *"Oh...thank you!* Thank you for every little thing!"

She wrapped the towel around the basket and hid it beneath her bed, tucking it behind the treasure chest. At her bedroom door she paused, listening to scraps of an argument between her mother and Rob Novak, the tone of the adults sounding equal parts belligerent and bored. The girl frowned, pushing away a vague thought that conflict was a desired state for her mother, a less hollow way to pass the time. Her stomach turned over and she hovered in the hallway, unable to pinpoint the source of her concern. Finally, she folded her arms and went out the back way, closing the door so it didn't make a sound.

When Alice reached Anderson's chicken coop, Remy was nowhere to be seen. Ichabod, on the other hand, paced in front of the henhouse, his chest thrust forward and tail spread out like a giant fan.

"Remy?" she called, looking around.

"Over here!" hissed the boy, poking a feather through a crack in the henhouse door.

"Oh, there you are!" exclaimed the girl, squinting as if deeply perplexed, "What on earth are you doing in the henhouse?" There was the faintest hint of a smile on her lips.

"What am I doing?!" sputtered Remy, "What does it *look* like I'm doing? This here's a hostage situation and that stupid bird intends to do me in!"

"Poor little guy," crooned Alice, "So misunderstood. He's just a regular turkey who wants to be loved."

"Ha ha, *very* funny. Now get me outta here!"

"One hug. Is it too much to ask? Beneath that wattle lives a lonely, tormented soul."

"Alice, so help me."

The girl clapped her hands and laughed. She skipped to the far end of the coop, rattling a stick along the wire.

"Yoo hoo, Ichabod!" she sang, showering a handful of pebbles into the water trough.

Incensed by this breach of territory, Ichabod turned and

made a beeline for the girl. Remy slipped out of the henhouse and scurried across the yard, carrying a bucket of eggs. He exited the coop and closed the door before the turkey could realize his captive was on the run.

"How does it feel to be rescued?" Alice asked the boy, who was checking to see if the eggs were still intact.

"I'm glad my brush with death could amuse you," he replied.

Alice threw back her head and laughed.

"I'm sorry, but I can't help it," she said, "I'm just so happy because Pip drank some water from the medicine dropper! I think he's going to make it, after all!"

"He did? That's great, Alice. That's a really good sign."

"It *is* a good sign," said the girl, nodding, "C'mon, let's go. I need to get back and check on him."

"I doubt he's going anywhere," said Remy.

"I know," she said, looking vaguely troubled, "But I need to get back there."

They set the eggs on Anderson's porch and started off across the pasture, Alice leading the way.

"Wait," said the boy, stopping to pick some Indian paint.

"Remy, we need to hurry."

"This'll just take a second," he said, drawing an intricate pattern of lines on her face and standing back to survey his work, "There, now you look like an ancient warrior."

The girl made a grimace, deeply pleased.

"Here, now let me do you," she said, plucking a stalk and returning the favor.

The children smiled at each other. A breeze came through the grass and Alice turned, lunging at an imaginary foe.

"I'd save you from a thousand turkeys!" she exclaimed.

"Very funny," said Remy, not minding at all.

"Come on," said the girl, resuming their walk, "Do you want to play the story game?"

"That depends," he said.

"Do you even know what it is?"

"No, but I'm betting you can't wait to tell me."

Alice made a face and gave the boy a little push.

"For your information, it's where the first person starts telling a story and when she stops, the second person has to pick up where she left off. You trade back and forth that way, making it up as you go."

"Let me guess: *you're* the first person."

"Unless you want to go first."

"No, you start."

"Okay," said Alice, walking lightly on her toes, "Once upon a time there was a girl who lived all alone in a cottage at the edge of a dark and forbidding forest…"

"Then one day this boy came along who was so extra cool

she practically begged him to be her friend," said Remy.

"Remy! That's not how it goes!" she protested.

"Why not? You said we could make up whatever we wanted."

"But it wasn't your turn yet. And besides, your story was…"

"What?"

The girl waved her hands in the air, attempting to conjure a response.

"You didn't even…*try*," she finally said.

"Who says?" sputtered the boy.

"Remy, you were turning it into a joke and you know it."

"A joke?! Alice, how could you? I'm crushed!"

"For crying out loud," said the girl.

"Don't worry, I forgive you. Keep going with your story."

Alice stared at the boy until he had the decency to look away.

"Honestly," she said and walked on, speaking in low, urgent tones. "The cottage was enchanted, protected by an old magic. As long as the girl stayed within its walls, no harm could come to her. When she looked out the back window, she saw the endless forest where all manner of danger was known to lurk. When she looked out the front, a patch of meadow sloped down to an emerald green lake. The water sparkled in the sunlight, beckoning to the girl, but she didn't dare go outside because there was a great, terrible…"

Here Alice broke off and looked at the boy expectantly.

He returned her gaze with an identical expression.

"A terrible *what?*" he said.

"It's *your* turn. You're supposed to make it up from here."

"No, you keep going. It's starting to get really good."

"But that's the whole point of the game! Taking turns to make up a story."

"Forget about the game! I just wanna hear *your* story."

Alice pursed her lips against a smile.

"Fine," she said, "But you'll have to wait–we're getting close to home. Let's go see if Pip will drink some sugar water."

"A terrible *what?!*" he repeated, but the girl tossed her head and kept walking.

The children went quietly into the bungalow, passing through the living room where Penny and Rob Novak lay sprawled across the couch. The TV was on but the house felt oddly quiet–subdued, perhaps, by a pungent haze in the air. Rob watched the girl through lidded eyes, enjoying the buzz from a half-smoked joint.

"You make a better door than a window," he drawled, thinking he said something funny. Ignoring him, Alice led Remy to her bedroom and shut the door.

"Hey!" yelled Rob from the couch.

For a moment, the children did not speak or move. They did not look at each other or acknowledge the outburst but each knew to freeze, to wait, to make sure some precarious scaffolding remained in place before they could breathe and carry on.

"Where's Pip?" asked Remy, breaking the silence.

The girl blinked at the boy, coming back to the moment.

"I hid him."

She got down on her knees and crawled beneath the bed, pushing her treasure chest aside. The boy saw her body stiffen and remain still.

"Everything okay?" he asked.

Alice squirmed out and scrambled to her feet, staring at the bed.

"What's wrong?"

"He's gone. Pip is gone."

"He got out of the basket?"

"No, the basket's gone, too."

Alice stood with her hand to her mouth, then turned and darted into the hallway.

"Where is he?!" she demanded, rushing into the living room.

"Where's *what*? Thought you said you didn't have nothing," said Rob Novak, smirking with an authority he wore like an ill-fitting coat.

"Alice," began Penny, staring at her cigarette, "You can't just..."

"Where is he?" repeated the girl. She did not speak loudly,

but her voice seethed with a terrible calm.

"I took care of him," muttered the man, shrugging his shoulders, "You shouldn'a brought that thing inside in the first place. It's filthy, carries all kinda disease."

Alice shook her head.

"What do you mean–*took care of him?*"

"He was never gonna make it anyway."

"What did you do to him?"

Rob stared at the television and swore.

"You're in the way," he said, annoyed at how many things were piling up in his head at once.

"I said, *what did you do to him?!*"

The man squirmed fitfully, telling himself he would deal with the girl's insolence another time.

"I took him down to the creek."

"Alice, it was the merciful thing to do," began Penny, holding out an arm that fell to one side as the girl pushed past her and ran out the door.

Alice scrambled down the bank, the boy close behind her. A light rain was beginning to fall, its soft patter lost in the roar of the creek that churned and boiled, carrying the melt from the spring thaw. The noise was deafening as the girl spun around, looking blindly in every direction–the water, trees, and undergrowth blurring together in one dark, continuous streak.

"Look!" yelled Remy, pointing to a scrap of white in the bushes. Alice lunged, recognizing the tea towel, and beyond it in a patch of weeds she found the berry basket.

"Pip!" she cried, falling to her knees. The basket was empty, glistening with mercurial drops of rain. She searched through the tall grass, parting it gently, the Indian paint running down her cheeks. There was a sound in her ears like a muffled wail, and she did not know it was her own voice. After a time she sat back on her heels, breathing heavily, then got up and turned to face the creek.

The creek was huge and swollen, unrecognizable at this time of the year. It thundered through the valley like a marauding invader, its current seething with the heavy runoff of melted snow. Alice fought the urge to close her eyes, to stop having to know what she could not bear to be true.

"Pip," she whispered, feeling something break off inside her and swirl away. Remy went downstream to scour the terrain, making his way back through the clinging weeds. He used a stick to dislodge the debris caught in the willow roots along the bank, keeping an eye on the girl as he drew near. She was not searching anymore but stood facing the water, her shoulders slumped and small.

"I couldn't find nothing," he yelled, shaking his head, "Current's too strong!"

The girl did not respond and when he touched her arm she felt off-balance, like a statue on uneven ground.

"Alice."

"I wish it was me," she said, staring blindly.

The boy leaned forward, half-catching her words.

"What did you say?"

"I wish I was the one gone."

The girl's face hung heavy and the boy stared at her, uncomprehending at first, then he grabbed her by the arm and gave it a rough shake.

"Hey, don't you talk like that, you hear me?! You don't say those things!"

He pulled her away from the bank and she stumbled after him, eyelids fluttering. Thunder growled overhead and in the hills beyond Anderson's pasture lightning struck, a blinding fork that ripped across the sky. Alice stood stiffly as Remy bent to retrieve the tea towel, folding it carefully and placing it in the basket. A torrential rain beat down upon the children, but the girl did not flinch and the boy did not try to coax her to shelter.

"How did he get ahold of Pip in the first place?" he finally said, uttering the concern that had been lurking in his mind all along, "I thought you said you hid him under your bed."

"I did," said the girl, her voice empty and flat.

Remy looked over his shoulder at the outline of the bungalow, dim against the roiling clouds. The sound of the creek roared in his ears as a shadow crossed his face, saddling the boy with the weight of a dark and terrible unease.

CHAPTER
18

"May Day is coming," said Ms. Kemp as the children sat copying out their spelling words for the week, "And we need to choose three students from our class to participate in the annual Maypole dance."

The announcement had an electrifying effect upon the girls in the room, who dropped their pencils and sat up straight, quivering in their seats. The boys, knowing the offer amounted to little more than a death wish at the hands of their peers, continued writing with unprecedented concentration.

"Three lucky children," sang the teacher, pacing back and forth in front of the chalkboard, "Do I have any volunteers?"

A sea of hands shot up, waving in the air.

Ms. Kemp looked over the classroom, her eyebrows arched.

"No boys?" she asked in mock surprise. It was the same joke, every year.

"Let me see," continued the teacher, stroking her chin as if this was a matter of serious deliberation, "Corinne LeRoy. You may be one of the dancers."

Corinne squealed and turned around in her desk to receive the congratulations of her peers, none of which were forthcoming. The LeRoy family was one of Starling's more prominent clans, and the deference accorded them was both predictable and resented.

"Nikki Kilchuk. You may be a dancer, as well."

Nikki sat back, a triumphant smirk on her face. She did not look around to solicit anyone's well wishes because she didn't care if they were happy for her or not. Nikki Kilchuck was something of a big fish in a little pond. She had ambition, dreams for her life that did not entail sticking around this backwater dump any longer than she had to. Her older cousin lived up in Prince George and made good money working in the hotels. Nikki was biding her time, counting down the days until her fifteenth birthday, when she would hitch a ride from some guy in a van and never make it to the place where she and her cousin had been planning to meet.

The tension in the room was mounting. Cries of *'pick me!'* filled the air as the remaining girls waved their hands, nearly levitating in their seats. Alice did not raise her hand. The notion of the dance was enticing to be sure, but she had long since learned the survival skill of not calling attention to herself and therefore sat quietly, copying down her words. Ms. Kemp looked at her and saw through the ruse.

"Why not Alice Quinn?!" she exclaimed, clapping her hands as if suddenly and intensely amused, "Certainly no one could accuse me of playing favorites!"

There was a collective groan as the other girls slumped in their desks, casting dirty looks at the chosen few and brewing feelings of ill will toward them.

"Wait a minute!" called the teacher, waving her hands as if to restore order, "We may have a little problem: I forgot to mention the participants will need to wear a white dress for the dance."

Her words hung in the air as a fervent hum renewed itself and spread throughout the room. Corinne and Nikki looked at each other and shrugged, while Alice gazed at her pencil, twisting it in her hands.

"Will that be a problem for anyone?" asked Ms. Kemp.

"No," said Corinne and Nikki in unison.

"Alice?" prodded the teacher, syrupy with concern.

A hush fell over the students as the girl looked up, a curious set to her expression.

"No," she said.

"No…*what?* You don't have a dress or it won't be a problem?"

"It won't be a problem."

Ms. Kemp stared at the girl, her fingernails poised against the surface of her lectern. She leaned forward and took a deep breath to calm herself, to slow down and enjoy the pleasure of the hunt.

"Do you own a white dress?"

The teacher had her fish on a hook and knew it, but she was in no rush to reel it in.

"Yes," replied the girl after a moment, her mouth slightly ajar.

"Really? That's funny. I've never seen you wear it. Come to think of it, I've never seen you wear any dress besides the one you have on at this very moment. Stand up, will you, and give us a little peek."

Alice did not move.

"Did you hear what I said? *Stand up.*" Ms. Kemp was straining like a dog on a leash.

The girl got to her feet, her shoulders hunched as if they had already absorbed a blow.

The teacher pressed her lips together and used the lectern for support; she felt weak with the rapture of being alive.

"No, that won't do," she said, shaking her head, "Come to the front of the room so we can all have a look."

Alice made her way to the chalkboard. Her expression was vacant, as if she wasn't there, so that Remy could hardly recognize the girl.

"What would you call this?" asked Ms. Kemp, walking around Alice and picking at the fabric of her sleeve, "Is it even a proper dress?"

"It's a Brownie uniform," mumbled Alice.

"A what?"

"A Brownie uniform."

"Are you a Brownie?"

"Not at the moment."

"I *see*."

The students sat in silence, paralyzed by this exchange. They were accustomed to blatant, unbridled expressions of anger–to coarse language, violent tempers, and having the living daylights knocked out of them, but this was cruelty on another level, a higher plane. It was strange and seductive, a subtle game of cat and mouse, and they were breathless to see it on display. Only Remy sat with his fists clenched, wishing he had a grenade to lob at the teacher.

Ms. Kemp cocked her head and studied the girl.

"I don't think you do have a white dress," she said softly, the trace of a smile on her lips.

Alice closed her eyes, prepared to surrender, but in the end she could not bring herself to do it. There was a grim futility in the way Ms. Kemp bore down upon her, as if no triumph could be enough, as if the teacher had an insatiable hunger for something the girl did not know how to supply. She swayed wearily on her feet so that when the words came out of her mouth, it was as much to her own surprise as it was to anyone else in the room. The girl spoke faintly at first, her voice gathering strength in the way sunlight peeks through the clouds before bursting into full view, and the children leaned forward in their desks, eager to be warmed by its sound.

"I have a closet full of dresses, in colors the shades of the sky."

"I beg your pardon?"

"Sunrise, sunset, stormy weather, snowfall, and endless blue in its pale hues of dawn, deepening into the night," intoned the girl, gazing past her teacher at a vision she alone could see.

Ms. Kemp stared at Alice, the euphoria of the past few moments deflating like a punctured balloon, and she fought like it was her last breath to regain the high.

"Well…my stars!" she sputtered, her voice tight and shrill, "What marvelous air you must breathe! How rare! Of course, I'm more than happy to take you at your word, Miss Quinn. Perhaps you'll grace us with a fashion show one of these days?"

Alice blinked and the teacher's face rushed back into focus.

"How about tomorrow?" said Ms. Kemp, fixing the girl with a hostile stare.

The children sat up, rapt with attention.

"I'm not allowed to wear them to school," Alice said, addressing the pencil in her hands.

"What's that? I couldn't hear you."

The girl did not look up.

"I said, I'm not allowed to wear them to school."

"Ohhh. Of *course* you're not," replied the teacher, reeling in her line then letting it back out again.

That afternoon, as the children walked home from the bus stop, Remy kept looking at Alice from the corner of his eye. The girl took deliberate strides, refusing to acknowledge his attention.

"Why'd you do that?" he finally asked.

"Do what?" said the girl, scuffing the gravel with steadfast intent.

"You know. Why did you say that thing about the dresses?"

Alice looked up at the sky.

"I have one as white as those clouds," she said, nodding, "Made of pure silk, with miles and miles of lace."

"Alice, you don't have to talk that way to me," said Remy, "I've seen your closet."

"So what? Just because *you* can't see the dress doesn't mean it's not real."

"And just because you *can* see it doesn't mean it *is* real."

"It's real to *me*."

"Yeah, well that's not the same thing as showing up to school on May Day wearing a dress everyone else can see, now is it?"

The girl looked at him, stricken, and Remy bit his lip, wishing he could take it back.

"I'm sorry, I didn't mean it like that. I'm just trying to help."

"I know," she said, stopping to crouch over a shiny black beetle that was turned upside down, its legs waving furiously in the air. She plucked a stalk of grass and coaxed it to its feet, watching the metallic creature totter off through the weeds, then brushed her hands together and walked quietly the rest of the way home.

That night Alice lay in bed staring out the window. Penny was at the glass plant, working the graveyard shift, but the girl did not mind being alone. If anything, she embraced the solitude, finding within it a reliable presence. She curled into a ball and closed her eyes, waiting for the ambient hum of the bungalow to ease her churning thoughts. When that didn't work she got out of bed and drew a picture of a girl in a long, white dress floating through the sky. She stared at the drawing until she felt a heavy pressure in her head, then crawled under the covers and turned to face the wall.

The next morning she woke up early and reached for the petrified wood beneath her pillow, running her thumb over its smooth, worn ridge. As the room emerged from the shadows she opened her Bible, hovering over its pages in the faint light: *He telleth the number of the stars; he calleth them all by their names.* Alice clenched the piece of wood and looked out the window, gazing at the coral streaks of dawn. The sound of Penny's car coming down the lane made the girl blink with the recollection of her mother's absence. She stood and tiptoed to her closet, pausing to take a deep breath before opening the door.

The Brownie uniform hung there, limp and alone. Alice stared at the dress then moved past it, reaching to graze her fingers along the gowns of oyster, jade, and lavender that rustled softly in the corridors of her mind.

When the girl showed up to school that morning, Ms. Kemp looked her over from head to toe.

"What a pity!" she exclaimed, raising an eyebrow, "I thought we were to be graced with one of your technicolor frocks?"

Alice froze, lowering her head.

"I'm not allowed to wear them to school," she began.

"Oh, yes. How silly of me to forget!"

The girl hurried to her desk and sat down.

"Miss Quinn."

Alice looked up.

"You *do* realize the May Day dress needs to exist in more than just your imagination…?"

A titter ran through the class, fueled by the girls who were still vexed at their exclusion from the dance, that curious practice of identifying with the predator rather than the prey. Alice did not notice their laughter; it sounded muffled and distant, as if she was down the hall or in another room. She bent over a piece of paper and wrote her name in careful loops, mesmerized by the tip of her freshly sharpened pencil.

On Friday there was a rehearsal for the Maypole dance on the playground after school. Alice attended, skipping and weaving her ribbon through the circle of children, her laughter lighter than air. Remy leaned against a nearby tree, watching the girl vanish and reappear through shafts of afternoon sunlight. He closed his eyes and saw her still, turning away to keep his expression to himself.

When the rehearsal was over the children walked home along the creek, stopping to do the chores at Anderson's farm.

"Is that the Gorsma's place?" asked Alice, nodding to a dilapidated house and series of sheds across the creek from where they stood.

"Yeah, one of 'em," said Remy, scowling.

Alice shivered.

"Are we really trespassing?" she asked.

"No. Mona's full of it. This side belongs to Anderson."

The children continued walking home, legions of grasshoppers scattering before them with each step. The sun was gentle and warm, the breeze scented by a thousand wildflowers, and the grass teemed with the rustle and hum of tiny creatures, intent on living out the full measure of their existence.

"You wanna go see if there's any frogs in Anderson's pond?"

"What pond?" said Alice.

"Over there," replied Remy, pointing to a cluster of cattails next to a maple tree at the far end of the pasture, "It's more of a marsh, really, but it gets deep in some places."

"I can't believe you never showed it to me," said the girl.

"It's been there all this time. I can't believe *you* never noticed."

There was a brief silence as the children walked on.

"I know you're smiling," she said, "I can hear it."

"Oh, really? You can *hear* me smiling? That's pretty sharp for a girl who managed to overlook a whole, entire pond."

"You're doing it louder now."

The boy laughed.

Alice pushed him and took off running, lopsided beneath her knapsack.

Remy watched her go, shaking his head. When she looked over her shoulder he gamely gave chase, zig-zagging across the field as the girl shrieked with laughter, alternately commanding then begging him to stop. He relented as they neared the lone maple on the slope overlooking the pond. Alice walked backward, keeping an eye on the boy, laughing and holding out her hand.

"I call home base," she said, touching the tree.

"Okay, home base. Let's leave our knapsacks here," he said.

Alice set her bag against the trunk and sat down, trying to catch her breath.

"What a perfect climbing tree!" she exclaimed, looking up at the latticework of branches interwoven with the leaves and sky.

The children went down to the pond, stepping carefully as the ground began to soften underfoot. Birds sang in soaring trills and dragonflies dove like fighter pilots, young and delirious with flight. Clouds of gnats hovered in the air, skeeter bugs shot across the water, and bees droned in the wildflowers along the shoreline.

"It's a miniature utopia," said the girl, transfixed.

"What's a utopia?" asked the boy.

"A place where everything's perfect," she replied, "Perfect, happy and…free."

"Look!" said Remy.

A tiny frog struggled through a patch of grass, heading for the water. The boy crouched down and scooped it up.

"You got him!" said Alice, coming close and peering into his cupped hands.

The frog was no bigger than a penny. He was speckled olive green, his face tense and alert, gazing evasively from his captors through bulging, amber eyes.

"So perfect!" breathed the girl, "How could there be such a tiny, perfect thing?"

"You wanna keep him?" asked Remy, offering the frog to Alice.

A light passed over her face then quickly disappeared.

"No, that's okay," she said softly, touching her fingers to his hand, "I think he's better off in this place."

"Let's keep him a little while," pressed the boy, watching her, "Just a few hours, then we can let him go. An afternoon pet. You wait here while I run back to Anderson's barn for a bucket. How about that?"

A smile tugged at the girl's lips.

"Okay," she relented, holding out her hands.

Remy hurried up the slope, pausing at the tree. He turned to see Alice huddled over the frog, holding it close. She cocked her head, speaking softly. The boy stood still and forgot his errand, filled with a sensation that made his chest ache.

"*Utopia*," he whispered, trying the word on for size. He could not make sense of the feeling–how much he wanted it never to end and how much it scared him to know this.

CHAPTER 19

On Saturday morning Alice awoke with a start. She sat up and looked about the room, her heart racing. It had rained during the night and clouds hung low over the valley, making the air smell musty and dank. Her closet door stood open, revealing the shadow of the brown dress–a limp, defeated cipher against the wall. Alice gazed at it, feeling a lump form in her throat.

"You're just a stupid, old thing," she whispered, piercing her soul with the words. She flopped down against her pillow, causing the drawing of the girl in the white dress to slip from the milk crate and waft to the ground. Alice leaned over the mattress and gazed at the sketch, staring with new concentration. She stood up quickly and tugged at her bed sheet, pulling it free, her face set with an expression that was curiously bright.

Ten minutes later a blizzard of fabric littered the room

as Alice cut the sheet into pieces, stitching and pinning with feverish zeal. When the creation was complete she tried it on and stood before the mirror, cocking her head this way and that. There was a moment of silence wherein she wavered before two pathways of thought. The results were not quite what she'd envisioned but it *could* be considered a dress and it *was* white, and therefore the girl was determined to be content. She set her face to this resolve and curtsied before her reflection, dancing around the room until the sound of her mother and Rob Novak raising their voices in the kitchen shattered her play. Alice froze, listening intently. She crept to the closet and got changed, stowing the dress in a brown paper bag. The adults were still arguing when she tiptoed into the hallway and left by the back door.

It was chilly outside but the girl pressed forward, unwilling to return for a sweater. She stopped at a puddle, leaning in to peer at her reflection. The girl gazing back looked squeamish and pale.

"Hello," she whispered. A raindrop fell, rippling the surface, and Alice straightened up quickly. There was a flash of movement in the distance and she stared without breathing. A figure disappeared into the willows along the lane and the girl hurried forward, her limbs tense and stiff.

"Remy, is that you?" she called, picking her way through the wet grass, "What are you doing out here?"

The boy leaned against a tree trunk, his fists clenched. Alice watched a tear drip off his chin.

"What happened?"

Remy turned away, his body so rigid it trembled, a sound from deep within unable to rise to the surface.

The girl stepped forward, holding out her hand.

"Hey," she whispered.

There was no response and she watched him, sick with the dread of only half-knowing what was wrong. She folded her arms and noticed his shoes, soaked and covered in mud.

"Remy," she said, "You don't have to talk. You don't have to say a thing. But I'm not going anywhere, just in case you do."

The children stood by the tree, a haphazard staccato of raindrops dripping from its branches. The clouds began to dissipate and roam across the sky, allowing the sun a furtive glimpse into the valley. Presently the birds began to twitter, rehearsing their simple fugues, and the air took on a scent that was fresh and sweet.

"Do you want to go for a walk?" asked Alice.

The boy did not respond.

"Remy," she said pleadingly.

He shook his head imperceptibly, as if it was too heavy to move. His features twisted together and he hunched into himself like a gargoyle racked with pain.

Alice felt weightless with fear, knowing only she must stay and bear this moment with him. An immense ache spread through her chest, lodging in her throat and making her ears ring. She reached out slowly, tracing the boy's brow with her finger and wiping the tears from his cheeks. She brushed the hair from his forehead, discovering the place where blood matted his locks and a swollen knot had formed. The girl began to tremble but she held her ground and traced his features over and over until the tension softened and some semblance of familiarity returned to his face.

"I see you've found my favorite hiding place."

Alice looked up. Madame Voisine stood across the lane, wearing a long, green dress that shimmered in the light.

"Most people don't know it, but some trees have special powers," she continued, "One is to protect. I come to this very willow myself for safe haven."

The woman moved toward them, her dress flashing like the facets of a gem.

"Something is needed here," she said, regarding the children through darkly ringed eyes, "A sign or wonder, perhaps, but failing that there is much to be gained from the telling of a good story."

From her pocket she withdrew a small paper sack and offered it to the girl, who peeked at its contents.

"Peppermint," said the woman, "For clarity."

Alice took a candy and popped it into her mouth, tasting the cool, sharp zest. She offered one to Remy, who ignored her, but this time she shook her head and kept her hand outstretched.

"Take it," she said evenly, a new fortification in her voice.

The boy did not look up, but took the candy and put it in his mouth.

"That's better," said Madame Voisine, "Now make yourselves comfortable and listen to what I have to say."

The clouds broke into patches across the sky and the sun burst forth with a sudden radiance, dappling the children through the branches of the tree. Alice and Remy sat down, finding the ground to be remarkably dry as the woman arranged herself on a nearby stump, her dress fanning out like a mermaid's tail.

She stared into space until her eyelids began to flutter, then took a deep breath and began.

"Once there was a girl who lived all by herself on an island shaped like a pearl, out in the middle of the sea. How she came to be there in the first place is a story for another day, but it involves pirates, a shipwreck, and an escape through shark-infested waters in the middle of a moonless night.

The girl didn't mind being alone; indeed, she didn't think of it as such! How could one feel lonely on an island that was home to lustrous beetles and silvery ribbon snakes, with mango trees and cliffs where birds built nests and filled them with eggs of every color, some no bigger than mung beans, and others like stones from the sea? By day she swam along the reef, collecting conch shells that whispered secrets in her ear. She made friends with the dolphins and tried to understand the curious ways of the seahorse.

In the heat of the afternoon, she wandered through the tall grass to a giant banyan tree that stood on a hill overlooking the bay. The tree had a way of beckoning to the girl and as she drew near her breathing grew even, her heartbeat more calm. She reached for the branches and it seemed as if they obliged, lifting her to a place that was hidden and safe.

Early one morning a ship cut through the fog and sailed into the bay. It was a scabby looking vessel, listing to one side, with a tattered flag fluttering like claw marks in the air. The girl's blood ran cold; she knew trouble when she saw it.

She grabbed her conch shell and hurried up the path, stopping in places to crouch behind rocks and peer at the ship below. The crew had dropped anchor and was boiling up from the berth, swarming over the deck like a ruinous plague. They climbed into longboats and headed for shore.

The girl ran to the banyan tree. Up she climbed, its branches closing like a fortress behind her until she was tucked away in its very heart, safe from the outside world.

In the longboats there was one figure smaller than the rest, and while the others looked to shore, he turned and fixed his gaze in the direction of the tree.

For the next several days the girl stayed where she was, cozy as you please. She had the conch shell to tell her secrets and the company of an old cormorant who circled overhead, dropping mangoes into her hands. The beetles brought her rose petals covered *in dew and the ribbon snakes curled around her arms like bracelets to make her smile. At night the tree cradled the girl in its branches, rocking her to sleep, the wind like a lullaby in the leaves.*

The pirates, for that is what they were, camped on the beach and stayed up through the night drinking rum and fighting with swords, dancing around bonfires that licked at the stars in the sky. By day they slept like corpses in the sand. When they ran out of things to drink they looked over the island and settled upon a place to bury their treasure. Then they patched up their ship and set off, bound for more mayhem and plunder.

When it seemed the coast was clear, the girl peered through the leaves and saw, to her astonishment, a boy standing at the foot of the tree. What could this mean?! The snakes around her wrists were incandescent and the beetles glowed as never before. She looked again. The boy was dirty and unkempt, but he stood as if he knew how to keep his balance. He did not say anything nor even look in her direction but somehow, the girl knew he was waiting for her and would continue to do so until she was ready to come down.

A breeze came through the branches and the tree began to sway. The girl could feel her heart beating steadier now than ever before. She began to descend, knowing with each step she was leaving behind an old and trusted friend.

At the last branch she hesitated, staring at the boy. He returned her gaze as if he had always known her, and quite suddenly she could not bear to waste another moment up in the air. When he reached out she took his hand and jumped, and for the first time in her life she felt the ground good and solid beneath her feet."

Madame Voisine stopped talking and her eyes fell upon Remy and Alice. They rested against the tree looking different somehow, calm and untroubled, as perhaps children are meant to be. The woman took it in and smiled, tilting her face to the sun.

"*Magique,*" she whispered.

The three sat quietly, the soft hum of life floating through the space between them. The warmth of the sun came over the boy, filling his mind with an awareness that in this moment it was enough. He looked up and saw the woman was gone, wondering if he could have imagined the whole thing until he swallowed and recalled the taste of peppermint in his mouth.

"Alice," he said, "What are you going to do about a dress?"

The girl closed her eyes, lost in a world of luminous beetles, affectionate snakes, and seashells that whisper secrets in one's ear.

"For the Maypole dance," he continued, "It's on Monday."

She blinked and looked upward, stretching her arms to the sky.

"*Alice.*"

"I know. Don't worry. I've got it figured out."

"What's *that* supposed to mean?"

"It means…it's a *surprise.*"

"Tell me."

"No."

Remy scowled.

"Well, maybe I have a surprise, too," he said.

Alice leaned against the boy, nudging him off balance.

"Maybe you do," she replied.

Remy leaned over and nudged her back.

"Maybe I won't tell you what it is."

"Maybe I didn't ask you to."

She scrambled to her feet and ran a few steps down the lane, looking over her shoulder, willing him to follow suit.

Remy sat motionless, watching the girl go, then shook his head and got up. The children made their way to the creek and wandered downstream, returning to the bungalow when the last bit of light slipped behind the mountains. Alice cooked some rice and the children took it to her bedroom, eating in silence, thinking of a far-away island where they could stay for as long as they wanted, and no one could find them or even know they were gone.

CHAPTER 20

On Sunday morning Alice got dressed and went into the kitchen. She filled a pot with water, added two eggs, and set it on the stove to boil. Rob Novak came into the room and stood in a patch of sunshine, shirtless and scratching his chest. He yawned, looking like an overgrown fungus, pale and corpulent in the light. Alice turned away, studiously minding the eggs. Rob let his gaze linger over the girl, noting her flustered indifference and smiled, pleased to be the cause of it. When she reached into the cupboard for salt, a hole the size of a quarter revealed itself beneath the sleeve of her t-shirt. The man's eyes narrowed, feeling the rumblings of an appetite, and he moved through the sunlight toward her.

"You making those for me?" he asked, his gaze never shifting. Alice did not respond, as if by ignoring him the situation might disappear altogether.

Rob leaned closer, inhaling deeply.

"Mmm…something smells good," he said, poking his finger through the hole in her shirt, grazing her bare skin.

The girl froze as he pressed his body against her, his odor manifesting like a hand over her face. Time unraveled in its way of making such moments stand still: the hum of the refrigerator, the eggs jittering in the pot, the impossible knowledge that just beyond the window there existed a beautiful day. The man sighed and closed his eyes, unable to catch the groan in his throat, a wave of pleasure welling up inside him.

"You're a nice girl, aren't you?" he whispered, nuzzling her ear.

Alice did not speak or move. Rob Novak pressed forward, pinning the girl to the stove, rubbing against her and whispering things she could not understand. She closed her eyes against the bristling of chest hair across her face and her brain tugged as if it might detach from itself, fleeing the knowledge of things which cannot rightly register.

The petrified wood in her pocket pressed sharply against her leg. In the panicked flight of her mind the girl did not notice it at first; she could not see, hear, nor lay hold upon a single lucid thought. There was only darkness and escaping further into it, turning inside out and going deeper, still.

An airless silence came over the room and the house seemed to shudder at its very core. It was impossible to account for the interval of time since the man first stepped through the sunlight toward the girl but all the while, perhaps like the evolution of the fossil itself, an image of the petrified wood began to take shape in her mind. Imperceptible at first, it grew brighter and more distinct, emerging with such clarity it seemed she could reach out and touch it, this ancient shard that could not be destroyed. Somehow it became all the girl could think of, all she could see, an eon of resilience coursing through her body until there was nothing in her awareness but the assurance she would not break.

A deep, hacking cough sounded in the hallway and Rob Novak froze. The stove made a grating sound on the linoleum as he pushed away from the girl, the expression on his face like a fish slapped hard against a rock. Moments later Penny shuffled into the room looking as if she'd ridden out a storm. Her eyes were streaked with liner and her hair stuck out at odd angles, ravaged by a turbulent night of sleep.

"Where's my smokes?" she said, her voice rasping and low.

Rob turned away, fumbling, and Alice stared blindly at the eggs in the pot. The woman sat down at the table and took a pack of Luckies from the windowsill, tapping one out of the box and placing it between her lips. The spark-wheel on the lighter was stubborn so that it took a few attempts to ignite, and Penny's hands trembled to connect her cigarette with the flame. The moment wore on, a monstrosity of irrelevance, until it seemed as though the room would burst and splinter into shards of wood and glass. When the cigarette was lit she inhaled deeply and stared out the window, saying nothing.

Alice turned to her mother, her throat aching so badly it made her ears ring.

Penny glanced over and muttered, "What're you looking at?"

"Nothing," said the girl, who could not feel the ground beneath her feet.

She moved away, blinking. Her mother closed her eyes and coughed again, a violent spasm revealing the outline of her shoulders through a shapeless flannel shirt. Alice scooped the eggs from the pot and tied them in a tea towel, moving quickly to stay ahead of herself, of having to register the least degree of thought. She took her bundle and went out the back door, doubling over as she hurried up the lane to Madame Voisine's house.

"I brought you some breakfast," she said, waving the tea towel like a distress signal when the old woman came to the door.

Madame Voisine stood for a moment, squinting into the morning light. She was dressed in a silken robe, her hair gathered into a topknot and secured by an ornamental bird that regarded the girl with a glittering eye.

"Come in, child," she said.

Alice stepped into the kitchen and set her bundle on the counter. Her cheeks burned as she struggled with the knot and she fought the urge to put her hand over her mouth.

"Boiled eggs!" exclaimed Madame Voisine, "How divine!"

She put salt and pepper on the table, rummaging through the cupboard to produce a pair of dainty wooden cups resting on pedestals.

They sat down and the woman showed Alice how to remove the top of the egg by tapping the circumference of its shell with a knife. The girl went through the motions, flinching when the blade slipped from her fingers and clattered to the floor. The old woman looked at her curiously and bent to pick it up.

"How's your search coming?" she asked, setting the knife before the girl.

"Search?"

"I believe you were tracking down the Great Almighty when you last came to visit."

Madame Voisine went to the kitchen and returned to pour tea.

Alice bent over her cup, forgetting the question or even that it was her turn to speak, the pressure in her head so great she hardly knew she was there. The woman paused to watch, setting the kettle down as the girl closed her eyes and curled up like a dry leaf, waiting to blow away. Madame Voisine leaned forward and touched her shoulder.

"Child?"

Alice flinched and rattled the cup, sloshing tea across the table. She gaped at the woman as if she was a stranger and from beneath the potted mint, the cat opened an eye and mewed softly.

Madame Voisine shook her head slowly and fixed the girl with a searching gaze.

"What is this burden you carry," she murmured.

Alice turned to the window, beginning to tremble. She did not understand the woman's words but her tone soothed the girl in an alarming way, as if relief was unsafe, as if this ripple of warmth could break her into a thousand pieces.

"Come rest a moment on the couch, my dear. We must all take a break from our travels now and then."

Alice stood up like a sleepwalker, following Madame Voisine into the next room. She lay down stiffly on the chesterfield and the woman wrapped a blanket around her shoulders, plumping the cushions beneath her head.

"There," said Madame Voisine, surveying her work, "You are properly tucked in. Now I must tend to an errand that has been left long overdue."

As she turned to leave Alice whispered, "Please don't go."

The woman cocked her head, gazing out the window as if she hadn't heard the request, but when she turned back to the girl her face was gentle and kind.

"Would you like me to tell you a story?" she asked.

Alice nodded.

"Very well," she said, "There's always time to spin a little yarn."

Madame Voisine sat down in the armchair and withdrew some long wooden needles and a skein of wool from a basket on the floor. She began to knit, her fingers deft and sure, rows of neat, orderly stitches emerging in a mosaic of pattern. Alice watched the crystal pendants split the light from the window, checkering the wall with soft patches of color. The room felt smaller somehow, cozy and hidden away, and this was the girl's last thought as she closed her eyes, floating into a world conjured by the sound of the woman's voice.

"*Once there was a girl named Lin who lived in a house with a green door,*" said Madame Voisine, her words falling into place like the workings of an intricate timepiece, "*The door opened onto a busy street and the street ran down a hill through a vast and crowded city. The city stretched all the way to the ocean, with tall, grey buildings sprawling in the opposite direction as far as the eye could see.*

Each day Lin sat at the window, watching people pass by. Some struggled beneath heavy parcels, others hurried with their heads low to the ground. The people looked tired and driven, but they never stopped moving.

Lin's mother thought her simple, but in truth the girl was merely shy. If you were lucky enough to catch a glimpse of her at the window, you would know this for yourself. Her face looked out upon the world like a young fawn hidden in the forest. For this reason, though she was in plain sight, no one took notice of the girl. It was almost as if she didn't exist.

Lin spent most of her time on her own. Her mother was often gone, but when she returned her words were cold and distant so that the girl did not know which was worse: being alone and feeling lonely or feeling lonely yet not being alone. Such days were always rainy, and if anyone had bothered to look in the window they would have seen drops on the glass as if they were sliding down the girl's cheeks.

One day a package appeared on the front step of the house. Lin saw it and blinked. Had someone dropped it there by accident? Impossible! No one had come near the house all day. She leaned forward, her hands clutching the folds of her dress. The great wave of people surged down the street, greedily swallowing everything in its path. The girl turned from the window and hurried to the door.

There she stopped.

Lin regarded the doorknob, touching it with her finger. It was cool and smooth, and her reflection curved with the contour of the brass. She made a timid attempt to open the door and found it would not budge. For a moment she faltered, then grabbed the knob with both hands and gave it a mighty twist. The door swung open, carrying the girl with it.

The noise from the street boiled into the house—a thousand voices calling, laughing, shouting. Engines growled and machines hummed, fanning the clatter of life, and great waves rolled across the ocean like a distant, perpetual roar. Lin darted onto the step and grabbed the package, then hurried inside and shut the door.

The package itself was nothing to remark upon; wrapped in newsprint and tied with old twine, it did not suggest anything of great importance. Yet as Lin loosened the string, the paper fell away from its contents like the petals of a blossom opening to the sun.

The girl did not breathe.

A crystal egg rested upon a pedestal, about the size of a lemon and perfectly clear. Inside the egg there was a hill, and upon it stood an ivory pagoda with a golden roof and exquisitely carved jade green doors. From there, a winding path led to a garden where sakura trees, moss covered stones, and a pond were arranged in such a way that Lin felt her mind begin to soften and unfurl for the very first time.

Just then, the doors opened. A little old man came out and made his way to the garden. His shoulders were stooped and with each step it seemed he had reached his destination. He knelt at the bushes and trimmed a branch here and there with a pair of shears. He swept the mossy stones. He fed the koi in the pond. Then he sat on a bench and closed his eyes.

Lin leaned forward as if to hear his thoughts. Her breath left a foggy patch on the egg, which she wiped away with her finger.

The old man opened his eyes and looked up at the girl. He rose to his feet and offered a deep bow. Lin put a hand over her heart—never before had it leapt in this way!

That night Lin's mother came home long after the girl had gone to bed. She sang a line from a popular song over and over, tuneless and flat, until she collapsed on the couch and the house fell still.

Spring turned to summer. Autumn grew cold. The street, with its endless procession of people, carried the mother away for days at a time. But Lin did not wait at the window any longer; everything she cared for was inside the egg.

On a dark, wintery afternoon, the mother returned. She climbed the steps to the house and went inside. The rooms were cold and empty. There was nothing to eat, no electricity, and no girl. For a moment the woman stood there, the natural light beginning to fade. Then she turned to leave, ready to lose herself for good in the tide of humanity moving down the street like a hungry current, pulling out to sea.

But first she pawned the egg, failing to notice two tiny sets of footprints leading from the garden, past the koi pond, to the ivory pagoda with the golden roof and its exquisitely carved jade green doors."

Madame Voisine rested her head against the chair, her gaze wandering to the window. The winds were picking up, tossing the treetops so they bent and shuddered as if being punished for some grave, appalling wrong. Seeing the girl was asleep, she wrapped a shawl around her shoulders and stepped into the fray, her hair caught up and teased into shimmering flames held fast by the jeweled bird. The air seethed with the debris of twigs and leaves, of grit and spinning seeds, but Madame Voisine stood immune in the midst of it all, gliding down the lane like the figurehead of a great, wooden ship.

Rob Novak saw the old woman coming from a distance. He was alone in the house, Penny having gone to work, and he inhaled deeply on his joint, determined to ignore the visitor. But when several minutes passed without so much as a knock the man grew uneasy, twitching in the silence until he jumped up, cursing as he strode across the room.

"What d'ya want," he muttered, opening the door.

"I've come to warn you," said the woman.

"Warn me? What are you talking about, you crazy old hag?"

Rob swore, trying to laugh it off, but his face was flushed and he could not meet her gaze. He knew he should dismiss the rumors, the childhood speculations about the old woman and her curious ways, but whether his mind was weak to begin with or the drug had squandered his ability to make sense, he felt terror rush like ice water through his veins.

Madame Voisine reached out and put her hand on his arm. He yelped and tried to shake it off, but her grip was surprisingly strong.

"You don't belong here," she said.

Rob twisted and squirmed as his arm began to burn.

"How much darkness can one house bear? How much longer can rot remain standing? There's a blight upon this place–secrets that whisper through the walls, beckoning to me from down the lane. They come hissing and calling until the air hums with a terrible sound, and now I am bringing their message to you."

A gust of wind slammed the screen door against the house and Rob jerked back, letting out something of a whimper. Madame Voisine's hair shone like an inferno and she spoke in tones that pierced the fury and bore like the turning of a screw right into the middle of his head.

"*You don't belong here. Now get out before it's too late!*"

CHAPTER 21

Alice did not sleep that night. She sat in bed with her back to the wall, watching the door, paralyzed by thoughts that took her breath away. When the darkness washed into grey she got up, passing like a ghost through the hall. The bulb in the bathroom flickered and hummed and the girl stood there dumbly, forgetting her simple routine. She ran her hands over her face, pressing her fingernails into the flesh until she could feel herself, then clenched her fists and turned away. She got dressed and made her bed, hounded by the instinct to stay in motion, moving from one task to the next in a dull-witted stupor. When there was nothing left to be done she stood at the window, waiting for light to streak across the sky. She did not notice the boy's shadowy figure emerge from the trees even though he stood almost directly before her. Remy stopped walking, startled by the pallor of her skin, the blank stare, her body stiff and somehow vacant. He bent down to tie his shoe, hoping the movement would catch her attention, steadfast in this effort until she appeared beside him.

"Happy May Day," he said, nodding to the paper bag in her hand, "Is that it?"

"What?" she said.

"Your dress."

"What dress?"

"For your information, you're the only one who thinks that's funny," he said.

Alice stared into the distance and dropped her head, shivering as a cold warmth flooded her body. She started walking along the rutted tracks of the lane, not in the act of ignoring the boy but as if nothing had been said. Remy watched her go, his brow furrowed. He looked over his shoulder at the house, then back at the girl. Cursing under his breath, he hurried to catch up. The children did not speak again until they crossed the highway, heading for the bus stop.

"Alice," said the boy.

The girl shook her head and turned away.

"Look," she said, marking the dirt with her sandal, "This is where we met that first day when I found you trying to set your shoelace on fire. This is the exact spot."

She crouched down and scrutinized the ground, finding a rock that was smooth and grey which she picked up and put in her pocket.

"You probably saved me from getting blown to smithereens," said Remy.

Alice squinted in the sunlight, considering this.

"Then it's a good thing I didn't come by any later," she replied.

"You can say that again," nodded the boy.

Starling Elementary buzzed with a rare energy that morning, not in excitement for the heralding of spring but in tense anticipation of the costume contest to be held later on in the day. Most of the kids didn't bother to dress up, but there was a strange phenomenon in the area, a handful of local mothers who counted down the days to this event, circling it like a pack of territorial wolves. There were only so many ways one could establish a social pecking order in Starling, and the May Day costume contest ranked high on that list. Planning began months in advance and the ensuing secrecy between families rivaled that of a cold war, with more than one friendship coming to blows over accusations of espionage and intrigue.

No one dressed up beyond the fifth grade, thanks in part to a mutiny spearheaded years ago by a boy named Kyle Muntz, who got annoyed when his teacher kept pestering him about his plans for a costume. The boy finally said he'd look around and see what he could rustle up, coming to school the next day in a jacket festooned with butterflies impaled on safety pins, fluttering limply in a dismally gruesome swan song. As Kyle ran around the classroom flapping his arms, Cindy Frasier fainted, hitting a desk on her way down. The collision required fifteen stitches across her forehead though her uncle, an occasional tattoo artist, did it in ten. Kyle was marched down to the office for discipline, but it was too late to staunch the flow of collateral damage. The other boys, spurred by this act of rebellion, ran outside and tore off their own costumes, setting them ablaze in the middle of the schoolyard. There was a mass suspension of the fifth grade class that year and the following May Day, only the younger children were permitted to dress up. Kyle Muntz later dropped out of school, was known for his antics on a dirt bike, fathered a child or two, and went on to die in a grisly accident at the mill.

Banned from wearing costumes, the older girls established their own protocol for May Day attire. They came to school wearing sundresses that tied at the shoulder, and any boy reckless enough to yank a bow loose enjoyed a surge to his reputation like that of a rocket ship taking off for the moon. Of course this incurred the outrage of the so-called victim, who'd spent the entire day trying to position herself for that very offense to occur. Mona Gorsma made no such attempt at false modesty. She openly solicited the boys for a trade–a peek down her top in exchange for a cigarette–and when no one took her up on the offer, she made Kevin Olenski look anyway.

Shortly after lunch an announcement came over the intercom instructing the Maypole dancers to get into their costumes and meet at the library. Ms. Kemp, who'd spent the entire day floating between the teacher's lounge and Mr.

Bouchard's classroom, stopped for a smoke break in the supply closet and forgot all about the girl and her dress. Alice picked up her bag and slipped out of the room.

She followed Corinne LeRoy and Nikki Kilchuk down the hallway, listening to the girls argue over who'd gone to greater lengths to find a suitable dress. After an intense hunt in which three generations of LeRoy women had fanned out upon the town of Caribou, Corinne ended up ordering hers from the Sears catalogue. It was the kind of garment intended for a religious ceremony, but her mother made alterations until there wasn't the slightest chance it could be mistaken as such again. Nikki Kilchuk's mother drove two hours north to McBride where she found a shop selling prom attire, returning home with a dress that resembled an elaborate dessert.

"What about *your* dress?" said Nikki to Alice, leering over her shoulder.

"Oh…I couldn't find anything I liked," said the girl, "So I made one myself."

"You *made* your dress?" exclaimed Corinne, coming to a full stop, blinking for effect and letting out the slack in her jaw.

"Did I stutter?"

Corrine swore under her breath, triggering a loud guffaw from Nikki.

"No need to be so touchy," she said, "From the way you described your closet, I assumed you had *hundreds* of dresses to wear."

Alice ignored this and pushed into the bathroom, locking herself in a stall. She climbed onto the toilet tank and closed her eyes, trying to ignore the knots in her stomach.

"Wanna know how to tell if you have boobs?" Nikki was saying to Corrine, "Stick a pencil between'em and see if it stays there."

"You wish. Mine could hold a stapler," replied the girl.

Nikki cursed and Corinne responded by splitting the air with a cavernous belch, sending both girls into fits of hysterical laughter. Alice hunched over the bag in her lap and closed her eyes, drifting away from the commotion in the room.

"Hey, what's taking you so long?" yelled Nikki, banging on the door of her stall.

The girl looked up, startled.

"Just a minute," she said, jumping down from the toilet.

Alice reached into the bag, pulled out its contents, and stared. She had never seen this dress before in her life. She looked over her shoulder in case she was not alone, as if this might somehow be a prank with a hidden audience watching for her reaction. She picked up the bag and gave it a good shake. It was empty. The girl felt her skin begin to tingle and thought for one wild moment her imagination had come to life. *Could it be?* She closed her eyes and swallowed hard, trying to remain calm in case betraying her emotions might make it go away, as allowing herself to want something nearly always did. Breathing deeply, she turned to regard the dress.

It was made of a fine lace draped over layers of silk, light as gossamer, and in the softest shade of white. Handspun roses adorned the bodice, with tiny seed pearls stitched into the center of each bloom. Ribbons of velvet trimmed the hemline and waist, and little capped sleeves curved over the shoulder with a delicate puff. The dress rustled as if brimming with secrets and the girl leaned forward, hardly daring to breathe. In the dimness of the bathroom stall it seemed, impossibly, to glow.

"*God?*" she whispered, glancing up at the water-stained ceiling, the cork panel smashed open to reveal a gaping, black hole.

"Alice, *hurry!* We're gonna be late," called Nikki.

"Go ahead without me. I'll meet you on the field," she replied, having forgotten about the two girls altogether.

Alice put on the dress and came out of the stall, stopping short as she caught sight of her reflection in the mirror. There was something so open and artless about the girl gazing back that she looked away quickly, the color rising in her cheeks. It was as if all she had come to know about herself suddenly vanished, replaced with a truth that had been there all along and was at once both wondrous and mighty to behold. The girl in the mirror appeared to float in the air, her eyes softly bright as if she alone knew something no one else could guess or even dare to imagine. Alice covered her face in her hands and turned around slowly, the dress lifting gently like petals in the wind. She glanced a second time in the mirror and bowed her head, her heart aching with a mighty surge of hope. What more could she do than pin up her braids and lean into this moment, spinning in weightless circles as if she really might lift off the ground? It was the only way forward and she gave herself to it. Taking a deep breath, she opened the door and was swept up by a throng of children rushing down the hallway, eager to get outside.

Remy came around the corner just then and caught sight of the girl, stopping so abruptly the children behind him toppled like dominoes, cursing his ineptness.

"*Alice*," he whispered, a train roaring through his heart.

The crowd moved on and the girl saw him, her face bright.

"What do you think?" she asked, twirling around as he made his way toward her.

"You look like you fell from a star," he said, reaching out to touch the girl before he could think what he was doing.

"That could be closer to the truth than you know," she replied, the look on her face both earnest and serene.

There followed a brief silence wherein the boy failed to realize he was still staring, his mouth slightly ajar.

"Well, wish me luck," said Alice, making a curtsy, "I'd better get going."

"Wait a minute," he said, coming to his senses, "The dress is grand to be sure but it's missing something, don't you think?"

"Remy, I have to go."

"Just a final touch."

The boy reached into his pocket and pulled out her necklace, letting it glint and dangle from the chain.

Alice gasped.

"But how did you–?!"

"I said I'd get it back for you and I did," he replied, "Fixed the clasp, too."

Remy fastened the chain around the girl's neck.

"There," he said, a bit gruffly, standing back for the full effect, "Magic, just as you always say."

Alice gazed at the locket in her fingers, blinking. Suddenly, she threw her arms around the boy and held on tight, then turned and ran down the hallway without saying another word.

CHAPTER 22

Starling Elementary held its annual May Day celebration on the vacant lot next to the playground. By late morning the residents of the community began to trickle in, acknowledging each other with grunts and nods, as if chagrined to concede a social event entailed actually having to be social. The women were more boisterous, calling to friends over the crowd, hiking up their tank tops and sharing puffs of cigarettes. They took in every detail with feral acumen, noting new trinkets and hairstyles—a running tally being kept as to who was more or less a contender in the pursuit of status, that bright, coveted glory whose rays warm the chosen few. They made sly comments and crude jokes, their raucous laughter laid out like a set of tea leaves for the rising generation. The men kept quiet on account of being hung over, stubbing at the ground with their steel-toed boots. They appeared stand-offish, hindered from even the simplest attempts at self-expression, though caverns of longing lay buried within them beneath layers of anger, denial, and shame. They were bleary and unshaven, looking twice their age, their lungs and livers having clocked an excess of mileage, burning through life as if it was meant to be a sprint.

A handful of streamers hung from the swing sets and a makeshift stage had been erected next to the monkey bars for the costume contest to be held later on in the day. Mr. Redchenko presided over an arm wrestling booth where he was the undefeated champion going back as far as anyone could remember. His shirt was unbuttoned to reveal a broad, shaggy chest, and his mustache had been carefully waxed for the occasion. Ms. Benita showed up with a troupe of mimes, a sullen lot comprised of her unemployed fiancé and his friends who squatted in a series of trailers at the far end of her father's property. The mimes sat down and refused to budge, so that it was only Ms. Benita pretending to find her way out of an imaginary box. Mr. Bouchard brought a large jar filled with jellybeans to be awarded to the person who could most accurately guess the number of its contents.

Alice wandered through the crowd, entranced. She did not see the drabness of the decorations nor the fact the mimes were quite obviously stoned, but rather stared in wonder at children running by dressed as flowers and bugs, at the ring toss and the face painters, the table laden with sheet cakes and a large bowl of potato salad glistening in the sun. The school was selling boiled hotdogs and cans of root beer for a quarter apiece, and Derek Fleury was trying to blow wiener burps on all the girls. Alice passed by, writing down a number for the jellybean jar. When

Mr. Redchenko bowed low and said, "Regard the little Russian kukla!" it seemed as if her feet no longer touched the ground.

At the appointed moment she took her place with the other children around the Maypole, ribbon in hand. The music crackled over the loudspeaker as she closed her eyes and lifted her face to the sun, moving in time to the music and yet with a rhythm all her own, weaving and swaying with effortless grace. The people of Starling could not help but notice, remarking on the beauty of the girl who looked like a frost flower, drifting by as if carried on a breeze. Remy saw her and stopped breathing. He did not recognize the girl at first, for he had never quite seen her in this way. He blinked, trying to understand. It was as if something had fallen away, an invisible shield, and he was seeing what she looked like for the very first time.

When the sun caught Alice's dress, an extraordinary thing happened. It was so fleeting no one could say for sure, but the gown seemed to burst into color as a prism divides the light, glowing in shades of rose, pearl, sapphire, and gold. It was gone the next moment, leaving witnesses to rub their eyes and wonder if it wasn't an optical illusion or perhaps the lingering effects of too much drink.

Ms. Kemp was also watching, for she could not tear her gaze away from the girl, this incarnation of innocence and joy. For a moment she grimaced and bent over, feeling the stab of an inexplicable pain. It agitated her beyond reason yet she forced herself to straighten up and stare harder at the girl, as if by sheer contempt she could will the sensation away. Sunlight flashed in her eyes so that she blinked, then blinked again as she realized the glare was bouncing off a locket hanging around the child's neck.

A hideous sound gurgled up from the depths of the woman's being–a polluted, septic roar she barely managed to contain as she turned and pushed her way through the crowd. Making a beeline for the school, she broke into a hobbling sort of run spurred by a mounting, virulent rage. She lunged against the doors and charged inside, unable to restrain the noise any longer. It spewed forth into the empty hallway, a volcanic eruption of bitterness and hate, her face twisted beyond recognition and knuckles white like bare bone.

By the time she reached her classroom, Ms. Kemp was in a state of total disarray. Her blouse had come untucked and her hair looked like a wig on sideways. She hunched over, panting for breath, creamy curds of spittle thickening in the corners of her mouth. For a moment she paused at the doorway then rushed forward, howling as if to wake the dead. She got to her desk and ripped open the drawer where the locket had been kept, gaping at the scene before her.

A large, black crow lay in a clearing of pens and pencils, its beady eye shut and massive body still. A candy necklace hung from its neck, the pastel beads bright against its glossy plumage. Ms. Kemp's knees buckled and she began to shake. She could not bear to look another moment at this abomination, feeling the imminence of some great, unspeakable doom. Despite her revulsion or perhaps compelled by it, she leaned in closer and noticed a piece of paper tucked beneath the bird's wing. The woman drew a sharp breath and watched in horror as her trembling fingers reached out to withdraw the note, undoing its series of creases and folds.

DON'T MESS WITH THIS LOVEBIRD it said, written in red ink.

Ms. Kemp stumbled backward, dropping the slip of paper as if it was a coal from the ashes. She put her hands over her ears and cringed, the noise in her head roaring through her body with the fury of a tidal wave. But the motionless bird cast a strange spell over the woman, forcing her to return and look again as her jaw quivered from the pressure of her tightly clenched teeth.

Unable to breathe, she put forth her hand a second time, letting it hover like a specter in the air. Without knowing how it happened, she found herself touching the necklace, running her finger along the cool, lustrous beads. Such pretty colors! How sleek and smooth! A brittle smile spread like a fault line across Ms. Kemp's face and she began to hum a faint, dissonant tune. Suddenly, the crow's eye popped open and fixed her with a glittering stare. The woman gasped. The bird jerked its head, blinking, then reared back like a jackhammer and pecked her hard on the hand, breaking the skin.

A piercing cry shattered the air, so loud the woman felt as if her head would split in two. The crow struggled to its feet, still wearing the necklace, cawing and beating the air with its wings. Ms. Kemp ducked as it lunged off the desk and flew at her, a shower of black feathers exploding in every direction. The bird swooped around the room in a precarious pattern of flight, gaining then losing momentum, screeching its awful cacophony of sound. It grazed the window and demolished stacks of papers, splattering defecation across the chalkboard. Ms. Kemp fell to her knees and crawled beneath her desk, rivulets of blood coursing down her hand. The crow kept flying in circles and dive-bombing her shelter, coming close enough, almost, to pluck out her eye. The woman screamed and babbled incoherently, rocking back and forth with her head tucked between her knees. She failed to notice when the bird escaped the classroom because the ringing in her ears made it feel as if the world was on the verge of a complete and total collapse.

Out on the playground, the May Day festivities were coming to a close. April Bellamy won first prize for her costume of a hatching chick, in which her mother had painted the girl yellow and spackled her into a gigantic eggshell carved of styrofoam. It had been seventy-two hours since April had washed herself or sat on a toilet, but this was a small price to pay for victory as far as her mother was concerned. Mr. Redchenko won the arm wrestling competition for yet another year, though Peter Kowalski said it could not be considered a true triumph until he went up against his own wife. Some kid in the third grade guessed the right amount of jelly beans, and a group of fourth graders were already plotting to beat him up and steal his prize on the way home.

Alice meandered through the field with Remy, a dreamy look on her face.

"This has been the perfect day," she said, skipping beside the boy, "Too good for the bus. C'mon, let's walk home by the creek instead."

"Okay," said Remy, "Here, let me carry your knapsack so it doesn't mess up your dress." He shouldered her bag with his own and kept moving, eager to put distance between them and the school.

"Did you see me dance?" asked the girl, her arms aloft with the breezes in the air.

"Yeah," said the boy.

"How did I do?"

"Well," he spoke slowly, digging for the words, "I almost forgot I was standing there. It's like something inside me just left and floated away."

Alice stopped and turned to stare at the boy.

"I mean, it was *good*," he said, shrugging, turning to adjust his load.

The girl gazed at the locket, rubbing it between her fingers.

"I can't believe you got this back for me," she said, "Do you think Ms. Kemp will find out?"

"Yeah, I'm pretty sure she will."

Alice looked at Remy, suddenly fearful.

"What do you think she'll do?"

"I don't know. But she better think long and hard before she does it."

The children climbed over a fence and walked along the creek, crossing on stones where the water ran low. The air was golden, a perfumed bouquet of honeysuckle and rose, but the boy breathed easier once they reached the gate to Anderson's pasture. Alice let her hands drift over the tall grass, smiling when a baby grasshopper shot off a thistle–a miniature daredevil hurtling into the great unknown. She followed its trajectory, moving ahead of the boy who had stopped to inspect a large, distended earthworm writhing on the ground, the unfortunate picnic for an army of ants.

"Alice, you gotta see this," he called.

The earthworm flipped and turned, a feast from every angle.

"Alice."

Remy looked up but couldn't see beyond the tangled patch of growth. A large bird flew overhead, disappearing into the sun. Its shadow fell across the boy's face and was gone, but from high above a ragged caw drifted through the air. Remy scrambled to his feet and spun around, lopsided from the weight of the knapsacks. There was the girl, like a doll in the distance, surrounded by a sea of grass rolling toward her in great, shimmering waves.

"*Alice!*"

She didn't move.

Remy called her name again and when she failed to respond he began walking toward her, his pace quickening with each step. The grass coiled and parted before him, slashing his legs with thistles and quills, the velvety streak of Indian paint. The boy hurried on, feeling stiff in his joints, trying to reason away the sinking weight of fear. As he drew close the air became still and he stopped, comprehension draining all color from his face. Alice stood not ten feet from the Gorsma's dog who was crouched like a loaded spring, his massive jaws bared and nose pulled back in a hideous snarl.

"Alice," said Remy, speaking in quiet tones, "Don't move, okay? Let me get over there. Let me get in front of you."

The girl said nothing, her eyes round and riveted to the dog. The boy took a careful step toward her.

"It's gonna be okay, Alice. Don't move, I'm almost there."

But just then Dagger skittered sideways, barking like a machine gun, and the girl gave a little hiccup and pirouetted into the air. For a moment she seemed to float, as if offering the universe a chance to reconsider the grimness of its design, but when her feet touched the ground everything was still just as it had been and she took off like a shot, running across the field.

"No!" yelled Remy. He lurched forward and tripped, lost in an ecstasy of fumbling as he tried to wrench the knapsacks off his back. Dagger froze, momentarily distracted by this commotion before returning to the sight of the girl, her golden hair streaming in the sunlight, the dress billowing out like a great, white sail. A visceral moan, like the sound of a man weeping, lodged deep in the dog's throat and he stared without blinking, beads of saliva dangling from his jaw. For a second he hesitated, perhaps wrestling with the dregs of some gentler instinct, but the fleeing creature proved too irresistible and he lunged forward, yelping with the joy of the chase.

"*No!*" screamed the boy again, his voice cracking with the burden of comprehending everything had changed, horribly, in one instant. He wrenched his shoulder free of the first pack and started after the dog, throwing himself into the race as if by sheer will he could catapult himself across the distance. Over the field they flew, a pastoral scene on the brink of disaster–the girl in front, a wisp and shadow in the grass with Dagger in pursuit, flattened like an arrow and running low to the ground. Remy came last in an all-out sprint, tearing after the others as if his limbs might detach at any moment and cartwheel into the air, vaporizing with this immense expenditure of mind and matter.

Alice ran on, more certain with each step the dog would be upon her. She thought she could feel his breath on her heels and waited for his lunge, the splintering sound of his great, yellow teeth crushing her bones. She lifted her head, fixing her sights on the old maple by Anderson's pond and ran toward it as if nothing else existed, as if the tree was the only thing left upon the earth. Her dress dazzled in the sunlight and a sandal came loose, winging into the air. The girl kept running, her face set like china, impossibly white. Still, she was no competition for the dog and he whimpered as he closed the gap between them, knowing the end was near.

Alice flew down the slope and reached for the tree, leaping into its branches as if they awaited her with open arms. She struggled there a moment, trying to hoist herself onto the lowest limb. The sun was bright overhead as Dagger hurtled toward her and lunged, sailing through the last bit of empty space, his jaws frothing and wide open like a trap. The girl scarcely gained an inch as he passed beneath her, landing hard in the grass and wheeling around to snap at the crescent of heel dangling above him in mid-air. Alice clung to the branch, flailing as the dog lunged again, his breath hot and steamy against her skin.

Remy charged down the slope, his lungs stripped and burning, the ferric tang of blood in his throat. He slid the knapsack off his back, screaming a string of obscenities so incoherent it seemed as if the boy was speaking in tongues. Swinging the bag like a slingshot, he let it fly at the dog who yelped as ten pounds of textbooks caught him on the hind leg. Dagger spun around and froze. Something about the whiteness in the boy's eyes registered with the animal and he reared back and took off running. Remy gave chase, yelling war cries and following the dog to the edge of the pasture where he bent over, gasping for air. Dagger did not pause, crashing down the bank and into the creek. He cast a backward glance at the boy before making it to the other side, where he disappeared into the bushes for good.

When Remy got back to the maple tree, the girl was nowhere to be found.

"It's okay, Alice. He's gone now," called the boy, peering into the branches, "The coast is clear."

Up in the tree Alice could hear the boy but his voice sounded far away, drifting toward her as if from the end of a long tunnel. She climbed on with a strange fervor, gazing at a patch of sky peeking through the leaves overhead. The faster she climbed, the lighter she felt. The tree seemed to urge her on, its limbs steady and sure, the leaves brushing her body like a gentle caress. The girl began to hum, then sing traces of a song that came unbidden to her mind: *"The big wheel run by faith, and the little wheel run by the grace of God. A wheel within a wheel, a'rollin, way in the middle of the air."*

Alice stopped climbing. She could picture the woman who had taught her the song–tall and shapeless, with long, silvery hair and a strange way to her speech. There was a basement room filled with children, poorly lit and smelling of decay, though Alice could not remember the occasion nor why she'd been a part of it. She rested her head against the trunk, lost in these thoughts when she felt a sharp pain sear through her leg. The girl looked down, wincing, but could not see past the foliage at her waist. The leaves were dense as if to protect her from a knowledge of the truth and for a moment she held her breath, willing it to be so. But the pain was insistent and would not be ignored, so she took hold of the branch and pulled it out of the way.

Alice blinked, trying to comprehend the sight of her foot, lodged to the ankle in the depths of an enormous, tornado-shaped wasp nest. Feathery bits of paper floated in the air and a column of yellow jackets swarmed from the newly made rift. A rising hum filled her ears and she watched without moving as the wasps landed, crawling up her leg. There was fresh pain, and then more.

"*Help me*," she whispered.

She let go of the branch and fell out of the tree.

CHAPTER 23

Remy looked up to see the girl come crashing toward him. She bounced from limb to limb, her dress like tattered wings plummeting from the sky. He held out his arms and she landed against him with a thud, knocking him to the ground. The boy lay winded, unable to move, but Alice cried out, struggling.

"What happened?!" he gasped, trying to sit up and look at her, "You okay?"

He noticed a yellow jacket quivering on her arm and brushed it away.

"Get off her!" he exclaimed, swatting another wasp that emerged, inexplicably, from the neckline of her dress.

The girl cried out again, beating her hands against her body.

"What the–?!" said the boy, clapping his leg as a hot poker of pain shot through it. He looked up, a terrible comprehension dawning as a stream of yellow jackets poured from the tree, heading in their direction.

"Alice, we gotta go!" he cried, leaping to his feet. He grabbed the girl's hand and looked about wildly. The pond stretched before him, gleaming and deep. Remy took a step toward it then paused, recalling in a dark flash of memory the old account of Anderson's daughter who went into the water and never came back.

The girl began to cry, her sobs punctuating each new sting.

"We have to get outta here!" Remy turned, dragging her up the slope as she stumbled beside him, hunched and sobbing. The late afternoon sun beat down upon their heads and the creek, marked by the tree line, shimmered in the distance. A flock of starlings flew by, rolling and surging like a dark ocean swell as the girl tripped on a rock and fell to the ground. Yellow jackets roiled about the children, permeating the air with their furious hum.

Remy pulled off his shirt and beat at the wasps.

"Get off her!" he cried, his voice breaking, "Leave her alone!"

He bent over the girl who lay thrashing in the grass.

"Alice, listen to me. We have to keep moving. We have to get to the creek. Help me, will you? Just stand up and I'll carry you the rest of the way."

He pulled the girl to her feet, hoisting her into his arms. She huddled against him, shaking uncontrollably, making a noise as if she was crying deep within herself. Remy felt a burning sensation on his neck, then his shoulder, but he set his face in a grim line and pressed forward, staggering beneath the weight of the girl.

The arch of trees on either side of the creek formed a bower, the air beneath it cool and green. There was the occasional birdsong, a rustle in the bush, but a languid calm prevailed upon the place, like a hearkening to an ancient time. The current here was mild, feeding into a pool where the creek wrapped around a giant willow, the boy's favorite fishing hole. Remy appeared above the bank, the girl in his arms, their silhouette a dark brand against the sky.

He turned and stumbled sideways down the slope, crashing into the creek. Holding the girl with one arm and swatting at yellow jackets with the other, he floundered into the pool. The cold water, seeping over Alice's body, made her stir and moan.

"Take a deep breath," he whispered in her ear, "And hold on."

He wrapped his arms around her and ducked beneath the surface of the pool.

For a moment the shock of the water banished every other sensation. Alice opened her eyes and saw the sky rippling overhead like a living watercolor, the blurred outline of trees beckoning to her as if from a dream. She reached for the vision, willing it to be so, but the boy stood up in that moment and air rushed into her lungs. She coughed and flailed, crying at intervals between catching her breath. A feeble band of wasps came floating to the surface as a fresh swarm of replacements teemed overhead.

"Get away!" yelled the boy, swishing the castaways downstream.

"*What is going on here?!*"

Madame Voisine stood on the other side of the creek, looking frail and drawn. She wore a long, black dress and leaned against a tree as if clutching it for support.

"She got attacked by yellow jackets!" cried the boy, his voice breaking and eyes suddenly hot with tears, "I'm trying to get 'em off her!"

"You'll drown her first!" exclaimed the woman, "Bring the child over here–we must get her out of the water!"

"But there's too many! I can't get 'em off her!" The boy waved frantically, beating at the wasps in the air. Madame Voisine stared, blinking with comprehension. She turned her face to the sky and the boy heard her say something, though he could not be sure what it was.

A sudden gust of wind came through the trees, making a low, rustling sound. The branches overhead began to sway and for a moment it seemed as if the leaves came alive in a kaleidoscope of movement–shifting, darkening, then dispersing in every direction.

Remy looked up and beheld, in the plain light of day, the congregation of a hundred winged creatures darting through the air. He shook his head, trying to make sense of it all.

"*Bats!*" he whispered, and the word sent a surge of energy through his body.

The bats plunged into the clearing, dipping and swooping, feasting upon the yellow jackets with deadly expertise. The boy crouched beneath the ambush, watching with widened eyes as the woman held onto the tree, a look of wonder upon her face.

"Come, my boy!" she called, her voice nearly lost in the din, "There's not a moment to lose!"

Ducking low and holding Alice to his chest, he waded through the pool to the place where the woman stood. With surprising strength she grabbed the girl, pulling her out of the water as if she weighed no more than a fish.

"Help me carry her to my house," she said as the boy scrambled up the bank, "I have a poultice for the stings."

They picked up the girl and hobbled forth, following a path that wound through dense undergrowth, so thick the sky disappeared in places. Madame Voisine paused at a looming wall of ivy, unlatching a hidden gate that opened onto the far end of her property.

"This way," she said, ushering the children across the yard and up the steps to the bungalow. She strode across the living room and spread a blanket on the chesterfield, beckoning Remy to lay the girl down. Madame Voisine leaned forward and smoothed Alice's brow, making sounds like a sleepy hen. She suddenly became quiet and cocked her head, intent on a grim discovery.

"There's a bunch of them still caught in her hair!" she exclaimed, holding up a mass of curls tangled with yellow jackets. The bedraggled creatures, in a state of perpetual fury, had regained their wits and commenced once more to whine. Hearing this, the girl moaned in terror, flailing with her hands.

Madame Voisine hurried to her bedroom and returned with a brush, but the bristles lodged in the matted locks and would not to move. Alice began to struggle, crying out in fresh pain.

"They're still stinging her!" cried Remy, crazed by his inability to prevent this new assault, "We gotta do something!"

The woman clenched her hand and put it to her mouth.

"I see no way around it," she muttered, shaking her head, "Not with her this way."

She nodded to the basket on the floor beside the armchair.

"There's scissors inside," she said.

Remy rummaged through the contents, withdrawing a heavy set of shears. He handed them to Madame Voisine who took the offering, speaking to herself in French. The light from the window diverged through the crystals, splashing a constellation of color around the room. Remy knelt down and held Alice's hand as Madame Voisine gathered the girl's hair and began cutting through the tangle of wasps.

"Now we must get her out of these clothes," she said, setting the scissors down and moving briskly, "And her mother needs to be summoned."

"I'll go find her," said Remy. But he stared at the locks of hair on the floor, unable to move until the woman cast a look over her shoulder that sent him on his way.

By the time he returned with the news Penny Quinn was not at home, Madame Voisine had removed Alice's dress and placed her in a cotton shift. She'd applied a poultice to the stings and was administering sips of valerian tea.

Remy drew near to the girl, whose hair stuck out in bits and pieces around her face, her eyes swollen shut. She shook her head when Madame Voisine tried offering more tea.

"Why isn't she drinking?" he asked, agitated.

"She's taken a little, but she's travelling a dark path at the moment and with some mercy, will soon fall asleep."

"Remy!" moaned the girl, turning to the sound of his voice.

"I'm here," he said, kneeling beside her, "Alice, do you hear me? I'm right here beside you. Don't worry about a thing. You're safe now. You hear me? You're safe."

"Remy," she whispered, her voice barely audible. Tears ran down her cheeks and her lips moved, but she was lost in a world beyond his reach.

The boy dropped his head and clenched his teeth, feeling something deep inside him shudder as if it would tear apart.

"Is she going to be okay?" he asked, his voice at the breaking point.

Madame Voisine looked up, noticing for the first time the patchwork of welts on the boy's arms and legs. She set down the teacup and got to her feet.

"The road to recovery is not without its dips, but she'll make it all right. She'll do better if you're close by, that's plain as day. In all my years, I've seen no greater love."

Remy looked at the floor, feeling it begin to tilt and slide.

"Sit down, my boy," said the woman, gesturing to the armchair. She brought the poultice and spread it on his stings, then went into the kitchen and made some toast and a cup of tea.

"You're to make yourself at home," she said, setting the food beside him, "I'm going out to leave a note at Alice's house, then over to your place to have a word with your father." She wrapped herself in a shawl and left by the front door.

Remy sat in the chair, watching the girl. She was so still he got up, drawing closer until he could hear the sound of her breath. In the dim light he knelt down and beheld her battered, tear-stained face, a heaviness bearing down upon him as if he might drown in the shadows.

"Alice," he whispered. He took the girl's hand and bowed his head, touching his lips to her cheek. Something stirred and he half-remembered a time like this long ago, at the bedside of his mother. The boy closed his eyes, pushing the murky images from his mind until he could fight them no longer. Exhausted by the crossroads of memory, he slumped against the couch, empty and lost.

"Alice," he said again, to himself. The sound of her name flickered in the darkness, like a match being struck at the center of his soul.

The old woman returned when the house was quiet and still. Minou looked up in wordless greeting and the plants nodded together, keeping a drowsy vigil through the night. She stood for a moment to watch the sleeping children–Alice on the couch like a swaddled cocoon and the boy beside her, curled up on the floor.

CHAPTER 24

Remy woke up the next morning and looked at the girl, who was asleep. Her face was tender and bruised, the swelling still severe around her eyes. A rich aroma drifted in from the kitchen and he followed it to find Madame Voisine stirring a pot of oatmeal on the stove.

"How are you feeling today?" she said.

"I'm all right. Alice is sleeping."

"Yes. She had a rough patch during the night but has come through the worst of it now, I should think."

"Why didn't you wake me up?"

"Because you needed your sleep, child."

The woman spooned oatmeal into a bowl, adding berries, brown sugar, and cream. Handing this to Remy, she gestured and brought her own to the table. They sat down and began to eat, the boy devouring his food as if there was a famine in the land.

"Would you like more?" she asked and he nodded. When the second helping was gone he stared at the bowl until finally Madame Voisine said,

"Any moment now I expect it will crack."

He glanced at her, and the old woman smiled.

"You look as if there's something on your mind."

The boy frowned, still concentrating on the bowl.

"There *is* something I wanna know, now you mention it."

"And what might that be?"

"The bats."

"What about them?"

Remy folded his arms, and both he and the woman looked at each other expectantly.

"I've never seen 'em come out to hunt so early in the day."

"Nor have I," she replied, her gaze never faltering.

"What did you say to make it happen?" he blurted, abandoning all pretense of subtlety.

"What do you mean?"

"Before the bats came…you *said* something, and then they appeared."

Madame Voisine stared at him blankly.

"Are you asking: what did I say when you called my attention to the *yellow jackets?*"

"You said something and the bats came," repeated the boy stubbornly.

The old woman shook her head and leaned toward him.

"You want to believe in things more unlikely than the truth," she began, "What I said in a moment of desperation is best not repeated in the presence of a child, though I'd wager you've heard such language before."

"What's that supposed to mean?"

"It means I uttered a curse, yes–as in *profanity*, not some conjuring–no matter what you or anyone else might like to believe. Perception and reality are rarely the same thing, and it can be dangerous to confuse the two. For one so young, you'd do well to settle yourself on this point: leave behind what narrow minds whisper in airless rooms and hold onto the possibility of wonder with all your might. If there's any magic to be had in this world, *that* is where it begins."

Remy looked out the window, staring at the sky.

"Alice is like that," he said.

"Yes, I would agree."

The boy fell silent and the woman sipped her tea. Minou concentrated on a shaft of sunlight, pawing the air, his tail weaving back and forth amidst the plants.

A sound from the living room roused them both. Alice sat up, touching her face with her hands.

"What's wrong with my eyes?" she cried, "I can't see!"

Madame Voisine brought a damp cloth and began sponging the girl's brow.

"It's from the stings, my dear," she said, "The swelling has gone down since yesterday, but eyes are tender and take longer to heal. Let me bring you some ginger tea, it will help."

She returned to the kitchen, leaving the children alone.

"Remy, are you there?" said Alice, leaning against the pillow.

"Yeah, I'm right here."

"Are you okay? Did you get stung, too?"

"A few times…no big deal."

The boy came closer and sat on the edge of the chesterfield.

"Were you scared?" she whispered.

"Yeah."

"So was I."

She covered her face in her hands and the boy could see her tremble.

"Shhh, Alice. Don't cry," he said, "You were brave. You were so brave, Alice. You ran so fast, even Dagger couldn't catch you. You flew across that field, you really did. I swear you had wings."

The girl shuddered and turned away.

"Thank you for helping me," she cried into her pillow, "Thank you for saving my life!"

"Shhh," said the boy, "You were so brave. I never saw anyone as brave as you, Alice Quinn."

"I'm sorry you got stung, too," she said between sobs, "It's all my fault. I went up that tree."

"What are you talking about?! Are you crazy? Don't talk like that!" The boy leaned forward, choking on his words, "I would've taken'em all if I could."

He stopped, unable to say more, blinking furiously and looking at the floor.

Alice cried on, more softly now.

"There's no one like you," she whispered, "No one in the world."

Remy reached out and linked fingers with the girl, dropping his head.

Outside there was the crunch of gravel on the lane as a green hatchback turned in from the highway. Watching by the kitchen window Madame Voisine called out, "It's Alice's mother. Remy, go catch her if you can."

He hurried outside and ran across the yard, waving to the vehicle as it drove down the lane. Penny pulled over and unrolled her window, squinting into the sunlight as the boy gestured in broad motions, fumbling for the words to explain. Finally she got out of the car, scowling. She stepped on her cigarette and followed him to the bungalow.

Madame Voisine greeted her at the doorway.

"Come in," she said, "I'm very sorry to meet you under these circumstances. Alice is improving, but she's been through quite an ordeal. She will benefit greatly by the strength of your demeanor."

"By my *what?*" said Penny, shaking her head irritably as if the old woman was to blame, not just for her lack of comprehension, but for the overall inconvenience that had brought them together in the first place.

"I mean your reaction will affect her ability to heal, so a comforting presence is the order of the day."

Penny sniffed loudly, withdrawing her hands into the sleeves of her flannel shirt. Her eyes were blood-shot and her expression so slack it was possible to imagine it actually sliding off her face.

"Where's my kid?" she said.

Madame Voisine cocked her head, gazing at Alice's mother as if trying to make up her mind on some imperceptible point of concern.

"Right this way."

She ushered Penny into the living room, withdrawing to give the mother and daughter a moment alone. Remy hovered on the threshold, less inclined to see the wisdom of this arrangement.

Penny took one step forward and screamed, clapping her hands over her mouth and partially covering her eyes.

"What in the hell happened to you?!"

"Mom, I'm okay. It's just a few bee stings," said Alice, struggling to sit up.

"Just a few bee stings?!" The woman began to curse, gesturing elaborately to some invisible audience, "I'm your mother and even *I* can't recognize you! Why're your eyes all puffy like that? And *what did they do to your hair?!*"

"What are you talking about?" said the girl. She reached toward her head, patting tentatively. The composition of her features began to tremble as she touched her shoulders and neck, feeling her way to the truth.

"Alice, she had to cut it!" blurted Remy, unable to remain silent any longer, "Your hair was full of yellow jackets and we couldn't get 'em out. You were hurting so bad and they were still trying to sting you and…" here the boy faltered, his shoulders slumped, "There was no other way."

"No other way?!" cried Penny, "*No other way?!* Look at her–she's a *freak!* How dare you do something like that to my daughter without asking me?!"

"I came looking and you weren't home," said the boy evenly, meeting her gaze.

The woman stared at him, speechless, then crumpled into the armchair and buried her head in her hands.

"Mom," said the girl, beckoning from the couch, "Please don't cry."

But Penny ignored her, rocking back and forth while uttering loud, keening sobs.

"That's it. I guess I'm just a horrible mother, then!"

"No!" said the girl, her voice laced with alarm, "Don't say that. It's not true!"

"Yes, it is. I'm too needy. I can't do anything right."

"Mom, this was my fault. Please, it was just an accident."

But Penny was determined to have her moment.

Alice struggled off the couch and made her way toward her mother. She knelt down gingerly, putting an arm around her shoulders.

"Mom, I'm sorry. It was all my fault. Please don't cry."

The girl began crying softly herself.

From his vantage point Remy looked to Madame Voisine, desperate for an intervention, but the old woman attended to the tea, her face set like stone.

Penny began to cough, a wrenching bark that racked her body. She sniffed and wiped her face on her sleeve, a hollow attempt to rein herself in.

"Mom, don't worry. I'm going to be okay," said Alice, stroking her mother's arm. The woman stared at the ground, her fingers twitching for a cigarette. When she spoke, her voice trembled on the verge of recapitulation.

"Rob broke up with me yesterday."

The girl recoiled as if she'd been punched in the stomach.

"He said he needs his space."

Penny started crying again.

Alice opened her mouth but made no sound. She slumped beside the armchair as Madame Voisine came into the room bearing a tray of tea and cookies. The woman stopped short when she saw the girl on the floor.

"You should be laying down, my dear."

"How am I supposed to rest at a time like this?!" wailed Penny, importuning the universe with her hands.

Madame Voisine glanced at Remy, then offered the woman a cup of tea.

"Yes, anyone can see you've had a terrible shock. Please drink this, you'll find it quite soothing. Then perhaps you can go home to relax while I keep Alice a little while longer."

Penny took a sip of the tea and shook her head, addressing no one in particular.

"I don't know what I'm gonna do," she said, staring into space.

Alice sat on the floor, exhausted. She could partially see with one eye and the candy dish caught her attention, its ribbon sweets gleaming in the sun. Perched on top was a tiny ship carved from butterscotch, the exquisite detail of a brigantine with sails billowing in the wind. The figure of a man dressed in a crisp uniform stood on the deck, watching her through his telescope. The girl leaned forward, trying to focus but when she blinked, he was gone. Alice swayed gently as if she could hear the wind through the rigging, the great waves beckoning with their infinite, encompassing embrace. She longed to put her head down and let it all carry her away.

Penny heaved a sigh and her cup clattered against the end table, sloshing tea onto a doily made of lace. She stood abruptly, prompting the girl to scramble to her feet, whereupon her mother clung to her and whimpered, "I thought what we had was *real!*"

"Mom, what are you talking about? I'm your daughter. Of course it's real!"

"Then why is he asking for *space?!*"

Alice took a step backward, the bewilderment of her expression almost more than Remy could bear. He clenched his fists, trembling with murderous thoughts. He wanted to stand on a cliff and hoist a boulder over the edge, watching it whistle through the air and obliterate Penny Quinn in a cloud of dust.

"Why can't you come home now?" she whined, "I don't think it's good for me to be alone."

Madame Voisine opened her mouth to speak, but Alice nodded.

"Of course I can come. I'll make you some coffee and a nice bowl of pudding."

Penny let out a long, shuddering sigh and glanced around the room, taking none of it in.

"What I need is a smoke."

She grabbed her bag and walked past the old woman without saying a word. It was not until she reached the doorway that she seemed to recall what had brought her to the house in the first place.

"When it rains, it pours," muttered Penny, speaking in bitter, accusatory tones. She turned to Madame Voisine and paused, cognizant she held some degree of advantage yet having no idea how to use it. "You could've at least gotten my permission to cut her hair," she finally said, wiping her nose with a theatrical sniff. Appeased by this parting shot, she stalked off across the yard, rummaging in her bag for a cigarette.

CHAPTER 25

The door closed and everyone stared at the ground, as if by avoiding eye contact the events of the past half hour might ostensibly go unnoticed.

"I guess I should get going," said Alice, her voice trailing off as Remy lunged for the door, making himself a human barricade.

"No!" he exclaimed, "You're in no shape to go anywhere! Madame Voisine, tell her!"

The old woman looked at the girl.

"I do wish you'd stay," she said.

"But she needs me," replied Alice, giving a little shrug.

"Hey!" said Remy, noticing her bare feet, "You can't leave without your shoes! One of 'em's still in Anderson's field. Wait here until I find it."

He glanced sideways at Madame Voisine and went out the door, moving at a conspicuously unhurried pace.

The old woman turned to Alice and said, "Sit down, my dear. Try to drink some tea while I go fetch your things."

When she left the room, Alice slumped onto the chesterfield. Her gazed returned to the candy dish, the brigantine seeming smaller somehow, as if charting a course for departure. The girl closed her eyes and watched it sail off into the horizon.

Madame Voisine returned after a time, bearing the dress. It appeared smooth and pristine, remarkably untouched by the events of the previous day. Alice watched her lay the frock over the chair.

"It was you, wasn't it?" she said.

"Child?"

"The dress. It came from you."

Madame Voisine sat down on the couch. She gazed at the candy dish, reaching to adjust the little brigantine listing on the sugary waves.

"I once knew a girl who plucked every care from the universe," she began, "You remind me of her sometimes."

Alice did not respond but the woman went on.

"She put all her worries in a basket that grew heavier each day, tugging the smile from her face. After a time the burden became so great it pulled her head out of the clouds, which was indeed a pity, for that is where she was meant to be."

Alice rested against her pillow, staring at the floor.

"The world is filled with light and darkness," continued

Madame Voisine, "Most people prefer to keep their heads down, content to miss it all, while others only want to see what's wrong. There's a better balance to be had, my child. Look around and see it all, let it come and go. Take in every joy and sorrow, and be sure to gather beauty along the way. See the horizon and the details–the vast ocean and the tiny, perfect shell. And when there's trouble you cannot fix, don't keep it as your own. Everything will be okay; it all works out in the end."

Minou passed through the room, keeping his distance, and the ticking of a clock could be heard from somewhere in the house.

"Ever since I can remember," said Alice, her voice thin yet with a perceptible edge, "I've longed to hear someone say those words, *everything will be okay*, as if hearing them would somehow make it all come true. But I don't want to hear them anymore…I don't! It makes me sick to think I ever did. Some things are okay. But others *aren't*…and that's just the way it is."

Madame Voisine sat quietly, smoothing the girl's hair from her face.

"There's truth in what you say," she nodded, "But this much I can tell you–to turn from that longing creates a haven of sorts, but it comes at a high price.

"What's that supposed to mean?"

"Well, sometimes the more we seek for refuge, the stronger the shelter becomes until it refuses to release what it was summoned to protect."

"Then what happens?"

"It depends. The person either fights to break free, or forever remains in a place where nothing and no one can hurt her."

"Sounds good to me," The girl spoke harshly, wincing at her words.

"I know. That kind of safety can seem irresistible. But push and fight on as you can, my dear, to keep the best part of yourself free."

"What is that?"

"The part that allows you to feel. The part that allows you to *care*."

Alice took the dress into the bathroom and put it on. She kept her eyes averted, but at the last moment couldn't help herself and glanced in the mirror. The poultice had worked wonders, to be sure, but her face still looked like a lump of rising dough with a pile of straw stuck on top. Even so, there was something about the dress that stirred the girl, keeping her from the brink of encompassing despair. It rustled softly as if something extraordinary was about to happen and against all reason Alice straightened her shoulders and went into the kitchen to find the old woman watering her plants.

When Madame Voisine noticed the girl in the doorway, she stopped and stared.

"*Bonté divine*," she whispered.

"Do you like it?" asked Alice.

"You look like something from a dream," she said, "Like an echo at the end of a great hall."

"What kind of an echo?"

"Oh…music, I should think, and perhaps a little laughter."

The girl considered this, light and shadows playing across her face.

"And the necklace?" asked the woman, leaning forward, "I noticed it earlier. Was it a gift?"

Alice fingered the locket, hesitating.

"I found it at a bus station a long time ago," she confessed.

"However the piece came into your possession," said the old woman, her eyes earnest and bright, "Surely it must be an heirloom passed down through the ages, intended especially for you."

Alice looked sharply at the woman. Madame Voisine cocked her head and the two shared a smile that brought the girl more comfort than any words of reassurance ever could.

"It looks as if Remy has found your shoe," remarked Madame Voisine, peering out the window at the boy walking up the lane. He carried two knapsacks over his shoulder and held the sandal, dangling from a strap.

"It's a bit soggy," he said, coming into the kitchen.

"That's okay." Alice took the sandal and put it on.

Madame Voisine stood back and watched the girl, an inscrutable expression on her face. She withdrew from her chignon a delicate, jeweled pin and fastened it in Alice's hair.

"There," she said, patting the girl's cheeks, "A token for remembrance."

"Madame Voisine," began Alice, unable to say more.

"I'm here if you need me," replied the woman, nodding firmly. She returned to watering the plants and was soon lost behind a fern.

Penny was asleep by the time the children arrived at the bungalow. Alice tiptoed into the kitchen and made some rice pudding, setting a bowl aside for her mother. The children took their food into her bedroom and closed the door.

"I'm not very hungry," said Alice, setting her bowl on the milk crate, "You can have my share." She lay down on the bed and felt for the petrified wood beneath her pillow. Remy ate quickly, washing the dishes in the kitchen. He lingered in the doorway upon his return, seeing the girl's eyes were closed.

"About the ribbon dance," she murmured, as he turned to leave.

"Yeah?" he said, stepping into the room.

"It felt like I was floating, just as you said. Up in the clouds, as if I would never come down."

A wave of inexplicable anger rushed through the boy.

He clenched his fists against a sudden urge to tear down the bungalow, piece by piece, and watch the girl drift off into a pale, blue sky.

"You don't have to come down," he said, swallowing hard, "Keep floating…higher even. I'll find a way to go with you."

He sat on a milk crate, listening for the soft cadence of her breathing. When the room filled with shadows and the girl was fast asleep, he got up and let himself out the back door.

CHAPTER 26

By Monday, Alice's appearance had greatly improved. The swelling was all but gone and at her request Remy had evened out her haircut, trimming the unruly pieces with his jackknife until it curled in waves against her head.

Penny spent the weekend chasing down whiskey with cigarettes and ginger ale. She called in sick when it came time for her shift, sleeping all day and staring at the television through the night. She was easily agitated and given to tears, but with the start of the new week she got out of bed, drank a pot of coffee, and reported for duty at the glass plant.

Sitting at Ms. Kemp's desk that morning was an iron-haired brick of a woman named Mrs. Petroff. She worked as a substitute teacher at the school and was well known for her belief in corporal punishment, never hesitating to twist an ear or take a child over her knee to spank them with a paddle. Though such practices were generally abandoned in urban areas, they were not officially outlawed—a technicality Mrs. Petroff employed to her advantage with particular leeway in Starling.

When the second bell rang Mrs. Petroff got up from her desk and stood in front of the class.

"Your teacher has taken a leave of absence," she announced, regarding the children with dead eyes, her lips clamped together in a thin, sallow line, "And if anyone thinks it'd be a good idea to pull some monkey business while she's gone, they'd be sorely mistaken, indeed." Mrs. Petroff glared over the room, as if to ferret out anyone who might subscribe to just such a dim-witted notion. Kevin Olenski happened to be the very one, possessing the enviable gift of summoning farts on demand, and he couldn't think of a more fitting debut for his talent than at that very moment in time.

There were three weeks left in the school year. The warm air was a heady elixir and the children breathed it in deeply, zig-zagging around the schoolyard, playing robust games which nearly always resulted in bloodshed or tears. A mounting restlessness simmered in the classrooms and the whiff of anarchy blew through the halls. As if by some unwritten consensus the teachers began a subtle abdication of their own, manifested by permitting small insurgencies of students to use the bathroom at once, ignoring congregations at the pencil sharpener, and harboring a tendency to linger in the staff room long after the second bell had rung.

With two weeks to go, the children came to school whispering the news Kevin Olenski's big sister had been killed over the weekend. It was the age-old story: a carful of teens and some bottles of beer, resulting in a fiery collision that scattered the remnants of death forty yards down a wet highway in the cold, dark hours before dawn. There were no survivors, but the Gorsma twins reported visiting the accident site early the next morning and discovering a charred eyeball that hissed and exploded when they poked it with a stick.

On the last week of school Ms. Kemp returned, though it could be said the teacher never really came back. She did not raise her voice nor directly address anyone if she could help it. She kept to her desk or stayed away from the classroom altogether. Once, when Corinne LeRoy screamed because Peter Kowalski had picked his nose and was threatening to wipe the contents in her hair, Ms. Kemp flinched and turned the color of dried paste. The children, gripped by thoughts of imminent freedom, failed to notice their teacher had dwindled to a mere husk of her former self. Remy kept an eye on her in spite of this and was more careful than ever not to leave Alice alone.

When the final bell rang, heralding the end of the school year, the doors of Starling Elementary burst open and a throng of students poured into the yard. The younger children jostled into line to wait for the bus but the seventh graders had other plans, slipping into the woods beyond the playground where some of the boys lit up cigarettes and tried necking with Shannon Doucet, or whatever else she'd let them do. Mona Gorsma came along and against his better judgment, since he had none, Dennis Wiebe consented to make out with her. It went well enough until Mona tried adding her tongue into the mix and the boy pulled back, heaving on account of a delicate gag reflex.

"I won't always be this ugly, you know," said the girl, watching him vomit into a patch of weeds.

"Yes, you will," replied Dennis, wiping his mouth.

The neighborhood kids started down the road on a mass pilgrimage to Red's, kicking rocks, calling out insults–a jubilant throng in search of refined sugar to enhance their celebration of the day. Remy and Alice stood at the bike racks, letting the crowd pass by.

"What d'ya wanna do?" asked the boy.

Alice shrugged. Her report card, which had been handed out before the last bell, was something of a disappointment, the citizenship grade chief above all. Each year she held high hopes for this final evaluation of her character, yearning for her teacher's approval with a keen, immoderate desire. She kept her old report cards neatly stacked in her treasure chest, retrieving them often to read over the glowing comments from years past, even though she knew them all by heart. Despite her checkered history with Ms. Kemp, Alice could not squelch the delusional spark that the teacher might yet harbor some modicum of affection toward her. But when she opened her report card and scanned the column of grades, the space allotted for citizenship had been given a U for *unsatisfactory*, the lowest possible score, ground into the cardstock with vicious, red ink.

"C'mon," said Remy, "Let's go get some licorice whips from Red's and walk home along the tracks. It'll be fun."

"I don't have any money," said Alice.

"Well I do. And I earned it risking life and limb in Anderson's chicken coop, which is worthy of recognition in itself."

The girl shrugged again but nodded.

"That's more like it," said Remy, "And by the way, don't ever remind me of the proper term for Ichabod's nose flap again. I've managed to block it from my mind and for the sake of my sanity, I'm going to need your cooperation on this."

Alice gazed at her report card, ignoring the boy.

"I'm being serious, Alice. There's certain things civilized people just don't talk about. So you can say whatever you want, anything at all, but don't let it be *that*."

"Snood," she said softly.

The boy clutched his head, keeling over.

"Hey, do we speak the same language?! Do you need your hearing checked? I just told you *not* to tell me!"

"*Wattle.*"

Remy grimaced, nearly staggering into the ditch.

"Oh, you really did it this time, Alice Quinn!" he exclaimed, allowing himself to trip and roll down the embankment, "You see what this does to me?!"

The girl turned away, but not before Remy saw her smile. He scrambled to his feet and they continued onward, stopping for candy at the gas station and walking home along the train tracks, breathing air made sweet by clover and pine, laced with the exhilarating rush of freedom.

CHAPTER 27

June got off to a glorious start. The children picked berries in thickets by the lane, devouring the fruit until their stomachs ached and twisted in knots. They built a tree fort, swam in the creek, and slept beneath the stars on top of the old school bus. They set pennies on the train tracks and fished for trout, cooking their catch over the fire pit in Anderson's field. Remy found a set of moose antlers in the hills and hauled it back to display in their fort. Alice rescued some tadpoles otherwise doomed to languish in a dwindling ditch puddle, and in the pleasant warmth of the late afternoon they walked to the gas station and bought popsicles at Red's.

The fort was located in a willow tree by the creek. It was little more than a few wooden planks hammered between limbs, but the children constructed it with the same fervor as the great cathedral workers of old. They fashioned a precarious hammock from the remnants of Alice's bed sheets and strung it between two high branches. Remy stockpiled rocks from the creek in case it became necessary to discourage intruders. Alice picked wildflowers, festooning the antlers with braided grass and garlands of lupine and balsamroot. Willow branches hung in curtains all around, hiding the fort from the outside world.

The next day was Alice's birthday. Penny marked the occasion with a pile of change left on the kitchen table. As the girl stood contemplating this gift, there was a knock at the door and Remy stood on the front step, a knapsack slung over his shoulder.

"Let's go somewhere for your birthday," he said.

"What did you have in mind?" asked the girl.

"I dunno. Wherever the road takes us."

"How about Narnia?"

"Fine by me. Just make sure you have a sturdy pair of shoes."

The girl stared at Remy, her eyebrow raised, but he returned her gaze without blinking.

"Let me see what I can find," she finally said, ushering him inside.

Alice got dressed and brushed her hair, fastening it back with Madame Voisine's ornamental pin.

"How do I look?" she said, coming into the kitchen.

"Like a birthday girl," said Remy.

"Mona said my haircut makes me look like a boy."

"I don't think Mona Gorsma is in a position to criticize anyone's looks," he replied.

The children set off down the lane. When they got to the highway they stopped and looked around.

"Now what?" asked Alice.

"Let's follow the train tracks into Caribou."

"But that's over ten miles away!"

"So what? I wouldn't care if it was a million miles away."

"A *million* miles," scoffed Alice, "That would put us on Jupiter!"

"Fine by me," said the boy, kicking a rock.

They crossed the empty highway that narrowed in the distance, shimmering as if an invisible barrier had been thrown up to hedge their way. Before stepping onto the tracks, Alice hesitated and glanced over her shoulder at the LaPierre house. It was always her intention to ignore the place but somehow in the very act of doing so, she felt even more compelled to look. The slanted structure was watching and waiting as always, and though it was far enough in the distance she shivered and folded her arms.

"You okay?" asked Remy.

"Yeah."

Alice did not know what to say about the house or the dogs skulking around it. She did not know how to ask about the broken windows patched with tape or the crusted sauce pans stacked on the kitchen floor. The house had a way of worming into her thoughts, looming there unbidden until she found her heart racing and her mind tangled up like weeds at the bottom of a pond. She looked away from the dirty magazines, the beer cans and bottles of drink, and the holes punched into the wall. She tried not to breathe in its stench, turning from the old man at the table and the brother whose temper hung like a thunderclap in the air. She could not shake the feeling the house itself might try to catch her on its splinters and drag her somewhere deep within. Perhaps these were not reasonable thoughts, but the girl had long since lost the ability to dismiss a thought for being unreasonable. She did not know how to make sense or talk about any of these things, but she knew when Remy wasn't inside the house she somehow felt safer, too.

Alice shook her head and lifted her face to the sun, skipping down the tracks. Absorbed in this pursuit, she failed to notice a large, patterned snake weaving over the rail ties until it was nearly underfoot. The snake moved slowly in the morning sun, like a rivulet of water coursing along the path of least resistance.

"Oh!" she said, stopping short.

"What is it?" called Remy.

"A snake!"

"Lemme see."

He caught up to the girl and they hurried on, anxious to keep the creature in sight.

"It's only a gopher snake," said Remy, plucking a foxtail from the grass, "They're not poisonous."

"Maybe so," conceded the girl, "But I doubt he'll appreciate you touching him all the same."

"Don't worry, I won't hurt him."

"That would be the least of my concerns."

Remy leaned forward and brushed the snake with the fluffy end of the stalk.

The change was imperceptible, no more than an extra ripple added to its rhythm, but the snake gathered speed so that the children had to break into a trot to keep up. The markings on the serpent's back pulsed against the muscles beneath its skin, mesmerizing the children as they hurried along. They did not dare move faster and risk obtaining too great a proximity, nor could they bear to slow down and let such a magnificent specimen disappear altogether. They followed at this pace, breathless, until the snake slid over the tracks in one fluid movement and was gone.

"We lost him," said Alice, mournfully.

"He's just down there in the ditch," said the boy, pointing with the foxtail.

The ditch ran along the highway, separating the train tracks from the road. It provided drainage for the fields and pastures, burgeoning with all manner of refuse and debris.

"Oh, well," said Alice, gazing at the place where the snake had disappeared, "He's better off there, anyway."

Remy was first to notice the flattened patch of weeds. He waited as the girl moved ahead on the tracks then ventured close to investigate the dark, sunken shape hidden by cattails and fronds of burdock.

"*Dagger!*" he whispered.

"What did you find?" called the girl, who was balancing on the rail, her arms outstretched.

"Nothing," said the boy, straightening up. The dog had been dead for some time. His body was emaciated, revealing a grimaced jaw, a tufted hide stretched over ribs and thin, distended joints. The eyelid was shriveled and crawling with flies, peeled back to reveal the wedge of a milky blue orb. Remy turned to walk away. He took a few steps then hesitated, looking back over his shoulder. In one, swift motion he picked up a rock and lobbed it at the carcass. The rock sailed through the air, making a strange sound as it hit the dog's belly–a soft, wet, thud that caught the boy off guard. His eyes widened as he watched the rock disappear, sinking into the fur as if it was a pool of mud. There was a fraught silence and the boy, without knowing it, held his breath. It took him a moment to realize it was not quiet after all, but a sound was festering that had been there all along. The animal's skin began to wrinkle, then shiver as an eruption of maggots burst forth, spilling over the cusp of the wound and seething across the carcass like a blind, consumptive wave.

"Oh!"

The boy whirled around.

Alice stood behind him, her dark eyes enormous in her pale, peaked face. She looked smaller somehow and uncommonly alert, her presence so still it made the landscape around her seem to tremble and blur.

"Alice," he said, gesturing helplessly.

She stood motionless, not hearing the boy.

"C'mon, let's get out of here."

"Is that Dagger?" she said.

"Yeah."

"What happened to him?"

"Looks like he got hit by a car."

"But how would he have gotten all this way into the ditch?"

"I dunno. Maybe he got hit real hard, or maybe he just came here to die."

Alice stared at the dog, reliving both possibilities in her mind.

"Poor old boy," she whispered, blinking rapidly, the warmth of the day suddenly gone.

Wisps of pollen drifted by on a breeze and a lone coyote crossed the tracks in the distance. He stopped for a moment to watch the children, then vanished into a thicket. A column of ants kept to the shade beneath a rail tie, marching in splendid formation, and a little way off there was a rustling in the grass.

Two birds flew overhead, sparring in the sunlight, and a hundred furry caterpillars spun themselves into cocoons beneath the leaves of a wild rosebush. The children stood together in the midst of it all, surrounded by the buzz and hum of countless tiny creatures living to the fullest their brief and glorious spark.

"C'mon," said Remy, "Let's keep going. It's your birthday. You shouldn't be sad."

"*Wait.*" Alice broke away from the boy, sniffling. She roamed the bank, gathering an armful of baby's breath, then scrambled down the ditch and placed it next to the dog. She gestured for Remy to join her and when he did she said, "I think you should say something."

Remy glanced at the girl and saw she was serious. He squinted into the sun and shoved his hands in his pockets, clearing his throat several times.

"Uh, okay. Let's see…Dagger, you were not a good dog, but you *were* a dog, so I guess it wasn't all your fault. You can't help who you belonged to. Most dogs who are mean get that way for a reason. You gave us quite a scare the other day, but you couldn't catch Alice because she knows how to fly. Anyway… you're gone now, but no one deserves to die alone, in a ditch. Alice would say you're in a better place, but I don't know if that's true. For your sake, I hope she's right."

He stopped talking.

Alice stood quietly, bowing her head.

"Was that okay?" he asked, looking sideways at the girl.

She nodded.

"It was perfect."

Alice stared at the dog, struggling to grasp the brevity and permanence before her. In the end, it was too great to make sense of the thing. It was enough, simply, to be a witness.

CHAPTER 28

Over the weekend the bad dreams returned. The girl jerked out of sleep, breathless and thrashing in her blankets. In some far corner of her mind she knew she was awake, but the dream would not release her and she moaned in the darkness, rocking back and forth. An eerie glow in the sky caught her attention and she turned toward it, wondering if it was real. By degrees she discerned the entanglement of her bed sheets, the four walls of her room, and the light which still glowed through the window, making a rosy silhouette of the tree line along the creek between the bungalow and the highway.

Alice jumped out of bed and hurried to the window, fogging up the pane.

"No!" she whispered.

She slipped on her shoes and flew out the door, running through the night. The smell of smoke was upon her before she reached the highway and a blistering crackle seethed through the air. She emerged from the lane and stepped back, staggered by the impact of registering too much information at once.

The LaPierre house was on fire.

Engulfed in flames, the tilted abode had never appeared more upright than it did in that moment, a roaring inferno that seemed to beseech the heavens above. Here and there skeletal remnants emerged from the sparks, only to be reclaimed once more by the ravenous blaze. Alice crossed the highway and ran toward the house, darting past Starling's volunteer fire truck and the men standing beside it who were blackened and exhausted, beaten by the fire. One of them reached out and caught the girl by the arm so that she struggled against him, screaming Remy's name.

"Hush, little kukla! Where did you come from? What are you doing here?!"

It was Mr. Redchenko, covered in soot. Alice kicked at the man, lunging with all her might toward the shimmering blaze. He picked the girl up as if she was, indeed, a doll and carried her to the fire truck, sitting her on the top step.

"What are you doing here?" he said again, "Are you looking for the boy?"

He put his hands on her shoulders and regarded her closely, his grimy face obscured by the darkness.

Alice began to tremble and could not speak.

"The boy made it out. No one else." Mr. Redchenko crossed himself, muttering in his native tongue. He pointed down the highway toward Madame Voisine's bungalow. "He's that way."

"Which one?" said Alice, a raw pitch in her voice.

"The boy. He made it out."

"But there's two boys. Two of them!"

Mr. Redchenko stared at her, uncomprehending.

"Which one was it?! Which boy did you see?" she cried.

The man turned away and wiped his brow.

"This is no place for a child," he said.

Alice huddled on the step and did not move.

"What is your name, little one?"

"Alice."

The man nodded, "I am Viktor Redchenko. Please allow me to take you home."

There was nothing she could say to this, nor did it occur to her to try.

Mr. Redchenko offered his hand and she took it blindly, scrambling to the ground. In the distance the flashing lights of a fire truck from Caribou barreled down the highway toward them, its siren relentless and shrill. Alice turned to the Lapierre house and caught a glimpse of Remy's window, or the place where it had been. The fire raged on in garish shades of orange and red, the figures of men passing before it like shadow puppets on a stage.

"Come, kukla," yelled Mr. Redchenko, "Let's get you out of here!"

Alice turned to the man, her eyes round and imploring.

"Which one was it?" she cried, pulling her hand free.

Mr. Redchenko's shoulders sank and he shook his head, unable to look at her.

"No," said the girl, taking a step backward. She hovered there a moment, then spun in the gravel and was gone.

When Alice reached Madame Voisine's bungalow she charged toward it like a battering ram, recoiling at the last moment. She stared at the doorknob, frozen, but the old woman was suddenly on the threshold, ushering her inside.

"I knew you would come," she said.

Alice could not meet her gaze. She stood on the front step, unable to move.

"Child," said the woman, her face grim with sorrow.

The girl lurched past her, rushing through the bungalow to the figure on the couch.

It was Remy. He was wrapped in a blanket, his face a streak of ash and tears. Alice went to the far end of the chesterfield and sat down, inching closer to the boy until there was no discernible space between them. Madame Voisine appeared from the darkness, tucking a shawl around the girl. She sat in the armchair and the cat appeared, springing onto her lap. The sound of a clock could be heard, ticking softly, and moonlight from the window bathed the children in a faint, elusive glow.

CHAPTER 29

The next morning a white truck pulled into Madame Voisine's driveway. A man got out wearing a jacket with a badge on the sleeve. He announced himself as the chief inspector from the Caribou fire department, giving a name that was forgotten as soon as it was said. The man came into the bungalow, accepted Madame Voisine's offer for a cup of tea, and sat in the armchair facing the children.

"Very sorry for your loss," he said to Remy, nodding and repeating the condolence when the boy did not respond.

"I was over to the site with my men earlier this morning," he continued, "We've got a pretty good idea how the fire got started, but I wanted to get any further information you might have to help me complete my report."

"The child's been through a great ordeal," said Madame Voisine from her place in the doorway, "Can't your questions wait until he's had a chance to recover from the shock?"

The inspector peered into his cup.

"I understand and like I said, my condolences," he replied, "But it would be better if we could get this done while his memory is still fresh."

Remy looked down, his face impassive.

"What can you tell me, son?" said the man, "What do you remember? How did you manage to get out of the house?"

"I was asleep," the boy spoke slowly, his voice so hoarse the inspector had to lean forward in his chair, "But something woke me…a voice. Someone was calling my name, telling me to get up. *Get up and get out,* it said. I got out of bed and opened the door, but there was smoke everywhere. It came into the room and at first I couldn't tell if it was real or maybe just a dream. But when I couldn't breathe, I closed the door and went out the window."

"Where was your bedroom?"

"Upstairs."

The inspector took a notebook from his pocket and clicked his pen, frowning as he wrote.

"You say you went out the window of the second floor?" he asked, reviewing his notes.

"Yeah."

"How'd you manage that?"

"With a rope," said the boy, offering no further explanation.

"Then what happened?"

"I hit the ground pretty hard," he said.

"How's that?" asked the man.

"The rope wasn't long enough, so I had to let go."

"The rope wasn't long enough, so you had to let go," repeated the inspector, cocking his head as if to weigh this bit of information. He made another scribble in the notebook then looked up expectantly.

"Go on."

Remy leaned against the couch, looking hollow and grey.

"I fell on my back and couldn't breathe," he said, "But I got up as fast as I could and ran around the house, looking for my dad and Simon. I could hear the dogs barking inside. I tried to open the door but couldn't get close. It was burning everywhere I went, and the smoke kept coming at me so I couldn't see a thing."

The boy had a feverish look in his eyes and he seemed to be talking to no one but himself.

Madame Voisine spoke up from the doorway, "That's how I found him, running around the house, trying to get inside."

The inspector looked at the woman and clicked his pen.

"What alerted you to the fire?" he said.

"I saw it from my bedroom window."

"At what time?"

"Shortly after midnight. I called Viktor Redchenko, the

head of our local fire department, then hurried over to see what could be done. I found the boy outside in a state of shock. When the men arrived, we agreed I should take him home."

"I see," said the inspector, clicking his pen again. He looked at Remy. "Do you have any idea how the fire got started?"

The boy shook his head.

"He told you he was sleeping," said Madame Voisine.

"I know what he said," replied the inspector, "I'm just trying to collect enough information to submit my report." He made some further scribbles in the notebook. "We think the fire was sparked by a cigarette left on the downstairs couch, igniting gas cans on the main floor of the dwelling." He looked at Remy, as if waiting for him to corroborate this theory. The boy closed his eyes.

"Once the blaze got started, it went full tilt." The man shook his head and whistled, wrestling with an instinct to make plain his admiration for the fire, "That house was like a tinderbox, just waiting to go up. It's a miracle anyone made it out alive." He kept clicking the pen so that Alice longed to grab it from his hand and throw it across the room.

"One last thing," he said, looking over his notes, "You said you heard a voice that woke you up. Who was it?"

Remy did not open his eyes.

"Who alerted you to the fire? Who told you to get out?" pressed the man.

"I don't know," said the boy, shaking his head.

"Must've been your dad."

"I think that's enough," said Madame Voisine.

"Sure thing," said the inspector, standing up. He thanked her for the tea and paused to gather his thoughts for a concluding remark, but the woman maneuvered so that he found himself on the doorstep before he had a chance to speak or give his pen a final click.

The next visitor to arrive was Mr. Redchenko. He stepped into the bungalow with his head down, bowing beneath the weight of an emotion rarely on display. Upon seeing Remy, he strode through the house and clasped him in a silent, crushing hug. Mr. Redchenko's eyes were wet when he released the boy. He tried several times to speak then gave up, taking out a large handkerchief to wipe his face. Madame Voisine beckoned him into the kitchen where he took a cup of tea and drank it in silence.

Penny stopped by on her way home from work. She burst through the door, mascara streaming down her face, wondering aloud why she alone was crying, why she was the only one acting like she cared. Before she knew it Madame Voisine had escorted her back outside, patting her arm and remarking on her keen awareness for the suffering of others. The older woman persuaded her to go home and rest, or perhaps fetch a change of clothing for her daughter. It was the first suggestion that appealed to Penny as she drove down the lane, beside herself at the hardship of having to cope with all these trials now that her boyfriend was gone.

The visitors kept coming. Mr. and Mrs. Olenski stopped by with a box of clothing for Remy. They set it on the table as Mrs. Olenski wept softly, the silence in the room no longer a reason to think of something to say. Someone left a bucket of blueberries on the front step and Mrs. Kilchuk presented herself at the door, hoping to offer her butter tarts in exchange for details on the fire. A constable from the Caribou police department arrived to inform the boy his aunt had been notified of the deaths and was making plans to attend the funeral.

"Why would you tell her?" asked the boy.

"Because she's your next of kin."

"I've never seen her before in my life."

"Well, it's standard procedure in a case like this to notify the closest relative."

"Where does she live?"

"Halifax."

"That doesn't sound very close to me."

"I meant, she's your father's sister. The person you're most closely related to at this point in time."

Remy closed his eyes and did not respond.

At Madame Voisine's suggestion, Alice went home to change her clothes. She stood in front of the mirror and did not recognize the girl staring back, how the reflection moved when she did, disjointed and somehow adrift. She washed her face and went back up the lane, the smell of the fire still hanging in the air. The girl kept her head down, putting one foot in front of the other, afraid to look where the LaPierre house had been. When she reached Madame Voisine's bungalow and saw Remy wearing a shirt that had belonged to Kevin Olenski, she felt an overwhelming urge to turn around and close her eyes, willing it all to disappear.

That evening Madame Voisine made dinner for the children. She fried potatoes and cooked a steak, picking greens from her garden. When the light grew dim she set out blankets and poured cups of tea, her movements like the soft rush of wings in the darkness. Alice curled up in the armchair as the boy shuffled to the end of the chesterfield and sat down, occupying the least amount of space. Madame Voisine passed through the room and stopped, standing quietly in the shadows.

"I have a story to tell," she said, her voice resonant and low, "Once there was a boy who had a mountain to climb. So he did."

The clock ticked on, dispensing silence in delicate intervals, a revolution of stillness passing before the children realized the old woman was gone.

"It wasn't my dad telling me to get out of the house."

Remy spoke the first words between them since the fire, a seeming lifetime ago.

Alice sat up, startled by the sound of his voice.

"It was my mom."

She went over to the couch and knelt beside the boy.

"Remy," she said.

She picked up his hand, alarmed by the cold weight of it. The girl leaned against a cushion and closed her eyes, unable to say more. It was all she could do to breathe.

CHAPTER 30

Remy's aunt arrived from Halifax the following day. She stayed in Caribou, checking into the Lakeside Lodge which was neither by a lake nor bore any resemblance to a lodge. It had a local reputation for being rented by the hour, so that an unwitting tourist might think it a piece of good luck to find vacancy at the last minute when in fact, this was standard operating procedure. Mr. Redchenko took Remy to meet her that afternoon and Alice walked home from Madame Voisine's bungalow, shivering in the last week of June. She climbed into the bathtub and ran the water hot, sinking beneath the surface. Later she found herself standing at her bedroom window with no sense of how she got there. The sun sank behind the hills, burnishing the sky with persimmon and gold, a splendor worthy of odes and sonnets that went altogether unnoticed. Shadows swept across the room, creasing into oblivion and the moon appeared, cold and distant overhead. The girl got into bed and felt for the petrified wood beneath her pillow, leaving it be. She watched a faint wedge of light narrow to a sliver against the wall and when she blinked, it was gone.

Before sunrise the next morning, Alice got out of bed and tiptoed across the room. She opened her closet, sliding the door on its crooked, dissolute track. The white dress hung there, festive as ever, and the girl touched her cheek, feeling unsteady and hot. In spite of this she reached for the dress and put it on, smoothing her hands over the layers of silk. She lay on the bed to rest a moment and when a noise roused her from the kitchen she sat up, confused, having to remember what had happened all over again.

"Where're you going in that get-up?" said Penny, sitting at the table with her coffee and cigarette.

"The funeral's today."

"At this hour?"

"No, later this afternoon."

"So what's your rush?"

"I'm not going *yet*."

"Well…here's to the early bird." Penny took a drag from her cigarette and exhaled, smoke curling in plumes from her nose.

Alice looked out the window, staring at the sky.

"Have I seen that dress before?" asked her mother, squinting through the haze.

"I don't think so," said the girl.

She put on her sandals and went out the door.

Summer was in bloom and it was shaping up to be a glorious day, but the sun felt cold on Alice's neck as she went down to the creek, picking her way through skunk cabbage and nettles to the firm, dry ground of the willow tree. Clouds of gnats hovered in the air, engaged in their tiny furies, and an old trout dozed in an amber shaft of light at the bottom of the pool. The girl jumped and caught hold of a limb, hoisting herself into the tree. She climbed to the fort and sat down, huddling against the trunk, the dress arrayed about her like a luminous shield. Sunlight peeked through the leaves, casting patterns across her feet, but Alice stared without seeing until she forgot she was there. The creek chattered on, content with its own company, and songbirds announced themselves at intervals, repetitious and bright. The scent of dogwood floated by on the breeze, mingled with warm pine and traces of freshly cut hay. The girl closed her eyes and leaned into the curve of the antlers, feeling its coolness against her cheek.

When Alice awoke the patterns of light were gone and she groped the air, tangled in the remnants of a dream. She blinked at the willow branches, piecing together fragments of thought until reality careened into focus and she lurched forward, scrambling out of the tree. It was the hottest part of the day but the girl's face was ashen as she hurried up the lane to Madame Voisine's bungalow.

"Am I late?" she cried, when the old woman came to the door.

Madame Voisine cocked her head, regarding the girl.

"You're right on time," she said, "Come in. I've been expecting you."

Madame Voisine cleared a place at the table and motioned for the girl to sit down, setting a bowl of fried potatoes before her with a glass of lemonade. Alice looked at the food and felt dizzy.

"I don't think I can eat right now," she said.

"That's exactly why you must," replied the woman.

She picked up her fork and ate every bite.

"Good," said Madame Voisine, joining her at the table.

"What's going to happen?" Alice kept her head down, almost whispering the words.

"Whatever happens is less important than knowing you'll get through it."

A shudder ran through the girl and she pressed her fingers against the seat of her chair. She did not dare tell Madame Voisine, nor acknowledge it herself, that the woman had just uttered one of her deepest, darkest fears.

When it came time to leave Alice went outside and picked a bouquet of lilacs, feeling her stomach sink when some of the blossoms, past their prime, fell to pieces and spiraled to the ground. Madame Voisine disappeared into a shed at the edge of her property and emerged driving a truck pieced together from spare parts, like the checkering of a patchwork quilt.

"Get in," she said.

The girl climbed into the cab and stared at her flowers, the tissue blooms crumbling like faded decorations from an old dance. Madame Voisine pulled onto the highway, the silence like a cavern as they drove past the empty space where the LaPierre house had been. The blackened frame stood in stark relief against the sky like a belated supplication passed over and forsaken, a blistered patch of ash and dirt. Alice turned away, her throat tight as if a hand was closed around it. She pressed her forehead to the coolness of the window and the truck rolled on.

The old woman turned onto a paved road that passed through fields where the clover grew deep and corn patches stood tall enough to hide a young child. The road narrowed to a dirt lane as it entered the forest, winding through undergrowth and looming pines until it opened, rather abruptly, onto a rolling, green meadow. There was no gate or sign to designate Starling's cemetery, but Alice spotted a cluster of tombstones sagging at odd angles by a lone evergreen in the middle of the field. Madame Voisine parked at the edge of the clearing and got out of the truck without turning to look at the girl. Alice did not move. A giant moth landed on the windshield and the girl yanked the door handle, tumbling out of the cab. She picked herself up and hurried after the woman, feeling shaky on her feet.

A group of locals gathered near two piles of dirt, a grim sobriety stiffening their features so they appeared to the girl as strangers, though she'd seen them all before. Alice scanned the crowd until her eyes fell upon Remy, who stood at the graveside next to his aunt. His hair was wet and combed in the wrong direction, and he wore a borrowed suit that hung in folds around his shoulders. The distance, no more than thirty feet, stretched like a chasm between them. As if on cue Remy looked up, fixing the girl with a strange, owlish stare that made her turn away, terrified by the disappearance of this last familiar thing.

A priest from the St. James parish in Caribou pulled up in a dusty sedan, flustered at being the last to arrive. It was the fault of the church secretary for giving him bad directions, or so he told himself, preferring that version of events to the humiliation of admitting he'd missed a turn and steered erratically up the mountainside, a succession of dirt roads leading him deeper into the bush.

Though he looked little more than half his age Father Moran was thirty years old, fresh from the seminary and perhaps, one might say, not the most obvious fit for a man of the cloth. At the least provocation his skin would redden like wildfire, the souvenir of a childhood spent in the clutches of a mother whose penchant for drink left him not with a wealth of compassion, but rather a turbulent rage seething beneath the veneer of tightly wound control. No one had ever seen the full force of his anger, least of all the priest himself, who would have been terrified by its raw, unbridled power. But the blush was evidence enough and it attended him like a jealous lover, intimate with every inch of his body, tormenting the man until he longed for solitude, for the nothingness of being truly and completely alone.

Father Moran's robes were stiff and unhemmed, causing him to flounder through the grass as he made his way toward the gathering, the tips of his ears already tinged with pink. He was painfully aware of his oversized frock and the lack of authority this conveyed. It galled him to no end, his awareness of such details and how they throbbed in his head until he found it nearly impossible to rest a moment in his own skin.

His *skin!* The blush exploded in tiny pinpoints of sensation, as if by mere thought he could summon it anew. The priest avoided eye contact as he approached, trying to ignore the reddening of his face, a vain attempt at denial that was his signature line of defense.

In Father Moran's mind the crowd was unduly silent and he chafed at their advantage in watching him approach. Out here in the meadow there was no grand entrance to be made from behind a heavy curtain, no scented puff of smoke, but rather he must compete with the glories of nature, even stumble because of them, and he furtively scanned the gathered assembly as if expecting to see in their faces some confirmation of his own worst fears. He stood before them without speaking or smiling, in the way he had observed Father Shanley do at mass. To Father Moran's way of thinking, this pronounced pause served to reinforce authority, making clear the demarcation between shepherd and flock. It therefore unnerved the priest tremendously when he noticed everyone staring back at him with an expression that was, if anything, even more severe.

"No one knows why God allows bad things to happen to good people," he began, wincing as his voice cracked mid-sentence, catapulting a full octave into the air. He cleared his throat, stalling for time. For Father Moran, there was always a bleak moment wherein he could not deny the despondence he felt in not having a satisfactory answer for this question and indeed, in his deepening suspicion that one did not exist. He looked around the assembly, at their faces set likes bricks in a wall, and for one inconceivable moment he struggled with the impulse to throw his Bible into the air and take off running for the tree line. Why should he solve for these strangers what he could not make sense of himself?

"Yet to plague ourselves with doubt," he pressed on, obstinance being perhaps the greatest expression of his faith, "To falter in our belief at a time like this is to miss the opportunity to partake of His love as perhaps we never have before."

Someone snorted, followed by the distinct sound of a muttered curse. Father Moran fell silent, derailed by this unforeseen mutiny, a hot flush racing up his neck and illuminating the milky blondness of his hair. He took out a starched handkerchief and vigorously wiped his face, as if the color was something he could rub out of his skin. The result, of course, was a redness more vivid and alarming, like an open wound blistering in the sun.

"Go on, then," said an old ranch hand, a confirmed unbeliever who was sweating for a drink, "Finish what you've started."

"A reading from the Book of John," continued Father Moran at length, "*Peace I leave with you, my peace I give unto you: not as the world giveth, give I unto you. Let not your heart be troubled, neither let it be afraid.*"

Alice kept her eyes on the ground, not daring to look up and risk being met again with the boy's hollow stare. Somehow, nothing could be worse than that. The priest's words filtered past her and drifted away, and the shadows grew long, fanning out across the field. Father Moran circled the coffins, casting incense and muttering rites. It was his favorite part of the ceremony and he stared at the wisps of smoke curling into the air, his gaze inscrutable and skin like alabaster–unfettered, light, and free.

At the appointed moment, four men stepped forward and the pine boxes containing the remains of Gilles and Simon LaPierre were lowered into the ground. Without knowing it Father Moran held his breath, hopeful to the end, but the abrupt finality of the ritual left him feeling forsaken as ever, no closer to illumination for the great mystery of it all. He grit his teeth against this betrayal and the crowd, who was growing restless, generously interpreted his expression to mean the service was over. Jostling one another, they filed past the boy and shook hands, not a word exchanged between them. In small, straggling droves they tramped back across the meadow, anxious to return to the business of living.

Remy's aunt was crying loudly now. Father Moran hesitated, hoping the woman would regain composure, but if anything she was just getting started. Her bosom heaved like a great ocean swell and he stared without knowing it, feeling as if he was about to be sick. The priest reached out, resting his hand gingerly upon her shoulder, but when the woman drew a long, shuddering sob he yanked it back as if stung. Father Moran felt a headache of epic proportion coming on and he busied himself with the appearance of industry, packing his thurible as Remy helped his aunt to the car, rented for the occasion. They drove off in a cloud of low-lying dust and it was not long afterward that the priest took his leave, as well.

Alice stood motionless, a frozen look upon her face.

"Would you like to leave your lilacs?" asked Madame Voisine.

The girl turned to the mounds of dirt and blinked.

"I'm not putting flowers on those graves," she said.

Madame Voisine nodded as if this made perfect sense.

"Let's go home."

Alice followed the woman, lavender petals trailing in her wake, while overhead clouds made copper by the fading light streaked like ancient script across the sky.

When they reached Madame Voisine's bungalow, the girl got out of the truck.

"I guess I should be going now," she said.

"Oh? Are you sure?" asked the woman.

"Yes. Remy will be coming home soon. He'll be looking for me."

She did not face the woman as she spoke.

Madame Voisine contemplated these words, then nodded.

"I'm here if you need me. Always."

The girl walked down the lane, her arms tightly folded.

The bungalow was empty when Alice arrived, though for the first time she did not notice. She went to her bedroom and closed the door, standing at the window until a beam of headlights stabbed the darkness and swept across the wall. The girl pressed herself behind the curtain as a car drove up and stopped by the woodshed. The driver turned off the lights but did not kill the engine, letting it idle like a great, purring beast.

Alice opened the front door and stood on the threshold, her dress rustling in the shadows. The boy got out of the car and stood beside it but the girl hung back, unable to move. She gazed into the darkness as the silence stretched between them, until nothing seemed worse than letting it last a moment longer.

"Remy!" she breathed, flying down the steps toward him. He moved forward then stopped, bringing the girl to an abrupt halt where she seemed to hover in mid-air, frightened by this last bit of distance between them.

"Remy," she whispered again and he started to cry.

She reached for his arm but the boy shook his head, choking on his words.

"I have to go, Alice. I have to go back with my aunt to Halifax."

Alice stared at the boy, blinking. She felt submerged, as if she was sitting at the bottom of a pool, able to hear words yet failing to comprehend their meaning.

"What?"

"I have to go back with my aunt."

"What are you talking about? You mean for a visit?" The girl's voice grew louder, pitched in raw tones, jangling in her ears like a harsh cacophony of sound.

"No, Alice. Not a visit. I have to go back and live with her."

"What do you mean? What do you mean, you *have* to? You don't even know her! Remy, no. *No*, Remy! Don't go!"

"Alice." The boy hung his head, defeated.

"No. *No!*" Alice could not stop shaking her head, "Remy, don't leave me. Please don't go!"

Her voice crumpled and broke into a thousand pieces.

"You said you never would."

A cloud passed over the moon, plunging the night into oblivion. Remy stepped forward. He reached for the girl and they clung together, weeping softly.

"Alice, listen. Listen to me." He took a step back, his features contorted, choking as he spoke through his tears, "Nothing can keep us apart. Do you hear me? Doesn't matter where we go. Doesn't matter how long. This thing between us is stronger. You have to know it. *Tell* me you know it."

The girl blinked and closed her eyes, desperate for a way out. She wrapped her arms around her body, feeling a weight press against her chest so that she could hardly breathe.

"When are you leaving?" she asked, her tone hollow and flat.

"Tonight."

She flinched, swaying on her feet.

"Alice," said Remy, "Promise me you know it. *Please.*"

But the girl could not hear him. She closed her eyes, trembling at the fate that was rolling toward her. She could feel it coming, heralding its force with a swift and terrible speed. There was nowhere to run, no place to hide, no sleep or conjuring to pretend it all away. She stood, unable to feel herself, knowing only that this thing would happen, that it could not be imagined otherwise, that it would break her beneath its great wheel and roll on.

"Alice."

Remy reached for her hand.

She swayed as if in a trance and he waited, holding on. Suddenly the girl looked up, caught by an understanding that had eluded her in the past but was now, in this moment, as plain as anything she had ever known.

"Remy," She squeezed his hand, "I was wrong. You're not the falcon."

The boy regarded her blankly.

"From the poem. I thought maybe you were the falcon, but you're not. You're the ancient tower. That's what you are to me."

Remy was silent, staring at the ground.

"It's true," he nodded, speaking the truth as it welled up inside him, "I've been looking for you as long as I can remember, even when I didn't know it. You're the only thing that matters to me. The only real thing."

The children gazed at each other, slipping away from time to a place where such moments live on forever. The trees bowed their heads and the creek fell silent, flowing in hushed currents to its tributaries, branching out to the sea. Stars glimmered in delicate chains across the sky and the moon peeked through the clouds, bathing the valley in a soft, opalescent glow.

The car revved its engine, startling the boy, and he glanced over his shoulder, having forgotten it was there.

He turned back to Alice, dropping his head.

She stepped forward and threw her arms around him, pressing her face to his neck.

"There's no one like you," she whispered.

"I'll come for you, Alice. I'll find you again. I swear it."

Remy's voice broke. He shut his eyes against the momentum bearing down upon him and gripped the girl like a lifeline, trying to hold on.

"Let's get a move on!" called the aunt, rolling down her window.

Alice shuddered. A dark wave roared through the boy and he gasped at the pain of letting her go.

Somewhere in the universe a clock ticked on with soft, precise measurements, compelling the moon to rotate, the earth to spin, and every living thing upon it to sleep and awaken, moving against the odds through its relentless passage of time. The car drove off into the darkness, its brake lights hobbling down the lane. It paused at the highway then pulled out, spinning gravel, and was gone. No one saw the girl emerge from the shadows breathing deeply, relic in hand, her dress trailing shades of sunrise, sunset, stormy weather, snowfall, and endless blue in its pale hues of dawn, deepening into the night.

Printed in Great Britain
by Amazon